Seasons of the Sword #1

リス子

Risuko

A Kunoichi Tale

by

David Kudler

D0962714

Stillpoint/Atalanta

Stillpoint Digital Press
Mill Valley, California, USA

Cover design by James T. Egan of Bookfly Design

Publisher's Cataloging-in-Publication Data
provided by Five Rainbows Services
Kudler, David.
Risuko : a Kunoichi tale / David Kudler.
pages   cm. - (Seasons of the sword, bk. 1)
ISBN: 978-1-938808-32-6 (hardcover)
ISBN: 978-1-938808-34-0 (pbk.)
ISBN: 978-1-938808-33-3 (e-book)
1. Japan—History—Period of civil wars, 1480–1603—Fiction. 2. Ninja—Fiction. 3. Conspiracies—Fiction. 4. Determination (Personality trait)—Fiction. 5. Young adult fiction.   I. Title.
PZ7.1.K76 Ri 2016
[Fic]—dc23

LCCN: 2015918899

First edition, June 2016

Version 1.0

Also by David Kudler
The Seven Gods of Luck
Shlomo Travels to Warsaw
How Raven Brought Back the Light

Coming Soon!

Bright-Eyes (Seasons of the Sword #2)

Find out more on **Risuko.Net**

Follow on:
twitter.com/RisukoKunoichi • risuko-chan.tumblr.com
facebook.com/risuko.books • instagram.com/RisukoKunoichi
risuko.livejournal.com

For Sashako and Juju-chan

—

兵士,速く立下がり

白と緋色の戦い

地上にブロッサム

Provinces of Japan during Risuko

Contents

NOTE: In Japan, as in most of East Asia, a person's family name goes before the given name. In the following story, for example, *Kano Murasaki* is a girl named Murasaki from the Kano family.

Risuko

Prologue—Serenity

My name is Kano Murasaki, but everyone calls me *Risuko*. Squirrel.

I am from Serenity Province, though I was not born there.

My nation has been at war for a hundred years, Serenity is under attack and the Kano family is in disgrace, but some people think that I can bring victory. That I can be *a very special kind of woman.*

All I want to do is climb.

My name is Kano Murasaki, but everyone calls me Squirrel.

Risuko.

1—The Left-Hand Path

Serenity Province, Land of the Rising Sun, The Month of Leaves in the First Year of the Rule of Genki
(Totomi, Japan, late autumn, 1570 A.D.)

Spying on the lord of the province from the old pine was a bad idea. Risky. Stupid. That's why I didn't see what was coming. I knew it was a bad idea, but something about being there, high up in that pine, made me feel free.

And, of course, I was always fascinated by what happened in the castle. Can you blame me?

I watched where Lord Imagawa stood in his castle with a samurai, pointing at a piece of paper. Paper covered with splashes of color. Green, mostly. Blue and red shapes marking the edges.

It was a hundred paces away or more. I must have been squinting hard, trying to make out what they were pointing at. That's the only way to explain how I didn't notice the palanquin until it had almost reached my tree.

Below, two hulking men carried the shiny black box by the heavy bar between them. The thing scuttled like a beetle through the slanting morning shadows that darkened the woods. It was coming from the direction of the village.

Seeing it startled me—made my chest tight and my hands colder even than they already were.

I scooted to the top of the pine, hands chilled and sticky.

Half-way up the pine tree though I was, I had the urge to stomp on the dark, gleaming thing. Only nobles traveled by palanquin. And when had nobles ever done my family any favors?

I sensed danger in the steady, silent approach. Had they seen me spying on the castle?

"Risuko!" My sister called up to me. I could not even see the top of her head.

The black box crept closer, into the clearing below me. Then the palanquin stopped.

I scrambled to hide myself. The cold sap smelled sharp and raw as I pressed my nose to the bark. I gave a bird whistle—a warbler call, the one that I'd told Usako I'd use if she needed to hide.

I had actually been looking for birds' eggs, though it was the wrong season for it. Hunger and the desire to do something, as well as my own pleasure in climbing, had driven me up the tree. Mother had not fed us that morning. Once the weather turned cold, she could not always provide us with even a small bowl of rice a day. Also, the castle had been bustling like an ants' nest that's been prodded with a stick, and I had been curious....

Someone below me began talking. An old woman, I thought, her voice high and birdlike, though, again, I couldn't make out the words. Usako—my sister—stepped forward into view. I could see her head bowed, like a frightened rabbit. The old woman spoke again. After a pause, Usako-*chan's* face, open and small, turned toward my hiding place. She pointed up at me.

"*Risuko*," the old woman said, "come down now."

She and her men were at the bottom of the tree. I considered leaping across to one of the other pines, but there weren't any close enough and big enough to jump to. And I was worried that my hands were too cold to keep hold.

Usako scurried off on the trail toward home. *Thanks, sister,* I thought. *I'll get you for that later.* I wish that she had turned and waved. I wish that I had called out a good-bye.

If I was going to be grabbed at the bottom, I decided that I might as well come down with a flourish. I dropped from limb to limb, bark, needles, and sap flying from the branches as my hands and feet slapped at them, barely breaking my speed. Perhaps if I came down faster than they expected, I could make a run for it once I reached the ground.

My bare feet had no sooner hit the needles beneath the tree, however, than a large hand came to rest on my shoulder. The two huge servants had managed to place themselves exactly where I would land.

"What an interesting young girl you are," the grey-haired noblewoman said.

Somehow I didn't want to interest her. The two men stepped back at the wave of her hand. She stood there, still in her elegant robes, her wooden sandals barely sinking into the mud. "Do you climb things other than trees?" she asked, her deeply lined face bent in an icy smile, her eyes lacquer-black against her white-painted skin.

I nodded, testing my balance in this uncertain conversation. "That's why my mother calls me Risuko. I'm always climbing—our house, rocks, trees...." Her eyes brightened, cold as they were, and I started to let go and brag. "There's a cliff below the castle up there." I pointed to where Lord Imagawa's stone castle stood on the hill at the edge of the woods.

"Ah?" she said, looking pleased.

"I like to climb up the cliff."

"Oh?" she sniffed, "but certainly a skinny little girl like you couldn't get terribly far."

That stung. "Oh, yes, I've climbed all the way to the top of the cliff bunches of times, and up the walls too, to look in at the windows and see the beautiful clothes...."

I clamped my mouth shut and blushed. Noble as she clearly was, she could have had me flogged or beheaded for daring to do such a thing. I tensed.

But this odd old woman didn't have her enormous litter-carriers beat me with the wooden swords they carried in their belts. Instead, she truly smiled, and that terrifying smile was what let me know that my fate was sealed, that I couldn't run. "Yes," she said. "Very interesting. Risuko."

She motioned for the men to bring her palanquin. It was decorated, as were the coats of the men, with the lady's *mon*, her house's symbol: a plain, solid white circle.

They placed the box beside her, and she eased into it, barely seeming to move. "Come, walk beside me, Risuko. I have some more questions to ask you." Then she snapped, "Little Brother!"

"Yes, Lady!" called the servant who stood at the front of the palanquin, the larger of the two men. He gave a quiet sort of grunt and then, in perfect unison with his partner, lifted the box and began to march forward.

"Stay with me, girl!" the old lady ordered, and I scurried to keep up. I was surprised by the strength of the two men—they hardly seemed to notice the weight that they carried—but their speed was what took my breath away. As I scrambled to keep up, the mistress began to bark at me again. "What did I hear about your father? He taught you to write?"

How did she know my father? "Yes, he was a scribe." I wanted to add, but did not, And a samurai too.

"He can't have been much of a scribe," she sniffed. "No apprentice, so he teaches his daughter to use a brush? What a waste. And the rags you wear?"

"He... died. Mother has struggled...," I panted. "He was a good scribe... But there wasn't much... need for one here... What do farmers need with contracts or letters?"

We moved quickly, speeding right past the path that led back to my home. *Ah, well,* I thought, *we'll join up with the main road and come into the village the long way.*

"Yes," she said, looking pleased with herself, "I suppose Lord Imagawa would be about the only client worth having around here in this wilderness. Don't fall behind, child."

I was beginning to sweat, in spite of the cold. The smell of approaching snow was sour in the air.

The rear servant—the one who wasn't quite as enormous as the one the lady had called Little Brother—pulled even with me. Without turning his head, the man gave a low bark. Imperceptibly, the two men slowed to a pace that I could match. Grateful, I looked over toward the servant in the rear. I wasn't sure, but I could have sworn that he winked.

I could see the bulk of Lord Imagawa's castle though the open shutters of the palanquin. Banners flew from the roof that I'd never seen there before—blue and red. The old lady followed my gaze up the hill. "Yes, depressing old pile of rock, isn't it?"

I couldn't think of any way to answer that. I wasn't sure that she expected me too answer.

"You really climbed all the way up to the windows?" She was looking at me closely. I nodded. "Yes, very interesting." She clicked her tongue. "And today? I don't suppose you could have seen anything of interest today."

"Lord Imagawa," I panted. "Soldier. Pointing at... drawing."

Now her eyes widened. "You could see that from such a distance? Could you see what the drawing looked like?"

Green squares, surrounded by smaller squares of red and blue. What looked like little pine trees sticking out of the squares. I nodded.

The lady smiled again, looking like an old mother pig when it's found a nice puddle to wallow in. Somehow the smile was even more frightening.

At that moment, we met up with the main road. I was certain that we would turn right, back toward the village, to my house, my mother, and that some explanation for this peculiar line of questions would present itself.

Instead, the palanquin turned smoothly left.

Confused, I stopped in my tracks.

"Stop!" the lady yelled. Little Brother and the winking one came to a halt. "Come along, girl!"

"But...?"

"I told you to keep up with me, child." She wasn't even looking at me.

"But... the village is...?" I pointed back down the road I had been walking most of my life, to the bridge I could see just behind the spur of trees that led to my house.

"Silly Risuko. *Down!*" The two men lowered her to the crossroad. Now she looked at me. "You are not going back there. Your mother sold you to me this morning." She leaned out the window and barked at the carriers, *"Go!"*

2—Into the Circle

I began to back away. I was thinking—if I was thinking—that I could get underneath the bridge, in among the tangled beams where I had hidden so often before. No one had ever been able to find me there. Except, of course, my father.

Before I had managed even to stagger back to the small road leading to the bridge and to my home, a hand as big as a melon closed around my wrist. The giant called Little Brother's expression was hardly threatening, but far from friendly. With his free hand he untied the belt at his waist, which turned out to be a thick length of smooth cord. He let his polished wooden sword fall to the road. Turning back to the palanquin, he grunted. "Wrists?"

"That depends," said the old woman. She smirked at me. "We can do this any one of a number of ways, Risuko. You may come as my guest, in which case he will simply tie the rope around your waist so that you don't... get lost. You may come as my prisoner, in which case he will bind your hands to keep you from escaping too easily. Or you may come as my possession, in which case he will hog-tie you and carry you on the bar to my palanquin here. Now. Which shall it be?" Her face seemed almost kindly despite the obvious threat, and yet I felt her eyes boring into me. "Well?"

I looked up at the two men, whose faces were stone, and glanced desperately down the path to the village. Little Brother's hand remained on my wrist, and I knew that I could not possibly have escaped his grasp. My throat was thick, but a kind of awful, resigned relief settled on me. I looked to the lady again, whose made-up face seemed hardly to have moved, and then, finally back up into the warm, boulder-like face of Little Brother. I slumped. "Guest."

"Excellent," said the lady, as Little Brother tied one end of the long cord around my waist, picked up his sword, and handed the other end of the leash to his fellow, who favored me with a grimace that may have been another smile. "Enough of these delays," barked the noblewoman. "We have a delivery to make. *Go!*"

Down the path to Pineshore and away from my home they went, and I stumbled along behind them, down into the valley, watching the clouds thickening the sky above us, blotting out the thin midday sun.

———

I couldn't feel my feet, and it was not because of the cold—or not only because of the cold. Mother had sold me. I would never see her or Usako again. As I stumbled beside the palanquin, my shock began to turn to cold rage, and then to fear. Who was this lady who now owned me?

An Imagawa rider galloped by us in the opposite direction, splattering slushy mud onto my already cold, already filthy legs.

My stomach rumbled against the rope bound around my waist. Between climbing and walking I was tired and even hungrier than I had been.

We walked along the main street in Pineshore some time later, I saw some boys a little older than me carrying baskets of dried fish up the road. They stopped and bowed as we walked past them, and the look in their eyes was one of pure awe. For a moment I woke to myself, and thought what a remarkable picture we made: the two enormous servants carrying the elegant lady in the box, with the ragged, skinny girl shuffling along behind them at the end of a rope like a goat.

A gang of anxious-looking soldiers paid us no notice at all.

We approached an inn near the center of town. Two young women with the emblem of a white disk on their winter robes stepped out into the street and escorted us into the courtyard.

"Lady Chiyome," said the finer-featured of the two maids. "Welcome back. I see you have hunted well."

"Yes," said the lady, as Little Brother helped her out of the box, "I've managed to bag myself a squirrel."

The maids gazed at me as if I were indeed a trophy from some exotic hunt.

"Her name's Risuko," the lady laughed, hollowly. "Little Brother, you can untie her. I'm sure that our guest won't bolt."

The smaller carrier walked over to me and undid the knotted cord around my waist. Now he favored me with what was clearly a smile.

The courtyard walls were tall, but timbered; if I had been alone, I could have gotten to the roof, but—

"I want to get out of here. The Imagawa are nervous. We're leaving immediately, as soon as I have had a bit to eat. Mieko, give her something more presentable to wear than those rags, then take her to the others and feed her."

Food.

The maid nodded, and then Lady Chiyome looked at me, impaling me with that cold, level stare that I had encountered in the woods. "Don't be boring and decide to behave like a possession rather than a guest. Tonight, once we reach our destination, Mieko here will bring you to me, and we will see how fine a prize you actually are."

I bowed and began to back away, but her voice stopped me. "Kano Murasaki, you may not realize it, but I have done you a great favor. I have it in my power to give you a gift that you don't even realize you desire. Make yourself worth my trouble, and you will be glad of it. Disappoint me, and you will be very, very sorry."

I had no idea what she was talking about. To be honest, I was stunned that she had used my full, true name. No one had called me that since Father went away. I looked up into her face, but it was as empty and without answers as a blank-faced Jizo statue's. "Kuniko, I want a bath," she snapped. Then she turned and walked into the inn, followed by one of her maids.

"Come, Risuko-*chan*," Mieko said, "follow me." She turned smoothly around and began to walk across the courtyard, her tall wooden sandals clopping on the stones like horse hooves, a sound made hollow by the snowfall.

As I stumbled behind her, my body came back to me and I began to shiver—huge, uncontrollable vibrations. Tears began to roll down my face. At last.

She led me through the coin-sized flakes of snow. Though it must have been midday, the storm made it dark, and her form seemed to fade into the falling feathers of the crystal flakes. I danced across the cold stones, my bare feet fleeing from freezing stones to freezing air and back again, leaving me hopping like a mating crane next to Mieko's smooth stride. "We will get you changed and fed before we go," she said.

There was no one between me and the inn-yard entrance. I thought of bolting. But *food...*

We reached a wide door that looked like the entry to a stable. Mieko opened it and beckoned me in. "Come, Risuko."

I entered behind her and peered into the gloom. As my eyes adjusted, I could make out five figures, all seated around a tiny fire.

The room looked as if it were indeed intended to be a stable, but had been transformed into a sort of servant dormitory. Low, age-darkened beams crisscrossed, holding up the roof. Bedrolls lined one wall and a small, smoky fire-pit warmed the center of the space—almost.

The five figures stood and turned toward me. I felt the urge to climb up into the low rafters, just to get away. Too late to fly away, I realized.

I recognized the two bulkiest figures as Lady Chiyome's carriers. They glanced at me, bowed their heads, and then turned back to the fire, stirring rice in a pot.

The other three figures came toward me. As they stepped away from the fire, their black silhouettes softened and I could make out their features. They were older than me, but definitely children. The biggest was a boy, with a doughy, smiling face. The middle one had a smile too, but it wasn't a friendly one at all. And the smallest one, who was just a little bigger than me, wore the most ridiculous frown on her face that I've ever seen.

"Children," said Mieko, a hand resting gently on my shoulder, "come and introduce yourselves to our newest companion, Kano Murasaki."

"Kano." The middle girl's eyes narrowed. "So, *you're* the reason we've been waiting here," she spat.

I tried to step back, but Mieko's gentle grip held me in place.

The boy spoke as if the girl hadn't said a thing. "I'm Aimaru. And this is Emi." He gestured to the sad-faced girl.

"Hello," she said. Her voice was pleasant, but the scowl didn't break at all.

The boy was about to introduce the other girl, but she slapped away his hand. "I'm me," she said. "I don't care if you know who I am or not, but I want to know who you are, and why the lady was looking for a scrawny mouse like you."

"She's not a mouse, Toumi," said the frowning girl. "She's too big." I couldn't tell if she was joking, or just hadn't understood.

The girl called Toumi gave a dismissive snort and walked back to the tiny fire.

"There's food," said Aimaru. "Come."

"What's your name?" asked Emi.

I shuffled. I've never liked Mama's nickname for me, but that was how everyone seemed to know me there. "I'm called Risuko," I muttered, looking down.

"A squirrel's sort of like a mouse," said Emi, her face still twisted in a severe pout.

Is she simple? I wondered. *Is she making fun of me?* I somehow couldn't believe that either was true.

"Come, Risuko," said Mieko. "We can get you some clean things to wear and then you may eat."

Mieko grabbed some items from one of the bundles by the fire and led me into one of the empty stalls where I couldn't see the others. She gave a perfect, crescent-moon smile and held out her hand. "Come, give me your clothes."

Her polished sweetness was as impossible to disobey as Lady Chiyome's commands. Shaking uncontrollably, I pulled off my thin, wet jacket and trousers. I held them out to her, dripping on the straw-strewn floor.

Her smile froze on her face as she took the clothes by her fingertips. Holding them at arms' length, she draped them over the wall of the next stall. I never saw them again.

Then she handed me clean clothes: trousers and a jacket, both blue. On the back of the jacket was Lady Chiyome's white disk *mon*.

Mieko led me, newly branded, over to the fire, where there was a large pot of rice and a small platter with some slices of fish.

"I must go help pack up the lady's things," Mieko said quietly to me. Turning to the others, she said, "We will be leaving as soon as the lady has eaten. She wishes us to speed our mission and leave Imagawa territory as soon as possible. Please make sure that you are ready to go immediately."

The two large men nodded simply. Aimaru bobbed his head and Emi just stared. Toumi gave a snort.

With that, Mieko turned and glided out of the stable.

Aimaru and Emi picked up their half-finished meals. Toumi was wedged between the two carriers and the wall. She was mashing the fish into the rice with her fingers—but her eyes were still on me, glistening in the firelight. The big one whom Lady Chiyome had called Little Brother passed me a serving of rice and fish in a wooden bowl with a pair of battered chopsticks. I sat in the straw and started to eat.

Mother hadn't had food for us that morning, and I'd had a long, cold walk—not to mention the promise of more walking soon—so I was starving. I began to shovel rice and thin slices of fish into my mouth with the chopsticks. They might not have been clean, but I wasn't going to complain.

As I gulped down the food, barely tasting it but savoring it even so, the others began to gather up their belongings in preparation to leave.

I wasn't concerned; I had nothing to pack. I finished the last grain of rice, rinsed the bowl out with water from a bucket, the rest of which the younger of the carriers poured onto the dying embers of the fire.

"Does the meal meet with Lady Mouse's approval?" sneered Toumi from the wall.

"Don't be mean, Toumi," said Aimaru. "It's not her fault we had to wait here—"

"For three days!" snapped Toumi. "What makes the old lady think *you're* such a prize? Something special?" Her face darkened in the firelight.

I could feel the blood pounding in my ears. My fingertips were buzzing. Food and warmth had returned feeling to my limbs and to my soul. "I don't know! I don't know what she wants with me! She bought me off of my mother this morning." All of the rest of them—even the carriers, even Toumi—gaped at me. "One moment I'm climbing trees with my sister and the next moment I'm being marched off without even a chance to say goodbye to anyone!"

"You've got a mother," said Emi. "You've got a sister."

I gawped at her, her down-turned mouth looking even sadder than it had. I tried to speak but the miserable expression seemed so extreme—like my own sister's when her straw dollies would break, or she stubbed her toes, or after Father went away—that it struck me dumb.

Aimaru put his hand very softly on my arm. I realized I was gripping my chopsticks like a dagger. He said, in that same even voice of his, "It's not your fault that the rest of us are orphans."

"Orphans?" I responded.

Emi and Aimaru both nodded, solemnly. Aimaru said, "The lady found each of us. I grew up at a temple, I was left there with the monks when I was an infant. And Emi..."

"I lived in the capital's streets," said Emi. "I only remember my mother a little."

Toumi snorted again.

"Orphans?" I repeated. I could feel my eyes beginning to tear up, my throat filling. Why was I crying?

"Well, say what you want, my family's dead but I'm no orphan," snarled Toumi. "I *am* the Tarugu family. And no one would ever have been able to sell me like trash to a rag-picker."

3—Flying

I have no clear memory of what happened next, or why. I don't think I'd ever in my life tried to hit anyone before, not even my sister. Though I must admit I had considered it from time to time.

But something about Toumi's sneer—her brittle anger, even more than her insult, but also something familiar—pricked me to action. She hadn't even turned away from me when my open hand caught her cheek. We both stood there, frozen in shock. It must have lasted less than a heartbeat's time, but it felt as if a tree might have sprouted, grown, and fallen in the moment that we stood there, staring at each other.

The print of a red hand that matched the shape of my own began to darken against her pale skin. My palm burned.

In the same tree-slow time, I watched her eyes narrow with rage and knew that she now wanted to kill me—actually to kill me. And I knew that she was capable of it. She began to lean forward and I knew that she was getting ready to drive her hand into me.

Again, I have no idea how things happened next. I leaped backward and bounced against the wall. The boards had loose grooves that led straight up to the cat's-cradle of overhanging beams. I could see that the door was now open on the other side of the stable and that, if I got up into the rafters, I could climb over Toumi's head and escape out into the snow.

Toumi surged after me, snarling like a wild dog.

My arms and legs began to move without any conscious direction from me.

Before she could reach me, Toumi's charge was snapped short. Little Brother's enormous hand had fastened itself to the collar of her jacket and stopped her as surely as an iron chain. He held her at arm's length, her feet dangling. He turned his round tiger face up to me.

Somehow, without even being aware of it, I had carried out the first part of my plan. I was in the rafters, well above Little Brother's head, poised for escape.

Little Brother's face was, as always, blank and unreadable. So was his companion's, staring up at me from just inside the door, which he was blocking. I wouldn't have been able to get out that way after all.

"Come down," Little Brother said. His voice was as deep, slow earthquake rumble. "No one will be hurting anyone here today."

He gently placed Toumi back by the fire.

I dropped out of the rafters onto the straw-strewn dirt floor.

"Listen to me, both of you." He turned to the others, sitting around the fire. "All of you, listen to me. We face dangers enough. Do not add to them. You children are here out of Lady Chiyome's kindness, out of her greatness of heart. All of you belong to the lady. You are her guests—" He looked at me. "—but you are also her possessions. If you wish Lady Chiyome's kindness to continue, you are to treat all of her possessions respectfully." His calm gaze caught Toumi as her face contorted in a look of poisonous hatred, a look that was aimed at me. "If you feel the need to fight, to hit, you are to hit me. But if you hit me, expect to be hit back."

Toumi blinked, blinked again, and then turned away and strode out of the stable and into the snow.

Little Brother and his fellow giant stood, unmoving, not acknowledging her exit. I walked toward the fire, sat and tried to breathe. Their eyes followed me—the stares weren't threatening, but I felt unnerved, even so. I was ashamed to have given way to anger, to have struck another in spite of everything that my father had always taught. No harm.

Finally, their eyes let go of me, and they went outside—no doubt to search for Toumi.

Now I was aware that Emi and Aimaru were looking at me.

I was still feeling as if I were about to be attacked. "What?" I grumbled at them.

"You are a squirrel," said Emi.

"How did you do that?" said Aimaru, his face now looking more astonished than blissful.

"Do what?" I asked. Suddenly I felt hungry again.

"You climbed right up that wall like a spider," said Aimaru.

"Like a squirrel," corrected Emi.

"I've never seen a person climb like that," Aimaru continued.

"I... I don't know," I muttered. "I guess I've always been able to climb really well."

They both nodded, but I wasn't sure that they believed me.

"You know," I said, because I just felt as if I had to say something, "my name isn't really Risuko."

Aimaru raised both hands and smiled. Clearly it was all the same to him. His smile probably would have been just as Buddha-like if I'd said I was actually a *kitsune*, a fox-spirit who had come to steal all his food.

Emi, however, pouted at me and asked, "What is your name, then?"

"Oh," I said, because, even though that was the logical question to ask after what I'd said, I hadn't expected her to ask it. "It's... It's Murasaki."

Her sad face twisted into a confused smirk. "Isn't that a girl from some story? Some old story?"

"Yes," I said, "*The Tales of Genji*. The name of the writer, too. It's an old love story. It was my father's favorite."

Her mouth bowed even further down, and her eyes began to moisten. "Back when my mother was alive... she used to tell me stories from it."

I simply nodded that I understood, and watched as first Emi and then Aimaru shuffled away from the fire toward the door, bedrolls in their hands.

"They'll expect us to be ready to go," Aimaru apologetically.

I looked around to see if there was anything for me to bring, but of course, there wasn't anything. I was just considering hiding there in the stable, waiting for them all to go away, when I sensed a large, quiet presence behind me. I was not surprised to see Little Brother and his companion standing behind me like stone pillars.

I tried smiling at them. The younger one smiled back. "Please, sirs, I... What do I call you?"

"Little Brother," they both said, in unison.

The younger one, the one who had winked at me, now smiled fully. "It amuses the lady to call us that. All of her followers—the teachers and students at the Full Moon"—*Mochizuki*—"know us as the Little Brothers."

Teachers? Mochizuki? Is there a school on the full moon? I wondered in my bewilderment.

The larger one didn't seem to share his companion's amusement. "Lady Chiyome has informed us that we will be leaving immediately."

4—The Edge of the World

Around me, everyone was rushing back and forth across the courtyard, loading supplies on the two pack horses, putting on extra layers of clothing.

When I reached them, Emi smiled, a small grin, and handed me a warmer coat, and then a sleeping mat. "That's for tonight. Put it with ours on the white horse."

I was so surprised at the tiny smile that it took me a moment to accept the bundle from her.

When I had stowed my bedroll with everyone else's and pulled the padded jacket over the thin blue one, the younger Little Brother handed each of us a lumpy coat made of straw and a pair of straw boots. "We're going to be walking through snow," he said, placidly. "We can't afford to have you freeze your feet."

We each stepped into the boots, which gave me the unstable feeling of walking on a particularly scratchy pine branch. Then we pulled on the thick, long coats of woven straw. Emi and Aimaru started to snicker. I looked up; they looked like large, walking haystacks. Even Toumi gave a thin, embarrassed smile. That made me think of Usako, my little sister, and my heart twisted.

The entrance to the inn yard was once again unguarded. But in those boots....

Toumi batted at the straw hood and cloak that covered her body. "You look," she muttered, "like a bunch of cows in their winter coats."

"What does she think *she* looks like?" whispered Emi.

As the Little Brothers brought the beetle-black palanquin out of the stable where the horses had been kept, Lady Chiyome and Mieko stepped out of the inn. Kuniko, the maid with a face like a block of granite, followed the Little Brothers, holding what looked like a short sword attached to a pole as tall as she was. It was a weapon that I would later learn was called a glaive. I couldn't think what Kuniko was doing with it, nor why it fit so comfortably in her grip. I assumed that it was for one of the carriers.

The old noblewoman was dressed just as she had been earlier that day, in her dark, layered winter kimono. I had expected the maids to be in their elegant silk robes, but they too were dressed warmly in subdued blue winter robes bearing the plain, white circle. The Little Brothers set the palanquin immediately in front of Lady Chiyome, and once again she knelt into the box with that subtle movement that seemed to be no movement at all.

I waited for the two maids to get in with her. I hoped, I suppose, that their weight might slow down the speeding Little Brothers a bit.

Instead, however, the two young women came to us, Mieko with her unreal glide and Kuniko with her solid gait. Kuniko addressed us, gruff and direct, her glaive planted solidly beside her. "We will be walking for the next ten days, if the weather permits. Keep up. Do not whine." From the palanquin, Lady Chiyome's voice snapped, *"Go!"* The two Little Brothers picked up the box and, just as they had earlier that day, sped away, leading us out of the inn yard.

Kuniko strode forward behind them, leading the pack horses by their reins with one hand, swinging the glaive like a walking stick in the other, and we stumbled behind her. Mieko brought up the rear.

I have wondered, since, what would have happened if I simply hadn't followed—if, say, I had run into the streets of Pineshore and hidden in the woods behind the town. It didn't even occur to me in the moment to do anything other than fall into line and try as hard as I could to keep up.

As we headed north out of the inn along the main highway out of Pineshore. We walked quickly through the blizzard-barren streets of the town. A few shop-keepers and rag-pickers looked up, startled, as we passed.

A horse galloped past us, also heading north. It splashed mud—this time on our haystack coats—and disappeared ahead. I wondered if it were the same rider who'd splattered me earlier that day.

Watching the charger, I barely had the time to register the moment when I went further from home than I had ever been—past the shop of the rice merchant for whom Father had written a contract for his marriage with Jiro-*san*'s daughter Kana.

We walked steadily. Just beyond the edge of town, a bridge arced across the old, wide Weatherbank River. A clump of Lord Imagawa's soldiers stood guard, peering away from us, toward the north. The only one who was actually facing the town barely looked at us and waved us through.

Our pack horses' hooves rang hollowly against the wooden planks of the bridge. The river was much deeper and slower there than it was near our village, and I marched along near the side of the bridge, watching the dark green water swirl around the pilings, wishing it were summer and now the impulse to escape came, simply to leap the side of the bridge and swim back up to where the river passed near our house. However, the Little Brothers kept their quick, steady pace, taking us back onto solid ground and out into the open world along the Great Ocean Road, leaving my little world of pine, oak, and hemlock, creek and castle behind us.

———

The highway was wide, flat and very bare. Most of the time, we traveled just inland of the shore, where what trees there were had a twisted, wind-stunted shape. Even when we were traveling near to woods, the trees seemed to have been cleared back.

"Probably to keep travelers safe from bandits," suggested Aimaru when I pointed it out to him during a rare stop.

A group of Imagawa cavalry clattered past us, also heading north. The steam from the horses' nostrils flowed behind them like hair, like a single ghostly, white tail.

"Also," mumbled Emi, "makes it easier for us to stay out of the way of the troops."

I nodded, but mostly I didn't like it. My whole life had been spent surrounded by trees. Out there on the wide, flat road, I felt... naked.

As the sun began to dip toward the distant mountains, we discovered that sometimes even a highway isn't always wide enough to allow us to stay out of the way of troops.

As we approached a crossroads, we saw that the main road was blocked by what looked like a thicket of armed men—more Imagawa soldiers. Not on guard, these, with many of them lying down. Many bandaged. Many bleeding.

A samurai in battered armor stood as we approached him, one hand out and signaling us to stop, the other on his sword.

Kuniko released the reins of the pack animals and held her glaive in both hands—the point still up, not threatening, but ready.

Lady Chiyome leaned out of her palanquin. "What is it? Why are we slowing down?"

"Can't go this way, lady," said the samurai.

We all gathered behind Kuniko and the palanquin. Mieko stepped in front of Toumi, Emi and me.

"We need to head up this highway if we're to get past the fighting," the old lady grumbled.

The samurai gave a laugh that seemed totally without humor. "Not *this* way you won't," he said, pointing behind him with a jerk of his thumb. "Only way you'll get past the fighting down this highway is through the gate to the next world."

I shivered.

"There's a village a ways up that road," the samurai said, pointing to the smaller road that led inland. "Least, it was there a couple of days ago. You can spend the night there, then follow the road up the Little Nephew into Quick River Province. Don't think there's *too* much fighting up that way."

"But we have to—!"

"Lady, try to go down this highway and I'll kill you all myself. No civilians." He glanced at Kuniko. "Or... whatever."

"Bah!" Chiyome-*sama* slammed her window shut, which the Little Brothers took for a signal to head along the smaller road. As we began to march behind them, I could hear her growl from inside her box, "Ruffian!"

By the time we reached the village, it was nearly dark. Kuniko moved up to talk to the old noblewoman. I could hear the shrill sound of Chiyome-*sama*'s raised voice answering in anger, but I couldn't hear what she was saying.

The armed maid looked back at us, her jaw tight. I couldn't quite hear what she said to the lady, but I could make out the words *danger* and *enemy*.

On the other hand, when Chiyome-*sama* stuck her head out of the window, I could clearly hear her response, a disgusted snort. "Kuniko!" she hollered at her armed maid, who was still only an arm's-length away, and pointed at the only building in the village that had a sign. "Go see if that's an inn and get them to start the water boiling. I want a bath." And with that, she snapped the screen shut.

Making a show of maintaining her dignity, Kuniko handed the reins of the pack horses to one of the Little Brothers and sauntered off toward the building.

Mieko was standing right behind me. I turned to her and whispered, "Why was Lady Chiyome so upset?"

Mieko tilted her head to one side and asked, very quietly, "What did you see on the road during our walk today?"

I frowned for a moment. "Horsemen, riding back and forth."

"How many?"

"Um." I frowned again. Toumi scowled at me from under her straw hood. "One this morning, riding to the castle? Another as we were crossing the bridge out of Pineshore... and... a bunch when we stopped?"

Mieko raised an eyebrow and turned to Emi. "How many, Emi-*chan*?"

"Nine," answered Emi.

"Very good," Mieko said. She looked back to me. "A small group of cavalry like that is called a *squadron*. Why do you think there has been so much—?"

Toumi interrupted, "'Cause there's a damn battle going on, like that soldier said!"

Mieko's posture didn't change and her smile remained, but a hardness told us very clearly that she hadn't appreciated Toumi's interruption. After a moment she said, her eyes still on me, "Precisely. Back in Pineshore, there were rumors of a battle that might be taking place near here. Some of Lord Imagawa's men had set out to attack an outpost of... of Lord Takeda's. Chiyome-*sama* wanted to get past the danger before we stopped for the night."

"She expected us to get *further* than this?" I heard Emi mutter. For once, even Toumi had nothing to say. Looking at their faces, I could see that they were as exhausted and as cold as I was.

I shivered, thinking about something quite separate from my cold-parched lips and sore legs: those soldiers at the crossroad, so many of them wounded. A battle? It suddenly occurred to me that I was safer traveling with this peculiar band than if I were off on my own.

When Kuniko came back, she informed Lady Chiyome through the screen that the house was indeed an inn, that they were pleased to be honored by the lady's patronage, and that a bath was being prepared.

As we walked slowly down the street toward the inn, I saw a few faces peering out at us from behind curtains and doors. Several of the buildings' roofs had clearly been scorched—there was a layer of fire-blackened thatch beneath bright, new straw. Two houses were nothing but black skeletons.

The sign of the inn, too, was blackened, though it was hard to tell whether by dirt and age or by flame and soot. It carried a barely visible image of a cat with a raised paw.

We entered slowly. As unimposing as the inn that we had stayed at in Pineshore may have been, *this* place looked as though a good wind could blow it down. There was a wasp nest under the eves in the entryway, but even it looked ramshackle, as if the wasps had given it up for a lost cause.

"Welcome to the Mount Fuji Inn!" a dry voice warbled cheerfully. An old woman in a tatty kimono that had been elegant when her grandmother had worn it shuffled out of the front door and into the courtyard.

"Mount Fuji?" said Chiyome-*sama* as she stepped out of the palanquin. "We're two days travel from the mountain," she sniffed.

"Ah!" said the innkeeper, offering a stiff, deep bow, "but if the weather is clear tomorrow, you will be able to make out the holy mountain in the north." She looked around, pinkened, and added, "It is a bit distant, it's true, but you can make it out. On a clear day."

She clapped her hands together. "Well, honored lady, we will be happy to serve you and your party. I will lead you to your room. My husband will see to the horses." An old man, even more threadbare and tired-looking than his wife, stumbled forward, took the reins of the pack horses and led them into the inn's lone stable. Kuniko followed him.

"Room?" Lady Chiyome asked, looking for once more amused than imperious.

"Honored lady," said the innkeeper, "there have been very few visitors of late. It is the wrong season. And all the fighting... We have just one chamber available, on the ground floor."

"Ground floor!" said Lady Chiyome. "That will do for my servants," and she indicated us all with a negligent backhanded wave, "But I prefer something on the second floor."

The old woman hissed in apology. "*Eee*, so sorry, honored lady, the upper floor to our inn is... has been..." She looked at Lady Chiyome uncertainly. "You have noticed that the town has been ravaged by fire. The Takeda nearly burned the town to the ground last month before they were driven back by Lord Imagawa's men."

Both of the carriers straightened up, and Mieko raised a thin eyebrow, asking a question of the lady without speaking it. Clearly they were worried about being so close to all of the fighting that was going on in this district; it certainly frightened me. Lady Chiyome held her hand up to silence their unvoiced concern. "We will stay," she said, firmly. "The servants will sleep in the stable, or in the dining room."

The old innkeeper bowed rustily. "Yes, honorable lady."

Kuniko, who had just come back from stabling the horses, leaned in to whisper to Lady Chiyome. She smirked and said, "My maid informs me that the stables are barely habitable for the horses. My servants will stay in the dining room."

"Yes, honorable lady."

5—The Mount Fuji Inn

There were three rooms downstairs besides the dining room and kitchen, but the two closest to the front door were both closed off. The doors were edged with black soot. Lady Chiyome had the Little Brothers carry her chest to the rear room.

Mieko and Kuniko led Toumi, Emi and me to the dining room. I was surprised that Mieko left her own bedroll there in the room with us; I had expected her to spend the night with the lady, but she stayed with us and quietly took charge of the servants' quarters.

Once we had arranged our sleeping mats on one side of the large space, we filed over to the low tables on the other side. The tables seemed to have been made of fine wood, once upon a time, and what remained of the tapestries that hung on the walls showed that they had been lovely. Now, however, they were dingy and moth-eaten.

Dinner was a greasy stew of some sort of meat and a portion of rice that seemed as if it been cooked too quickly—one half was raw and the other half burnt. Yet we all ate it—even Lady Chiyome. We were starving after our long march. As we finished up, the old couple shuffled out to take our bowls, but Lady Chiyome held up her tiny, regal hand. "My servants will clean."

For a moment I was caught thinking what a kind, surprising gesture that was, when it suddenly occurred to me that I was one of the servants that Chiyome-*sama* expected to do the work. I looked around, and noticed that Aimaru and Emi had already stood and were beginning to gather bowls and chopsticks, and that even Toumi had begun to get up and clear the table with a look of angry determination.

I took my bowl and those of the Little Brothers, who were sitting to one side of me. Balancing them carefully, I joined the other girls and Aimaru carrying them toward the kitchen. The old woman waved her hands to stop us from going in. "Eeee, there is no need..."

"It is our pleasure," said Aimaru, with a quick bow of his head, and we walked through the patched curtain into the tiny kitchen.

There we found stacks of chipped and shattered bowls on cobwebbed shelves. The fire was smoldering, fading as we watched. The remains of the wood seemed clearly to have been shards of fine old furniture, and some unburned wisps of decorated fabric remained; a scrap of tapestry had clearly been used to start the flame. They had literally used their last resource to prepare our meal: the inn itself.

Emi grabbed a bucket and went outside to draw some water from the town well.

We began to clear away the cooking implements—a battered black wok, a frayed wooden spoon, and an extremely fragile-looking rice pot. "Pathetic," Toumi grumbled.

"Did any of us come from better circumstances?" Aimaru asked placidly.

Toumi bit her lip, and then muttered, "Maybe not, but better birthright." Then she set aggressively to scraping the food scraps from our bowls in the pot.

Emi came back. "At least the water's clean," she chirped, with a cheerfulness that as usual wasn't reflected in her face.

With a snort, Toumi picked up the pot full of burnt rice and small bones, to carry it out to the offal pit. "Unlike some of you, I wasn't born to this kind of filth."

"What do you know about what the rest of us were born to?" I said. Without thinking about it, I had stepped right behind her. She whirled around, and for an eye's-blink I was convinced that she was going to attack me with the pot. My hands rose to my face.

Very deliberately, with a knife-thin smile, Toumi lifted the pot over my head and emptied the greasy contents on me. I shrieked and was about to sink my nails into Toumi's face—which was probably what she wanted me to do—when I heard Mieko's quiet, calm voice from the doorway: "Clean it up. All four of you. Now."

Toumi and I locked eyes for a moment, each waiting for the other to start first. In that moment, I was beyond caring about anything that *Otō-san* had taught us about *doing no harm*; I wanted to kill. I could see-soaked rice dripping from my bangs. It was fortunate that the innkeepers were poor, and we were hungry: there had been little left in the pot.

Slowly, we each bent to clean the mess. Emi and Aimaru helped clean away the last of the dinner. Later, I washed my head in what was left of the clean water, relieved that my new clothing had not been noticeably stained. I was sure Lady Chiyome would not have approved.

When we were done, we all went to bed. I wanted to talk to Emi, to ask her so many questions. But she was snoring before I had even climbed beneath my covers.

I had to fight to keep silent, because I was weeping. Thinking of Usako and Mother. Of *Okā-san* having sold me. Of Usako wandering around in the woods without me.

Of the fact that, even were I to slip away that night, I wasn't altogether certain that I could find my way home, or whether I would be welcome if I did.

Before I was able to even try to calm myself enough to sleep, I heard a steady step coming across the *tatami*. "Kano Murasaki." It was Kuniko, her voice low. "Come now. The lady wishes to see you."

I stumbled out of my bedroll, suddenly very aware of how sore and tired my legs were, and how sticky my hair still was.

Kuniko led me from the dark dining room where we were all sleeping in to the cramped chamber where the lady was waiting.

She was seated on a cushion, her robes draped elegantly around her. The two Little Brothers stood behind either shoulder, massive and silent, and Mieko stood in the shadows to one side. In front of her was a low table, on which stood several objects, including sheets of fine rice paper, a bowl with the smoothest, blackest ink I'd ever seen, a box with six different colors of ink sticks, each in its own compartment, and a fine, sleek, red-handled brush.

Kuniko tapped me on the shoulder. I knelt and bowed.

"Come, Risuko," said Lady Chiyome, indicating with a small, pale hand that I should sit on the other side of the table from her.

I shuffled across the floor on my knees, feeling the rough *tatami* catching on the cloth of my new pants. In the end, I reached the table, still kneeling, still looking down.

"What *have* you done with your hair, child?"

I winced, still focusing on the mat and the table legs. "There was... an accident in the kitchen."

Lady Chiyome gave a husky sigh. "I suppose when I pluck urchins from treetops in the morning, it's too much to expect them to be ladies in the evening."

One of the Little Brothers gave a grunt that might have been a chuckle.

"Look up, child." The lady was either scowling at me, or smirking. She wiggled a thin finger at the writing implements before her.

The bowl that held the ink was eggshell thin, glazed a rich, deep blue that seemed to soak in the flickering light of the small fire and the candles that lit the room. A worn black ink stone lay beside it.

"I would like to see how well your father taught you, Risuko." She cocked her head to one side, like someone who was trying to look sly. "Write something."

Still barely lifting my head, I reached out and took a sheet of the rice paper. It was so thin I could barely feel it between my fingers. As I placed it before me, I imagined I could almost see the grain of the table through the paper.

"What should I write?" I asked.

"Whatever you like," she answered, dismissively waving her hand.

I chewed on the inside of my bottom lip for a second. I couldn't think of a thing. Then I remembered sitting next to Father, copying one of his poems, trying to match his flowing brushstrokes.

I reached out to pick up the brush, but my fingers were shaking. "The ink is really good."

Her nostrils flared. "Of course." She clearly thought it was the stupidest thing she had heard me say.

I took a deep breath, trying to gain time and steady my hand. I tried to visualize the words flowing from our father's brush, the three lines of Otō-san's favorite poem. Without even realizing that I had done it, I picked up the brush, wetted it in the ink, and let the tip flow black over the ice-white paper.

Soldiers falling fast

Battle of white and scarlet

Blossoms on the ground

Again, Lady Chiyome smirked, looking down at my calligraphy. This time, however, the smirk was definitely not disgust, but what I was beginning to recognize as the lady's sour amusement.

"Very nice," she said, eyebrows arched.

It was. Father would have been proud. It wasn't as good as his, but the lines flowed cleanly, evenly and easily.

"It's one of my father's poems."

"Yes," she said, "I know."

I was about to ask how she could possibly know that, but she held up a small, thin finger. Her face was still on the surface, but looked as if it were twisting underneath. "Poetry is very nice, but anyone can learn a bag full of haiku before breakfast. Show me something longer. Show me some prose."

I took a deep breath, and I immediately thought of that passage that *Otō-san* used to have us practice night after night. Again, I took out a clean sheet and picked up the brush. This time, I was calmer. With my left hand, I held back the cuff of my right sleeve.

"Keep your tongue in your mouth, child," tisked Lady Chiyome.

I sucked my tongue in. I hadn't even noticed that I was sticking it out. I could feel my fingers begin to shake again.

I took another deep breath, carefully wetted the brush once more, and began to write.

In the reign of a certain emperor there was a certain lady of the lower ranks whom the emperor loved more than any of the others. The great, ambitious ladies gazed on her resentfully. Because of this...

My concentration was broken by an odd sound—a wheezing, rolling, rasping sound. Alarmed, I looked up.

Lady Chiyome looked furious—her white-painted face was darkening and twisted. Then she let out the sound again, fuller and deeper, and I realized that she was laughing. Tears began to stream from her eyes and she was weeping, screaming, howling with laughter.

I knelt there, ink drying on my brush, afraid to move. I had no idea why she was laughing, and was afraid that anything I might do could turn her frightening good humor to anger.

She reached a hand out to Mieko, and from the look on the maid's face I realized that she was as shocked as I was. Mieko's perfect black eyebrows were arched so high they looked as if they might snap.

Lady Chiyome took a silk handkerchief from Mieko's sleeve, and began to wipe her eyes. I noticed that even the two bodyguards seemed astonished.

"Well, Mieko," the lady said to her maid, "there you are. I look up at the top of the most forsaken pine tree in forsaken Serenity Province, and I find the last great enthusiast of *The Tales of Genji*." She gave another rumbling laugh, and Mieko smiled, at least in sympathy if not in understanding. The old woman turned her streaked face to me again. "So, my little romance novelist. Your father did indeed teach you well." She blew her nose loudly.

"Here, Kuniko." She handed the wet silk rag to the other maid, whose face was a mask, and then turned back to me. "Now let me see how you can read."

Smoothly and so quickly that I didn't even see it happening, she plucked the brush from my hand. Holding it like a knife between her middle finger and thumb, she picked up fresh ink and poised to write on yet another sheet of beautiful, clean rice paper. She looked up, catching me with her gaze, as if to say, *Are you watching carefully?*

Like me, she pulled her sleeve back, but where my action had been a simple grab to keep my sleeve from trawling through the ink, hers was precise and elegant, like the motion of a dancer.

Her hand barely moved, but the brush slashed a character onto the paper—the phonetic *hiragana*, *ku* (く). Then came a sinuous curve—the phonetic *katakana*, *no* (ノ). Finally, another, horizontal slash—the Chinese *kanji* ideogram *ichi* (一).

She placed the brush down with the same deadly elegance, and looked up at me again. "Well?" she asked, indicating what she had written.

I was perplexed. I understood all of the pieces, but they made no sense. *Otō-san* said you weren't ever supposed to write katakana, hiragana and kanji in a single word. I turned my head, thinking perhaps that if I looked at it upside down I might understand it.

"Well," I said, "the first mark is *ku*, which means *nine*. And then there's *no*, which is... *of?* Or *on,* or sometimes *from*. And then that line looks like the kanji character meaning *one*." Then I sat back a bit, and the word came into focus, like an offshore island appearing through clearing fog. "But the whole thing... If you put the three strokes together it could be the *kanji* character for woman (女)."

Lady Chiyome smiled again, the frightening smile. "Yes, my squirrel, yes. A *kunoichi* is a very special kind of woman indeed." She looked to her two maids, and then back at me. "Perhaps, if you are fortunate, you will be such a woman yourself some day."

I stared at her.

"I have one last question for you, child."

"Yes, my lady?"

She picked up the brush and swirled it in a small bowl of water to clean it. Taking out yet another sheet of paper she said, "This morning, you told me that you could see the paper that Lord Imagawa and his commander were looking at."

I nodded.

She fixed me with a skeptical stare. "To have seen it from that distance, you'd have had to be a falcon, not a squirrel."

"But... I saw it, my lady."

"Hmmph. So you say. Do you think you could reproduce what you saw?"

Now it was my turn to frown once more. In my mind's eye the image was clear—the large blocks of green, with the smaller blocks of red and blue surrounding them. Lines like arrows sticking out of them. I nodded again.

She pushed the box of colored inks toward me and held out the brush once more. "Keep your tongue in, this time."

I sucked my tongue in. "Yes, Chiyome-*sama*." Then I reproduced the drawing I had seen as best I could.

When I looked up, Lady Chiyome's eyes were wide. "Are you sure this is what you saw?"

"Yes, my lady."

She grunted and turned to Kuniko. "We'll need to get out of here as quickly as possible tomorrow, Kuniko." Then she waved a hand at me. "Go to bed, girl. We will be traveling again in the morning." She favored me with a grin in which there was very little of lightness. "Pleasant dreams, Risuko."

My dreams that night were anything but.

6—Tea and Cakes

A rumble woke us all the next morning. It sounded like a peal of distant thunder. But Mieko and Kuniko were already on their feet before I could sit up and wipe the sleep from my eyes.

"What is it?" I asked Emi, who was rubbing her eyes next to me. "It's awfully cold for thunder and lightening, isn't it? And it doesn't feel like an earthquake...."

Emi shook her head and scowled. We both listened carefully as we pulled on our clothes—mine still slightly damp from the night before, smelling faintly of stale *shoyu* and burnt rice.

Another low rumble shook the morning silence. From where I had been sleeping near the kitchen, I could see a grey, thin light leaking beneath the outer kitchen door.

We began to fold away our bedding with a sense of uncertain urgency. I was about to ask again what that rumble might have been, when a new sound broke the silence and explained everything. It was a sharp, high crack. Musket fire. And not very far away, from the sound of it.

My legs went cold and I dropped my bedroll.

The battle had come to us.

Kuniko appeared at the front door, her face as stony as ever. To the younger Little Brother, she barked, "Go guard the rear gate." To the older one, she said, "Come with me to guard the lady." Then she and Mieko exchanged a look. It said: the lady's maid and the four children would have to fend for ourselves.

I caught Emi's eye, and I could see she shared the dry panic that was squeezing the breath out of me. Even Toumi looked pale and shaken.

There were several more gunshots, and the deep rumble sounded again—cannon fire.

Mieko turned to us, standing there in her thin robe as if she were waiting to sit for a portrait and not waiting for a battle. "Aimaru," she said, a hoarseness to her voice the only sign that she was nervous, "Aimaru, you take these young ladies to the kitchen. I will guard this door. You should be safe enough in there."

We all began to stumble toward the kitchen doorway.

"Aimaru!" Mieko called, her voice betraying more emotion than I had ever yet heard, "they are your responsibility, do you understand?"

He snapped a stiff, almost soldier-like bow, and led us into the kitchen.

There was another rumbling sound in the distance, longer and higher than the cannon's thunder. Horses were galloping in our direction.

Aimaru grabbed a curved chef's knife from the shelf next to the pots we had cleaned the night before. Its edge was nicked and scarred, but its point still looked lethal. He gave it a practice slash or two, and then looked up at the three of us. I realized that he was as terrified as we were. "There's a small pantry there. Can you three fit in it?"

I started to object, but he cut me off with uncharacteristic impatience. "Have you been trained to fight?" We all stood, silent. "Can you face a grown soldier?" Our shoulders sagged. He opened the door and pushed us in.

"Does he know how to fight?" Toumi muttered. Her shoulder pressed against my nose. I couldn't breathe.

The pantry was tiny. The shelves were bare except for a few cobwebs that fluttered as we squirmed to stay quiet.

Emi grunted and turned her head to try to get it away from Toumi's hair. "I was there when Lady Chiyome picked him up on Mount Hiei, rock-head. He was training to be a warrior-monk."

Toumi looked as though she might bite Emi, but a loud yell from the front of the inn snapped her to attention. "Who was that?"

There was an answering shout—"Get away from here!"—from a voice that I thought I recognized as Kuniko's.

"I think that's coming from the front gate," I whispered. I could hear our horses braying loudly. Then there was an explosion of noise: the shouting of many more voices, the sharp ring of steel meeting steel, and a wrenching snap that made the whole rickety inn tremble.

I heard the Little Brother outside the back door yell, "Come here, come here! It is a good day to die!" Several angry voices answered his.

There was no escape from the inn.

Now I was panicked—furious—at being trapped in the airless closet. *If I could only climb to the roof,* I thought, *I might jump to the next building...* Desperate to find some way out, I looked up.

Above, a crescent-moon sliver of light shone through the thatch roof. Before I had even considered, I had used Toumi's shoulder to push me up onto the flimsy shelves.

"Hey!" barked Toumi.

"Murasaki," Emi hissed, "come back down!"

"I just want to see," I whispered back, feeling a twinge of guilt at leaving them behind. "I'll be right back."

I could feel the brisk morning air blowing in through the sliver of space between the wall and the singed thatch, could smell the smoke of a thousand meals that had been cooked in the kitchen below. I pushed up, widening the opening by pressing between the straw and the wall.

As I squeezed up into the smoke hole, I heard Aimaru gasp below. "What are you doing?"

"Uh, just taking a look."

"Get down!"

"I will, I..." I didn't want to abandon him or Emi—it didn't seem fair. But I couldn't just sit there, locked up. I wriggled against the wall, pushing up into the smoke hole.

Looking up, all that I could see was the charred roof that covered the chimney, keeping rain out. Like all else in the inn, the cover had a moth-eaten look. The supports were charred and spindly, and it looked as if a stiff breeze might have blown it away like the ash from the previous night's fire.

But the sky beyond was blue—the bright, silver-blue of early morning— and I could just smell the distant tang of the sea through the thick odor of stale smoke. As I pushed up through the chimney, I was so feverish with relief at my soon-to-be-certain escape that I almost missed another scent, one that made the hair on my forearms stand up.

Gunpowder. Close by.

As soon as I raised my head through the smoke hole in the thatch, a thunder-storm of sounds burst over my ears. Gun shots. The *ping* of steel on steel. Screams.

As I peered around, looking for a nearby roof that I could escape to, I could see knots of dust, with occasional silver flashes. I tried to see any of our party, but the chimney was on the far side of the roof from the inn yard. I could hear the younger of the Little Brothers howling like an angry bear, but I could not see him; he must have been just out of sight, hidden by the edge of the roof. *Which way to go?* I wondered.

A puff of hay suddenly flew into my face. I couldn't imagine why—it wasn't windy, and so there was no reason for the roof to be blowing apart, ramshackle as it was.

I turned toward where the thatch had come from and saw a bright flash of red from the dust-filled street.

I did not hear the gunshot until the bullet had splintered the smoke-lathed support a hand's width from my ear. The support gave way, and the roof above me squealed as it began to lean and fall.

As I scampered back down into the pantry with a squeak, I could see relief and concern on Aimaru's round face.

"Well?" snapped Toumi.

"I... couldn't see anything," I murmured as I stood once again between them, trying not to tremble.

There was noise now in the corridor of the inn. The older Little Brother must have been fighting like a demon to protect Chiyome-*sama*.

I thought with terror of poor Mieko, standing frail and alone out in the dining room. Why hadn't she come back into the kitchen with us, or gone off with Kuniko? *She made a dreadful sacrifice for us,* I thought, *and made it with the quiet dignity of a samurai woman, just as our father had always hoped that my sister and I would conduct ourselves.* I was ready to call out to Mieko, to tell her to come in and hide with us, when I heard, through the clamor, two men entering the dining room.

Through the thin wall behind me, I heard one say, "Hey, Juro, look what we've found!"

"The pretty lady from the group at the crossroads, yesterday. Hey, pretty lady. Give a soldier a kiss?" I thought I recognized the voice of the samurai who had stopped us the previous evening.

I heard Mieko say, with that same polite tone that she seemed to use no matter what the occasion, "Please, gentlemen, go elsewhere. I do not wish to harm you."

*I do not wish to **harm** you?*

The two soldiers laughed grimly and we could hear the sound of tables being knocked aside. One thumped into the wall against which my back was pressed. I could feel Toumi, Emi and myself all try to take a sympathetic gasp of terror for Mieko, but the space was too confined—we simply pressed up against each other even more tightly.

From the dining hall, we heard the sound of a high shriek, and then what sounded like a sigh. There were two thuds, and then the room beyond the wall was silent.

Battle raged elsewhere. Grunts, shouts, the clang of metal—it was too much sound to give me a picture of what was going on outside.

Then a new sound drowned out all the others. It roared like a huge wave breaking on the shore, but instead of crashing and retreating, it kept thundering toward us from the same direction that the cannon fire had come from.

It was the sound of hundreds of galloping horses.

Otō-san told me once—only once—about witnessing the charge of the Takeda cavalry at Midriver Island. He said the thunder of their hooves was both the most beautiful and most terrifying thing he had ever witnessed— except for the births of my sister and me.

The sounds of fighting around us gave way to panicked shouts and the sounds of running feet.

There was more shouting, and then the roar of the horses' hooves came to a halt.

There was quiet for a few long moments, and then Emi gasped when the latch on the closet was raised. The door was flung open, and bright light blinded us. We all three—Emi, Toumi and myself—stiffened, ready to run, to fight for our lives if need be.

Aimaru stood in the door, his face as tense as ours must have been. "Good morning," he said.

From the back door, the Little Brother entered, looking much less good-humored than he usually did. His bald head had a large bleeding gash on it. "*Ssh!*" he ordered. "We don't know who those horsemen were." He looked at all of us. "Where is Mieko-*san?*"

Each of us gave a gasp—in our relief, we had forgotten what had happened to poor Mieko. We burst through the doorway back into the dining area to see if we could help her.

Mieko knelt, her hair loose around her lovely, sad face. She was wiping a long, thin blade with a rust-brown kerchief. Before her lay two soldiers whose armor bore the emblem of Lord Imagawa. The smaller was indeed the samurai who had ordered us up the side road the day before. Both were lifeless, their faces frozen in shock.

Her knife clean, Mieko slipped the blade into a small, flat sheath. With her left hand, she gathered her hair into a bun at the back of her head and then with her right slid the covered blade in so that it neatly held her tresses in place.

She did all of this with the modesty and ritual decorum of a shrine maiden preparing tea and cakes for the gods.

7—Wind

Mieko stood calmly and bowed to us.

From a small curtain at the end of the hall opposite the kitchen, we heard a whimper. Aimaru sprinted toward it, his battered knife still in his hand. With a yell, he yanked down the curtain, and revealed the old innkeepers, huddled on the floor of their small room.

After a moment of shocked silence, Aimaru bowed to them. "Pardon me for intruding," he said, as if he had merely turned in at the wrong door.

The old couple seemed barely to recognize that he was there.

We all stumbled out of the dining hall into the corridor. Two more Imagawa soldiers lay dead there, and the elder Little Brother was standing impassive above them. Emi and I started to run toward the front door to see who our rescuers might have been, but Lady Chiyome called out sharply, "Stay here, young idiots! We don't know who those horsemen are!"

Shamed, we shrunk back toward the back of the corridor, stopping just shy of the dead soldiers who had been piled at the bottom of the staircase.

The two Little Brothers lumbered up toward the front of the hall, blades at the ready. The door was hanging from a single hinge, and a shard of sunlight thrust against the corridor wall. The younger Little Brother, his head still bleeding, crept up to the door and peeked through.

"It's all right!" he shouted, "It's the Takeda cavalry."

I gasped at that: that our saviors should be the force that had been the nightmare of my father's warrior career, and the enemy of his second patron, once he became a scribe. *What have I gotten into?* I wondered.

With Lady Chiyome herding us from behind, we all began to make our way toward the exit. I was more than a little terrified. Father had said that the Takeda cavalry were the wind, a mighty tempest that swept away everything in its path. Toumi pushed at my back, or I would have been frozen to the spot.

When we were all in place, the elder Little Brother reached out to open the door, but before he could, the remaining hinge pulled out of the wall with a squeal, and the door slammed to the floor.

I let out a yelp, but then pulled my mouth shut, so that the teeth clicked.

A cold, nightmarish scene met us in the warm light of the new morning. In front of the stable, three Imagawa soldiers lay motionless on the ground in their own gore. In their midst lay the still form of Kuniko, her blood-streaked glaive still clutched in one hand. A sword was planted in her chest. Mieko and the two Little Brothers ran to her.

Lady Chiyome gave a low, growling curse.

At the entrance to the inn's yard, four cavalrymen sat gleaming on their black stallions. Each had a red flag on his back bearing a four-diamond insignia. The Takeda.

The foremost of the samurai, whose helmet was decorated with antlers, leapt from his horse and strode fiercely toward us.

Aimaru lifted his battered blade, but Chiyome-*sama* shouted again, "Put that down, boy. You'll get hurt."

The Takeda samurai knelt directly in front of Lady Chiyome and bowed deeply. "Chiyome-*sama*," he said, his voice respectfully low, "it is an honor to see you again. We were sent to find you. I didn't expect it to be so easy."

The old woman looked amused at his show of respect. "Easy indeed, Lieutenant Masugu. I had been told the Takeda army would be leaving Serenity Province to Lord Matsudaira's troops." She arched an eyebrow. "Who are, I believe, attacking from the other side of the province."

The samurai removed his helmet, revealing a sweat-stained cap and a sharp, wry face. He looked around at all of us. "The Imagawa seem finally to have realized that they were stuck between a pair of jaws, and they've started wriggling quite a bit." He gestured to the dead men on the ground. "They attacked our camp last night. When we scattered their charge, they ran back here, more interested in looting their own villages than defending their province."

Lady Chiyome looked down at the corpses with a look of utter contempt. "Ruffians," she said, and her tone made it clear that this was the lowest term she could have used.

Then she glanced over toward the stable door. Mieko sat, still cradling stony-faced Kuniko's head in her lap; she was not crying, but her face was blank with grief. The larger of the Younger Brothers shook his head, and Lady Chiyome gave something halfway between a grunt and a sigh.

Staring at the tableau, Lieutenant Masugu's mouth opened and closed. "Poor... I'm sorry." He turned back to Chiyome. "She... died well."

"She did."

What had Kuniko been doing out there? What had she been doing arming herself with the long glaive? Fighting well, clearly. Dying well.

Masugu gave an embarrassed wince and looked around at all of us. His eyes lit on Aimaru, Emi, Toumi and me standing there, still dressed for bed. "What are these?" he asked, a look of curiosity sharpening his frank gaze. "New shrine maidens?"

"Of course, Masugu," said Chiyome-*sama*. "The gods must be honored even in such times as these."

I blinked. *Shrine maidens?*

Chiyome-*sama* got a sly look on her face. "Lieutenant Masugu, let me introduce three young samurai maidens: Tarugu Toumi, Hanichi Emi, and Kano Murasaki." A little confused to hear my rank and formal name, I bowed politely, if stiffly. I could see the others do the same to my left.

"Kano...?" Masugu looked at us as if he were trying to think where he'd met us before. Then his brows sprang up, and he gave a sharp whistle of surprise. "Quite a pack!" he said. Then he jerked his thumb toward Aimaru. "Who's he? Go-Daigo's heir, come to life again?"

Lady Chiyome gave her thin smile. "No, he's just a spare." She glanced over toward where Mieko continued to rock Kuniko's head in her lap, while the two Little Brothers stood, looking impassive as statues. "Much needed spare, it seems," she sighed.

The Takeda samurai rubbed the top of his head through the cap, and looked around at us. "Chiyome-*sama*," he said, "we've come from the Mountain to bring you and your, um, cargo back to the Full Moon. Would you do us the honor of allowing us to escort you out of the battle zone?"

Lady Chiyome peered around at the scene, her acid gaze washing over the inn, now even more sad than it had been the day before, and our company, none of us even dressed for the day yet. "We will leave as soon as I am changed and packed," she proclaimed. Then she strode back toward the inn and her room. Mieko fell in silently behind her, and we all prepared to leave.

———

As quickly as our hands and feet could manage it, we were back in the courtyard. Lieutenant Masugu's troops now flooded out the inn-yard gate, an ocean of them, all on sleek black stallions, all with red Takeda flags on their backs. The horses' steaming breath was a glowing fog in the now-bright morning light.

The Imagawa corpses were all piled to one side of the courtyard.

In front of them, on a rough wooden platform, Kuniko's body lay wrapped in a dirty white shroud.

It felt odd. I had barely met the woman, had only known her for a day. I hadn't liked her very much. And yet I mourned her death far more than those of the pile of dead soldiers.

Lady Chiyome stood before the old couple that owned the inn. She handed the woman a small, heavy bag. "Let the proper rites be said for my woman." Then she looked to the broken door and sniffed. "And use what is left—what is *left*, mind you—to clean this place up."

The old couple muttered their thanks and promises, and touched their grey heads to the dirt.

Then Lady Chiyome turned and slid into her waiting palanquin. Next to me, Lieutenant Masugu extended his hand toward Mieko, offering to let her ride with him. But she stepped by without acknowledging his gesture. After the briefest expression of shock flickered across his face, Masugu turned and extended his hand toward me.

8—The Mountain

For three days, we rode quickly, without speaking until the mirror of the sun passed behind the mountains. On the first two days, we passed large groups of soldiers bearing the Takeda four-diamond banner marching toward the battles we had just left behind. By the third day, we might as well have been the only people in all of Worth Province —in all of Japan. We passed no one. Even the villages seemed empty.

Every night, the soldiers would make camp—in dry rice paddies or on the edges of fields. They would start preparing a simple meal, which Emi, Toumi, Aimaru and I would help clean up. The men would start talking to each other, and to the Little Brothers, occasionally. They would speak respectfully to Lady Chiyome occasionally, and even tease Aimaru and us three girls a bit.

None of them ever spoke to Mieko-*san*, though the lieutenant seemed always to know where she was.

Riding a horse turned out to be much more exhausting work than I would have expected, even if one was, as I was, merely a passenger.

I found to my surprise and dismay that I, who could climb the tallest tree or building without fear, felt profoundly unsteady on horseback. Every day, Masugu-*san* would very gently help me up onto his stallion, and each morning I had to work not to tear the poor creature's mane out in my terror. It felt to me as if I were sitting on the back of nothing less than an earthquake at rest.

The only consolation that I had was that Toumi seemed to hate it even more than I did.

At the end of the third long day, Masugu helped me down off of his horse, and I thanked him, embarrassed not to be able to manage it on my own. He smiled at me and shrugged.

Lady Chiyome was climbing out of her palanquin, muttering and grumbling as she always did. Steam rose from the Little Brothers, who didn't grumble at all.

The soldiers set up camp in the long-drained rice fields beside a lazy river.

As I had every evening, I looked south, seeing nothing homeward but mist.

For the first time, I turned to the north. The distant sight of a high peak struck me—a perfect, snow-capped cone, like the sand mountains that Usako and I had made when our mother brought us to the beach. Like the endless sketches our father had drawn on scraps of used paper or in the dust.

Mount Fuji.

"The Mountain," I whispered in awe.

"Yes," said Masugu from behind me. It was the first time he had spoken to me about something other than to tell me how to sit steady or when to get down since that horrible morning. We stood for a time, watching the sunlight disappear from the peak. "Do you know what our battle flag means—the four diamonds of Takeda?" Masugu asked.

I shook my head, still staring at the mountain, its white peak turning pink.

"It's the clan motto: Be swift as the wind, silent as the forest, fierce as fire, steady as a mountain. My lancers and the other companies like us are the wind, sweeping all enemies ahead of us. The infantry are the forest, impenetrable and overwhelming. And the heavy cavalry are the fire, consuming any obstacles an enemy might try to put in our way." He told it as if it were a bedtime story.

"And the mountain?" I asked.

"The mountain is Takeda Shingen himself. Like Fuji-*san*—" Masugu pointed at the peak. "—he is unmovable, untoppable. He has nerves stronger than any sword, and a mind as sharp. He can out-think any general." His voice was surprisingly soft, gentle.

As we watched the light fade from the distant mountaintop, I found myself thinking how strange it was that I had spent days riding in front of this stranger, this Takeda warrior, unable to see any part of him but his gauntleted hands, neither one of us speaking. And yet I found that I hoped for the first time that I would ride with him again the next day.

———

That night, we ate sitting around a campfire, watching the sparks float up to join the stars. The meal was mostly rice and pickled radish, but in that moment it tasted as good as any food I had ever had.

Masugu spent a long time speaking to Lady Chiyome, both of them very serious. Mieko seemed to be listening intently to them, but when Masugu glanced up at her, she looked away.

"Mieko-*san*?" I asked when a soldier who was carrying wood to the fire crossed to the other side of the circle before putting his logs down.

"Hmm?" She stared up into the night sky.

"Mieko-*san*, why don't the soldiers talk to you?" Then I considered. "Is it because of Kun—?"

Her finger sealed my lips gently but without compromise. "Do not use her name."

"Oh. Of course not." Mother had taught us that one should not use the name of the dead for forty-nine days after their departure, so that you don't call their spirit back from the journey to the next life. "I am sorry, Mieko-*san*."

Mieko gave me a sad smile. "No apology is needed, Risuko." She stroked my cheek gently, which made me feel the night's cold for some reason. "And Lieutenant Masugu's soldiers have been avoiding speaking to me since long before this ride." Saying no more, she rose and walked to Lady Chiyome's tent.

As she disappeared into the shadows, Emi took her place. "I can't decide if she is really nice, or kind of scary."

"Both," I sighed, and Emi nodded. We both turned away from the dark and warmed ourselves in the fire's light.

As the night closed in around us, we huddled closer together.

———

It rained as we climbed out of Worth Province, and I spent the next days with a rough blanket wrapped over my head to keep dry. At inns and villages, the people treated our party with great respect. I thought back to the way that the people in our village used to tease Lord Imagawa's soldiers. Clearly, in Lord Takeda's domain, his servants were treated with more deference—and fear.

As the days passed, my own awe began to lessen, and I began to talk with Lieutenant Masugu as we rode. We discussed the countryside, we discussed some of the books and poems *Otō-san* had made me try to read. I sang some of my mother's favorite songs. He told me stories about his cousins, and sailing boats, and chasing his father's horse when he was a boy. Often we would simply ride in a damp, thoughtful silence.

One misty morning after we had just begun riding, as we were still on the outskirts of the village we had stayed in, and the weather had trapped the smell of wet smoke close to the ground, curiosity overcame my awe. "Masugu-*san*?"

He grunted in response.

"What is this... Full Moon?" I felt sure that we could not actually be traveling to the moon—though it felt as if we had been climbing enough mountains to lead us to the heavens. "The school?"

"You don't know?"

"No." I was sorry now to have said anything.

"Oh" He was silent for a bit. I could hear him scratch his chin. "Yes. Chiyome-*sama*'s school for *miko*. That's where you're going." He cleared his throat. "I am so sorry. I assumed you knew."

I shook my head.

"Ah!" Masugu said, and cleared his throat again. "Yes. We are taking you to the school at the Full Moon. It is the great mission of Lady Chiyome's life since her husband died. There you will be trained to be a shrine attendant... and you will learn a few other skills, as well."

I absorbed this. "But why did she have to wander over half the country, through all the fighting and robbers and such, just to find girls to be *miko*? Aren't there enough unmarried girls near her home?"

"I guess not," Masugu mumbled.

A *miko*?

The Full Moon... Of course: Chiyome-*sama*'s symbol, which I bore like everyone else in her party.

I was silent for some time, but my mind was racing, reliving the conversations I'd had with Lady Chiyome and her servants. Had it been my imagination that I had been purchased away from my family for some purpose much more important than merely to be attendant at some local shrine? All this—sneaking about, taking me away from my home, marching across battle zones and snowy desolation—was so that I (and Emi and Toumi) could be trained to wear red and white robes, to learn sing and dance at weddings and festivals, and to serve tea and rice wine to the old forest gods?

That night I asked Emi and Aimaru about it. They were surprised, not by the news but by my reaction—like the lieutenant, they had assumed that I already knew.

A *miko*? It seemed... odd. But if that was what she had purchased me for, well, it wasn't the worst thing I could have been forced to do.

9—Worth

Up and up we rode, around a beautiful lake, and toward the mountain peaks.

A warbler sang from one of the trees and I whistled back. It was a funny time of year for the bird to be here.

"You do bird sounds?" Masugu asked.

I nodded.

"Can you do a loon?" We'd heard one that morning on the lake.

I grinned. That was one of my favorites. I raised my fingers to my hands and gave the loon's long, sad call.

"Well done!" Masugu laughed. "And how about... a nightingale?"

I turned around to look at him for a moment.

He laughed again. "Fine, fine, I was kidding." He stared down at me. "How about an owl. Can you hoot three times like an owl?"

"You're kidding again, right? That one's *easy.*" To prove my point, I raised my hands to my mouth again and gave three long hoots: one as a wood owl, one as a snowy owl and one as a Scops owl.

He whistled—not a bird sound for him, just a single note to let me know he was impressed. "Well, Murasaki-*san*, if you ever decide to give up being a—um—shrine maiden, you've got a future in the Takeda scouts." When I gawked him he said, "Well, that's one of the ways the scouts communicate. There's a whole bunch of codes. The loon call means *All clear.* But the three owl hoots mean *Danger—there's about to be an attack!*"

"Really?"

"Well," he said, "think about it. We're usually fighting in daylight. How often do you hear an owl hooting like that during the day?"

I nodded. It made sense to use that as a warning signal.

"Mind," chuckled Masugu, "I don't know what it would mean if the call were given by three *different* owls."

We both laughed and rode on into the mountains, the rest of the party trailing behind us.

As we climbed the winding, narrow road up toward the pass, the air grew steadily colder, and the bare-limbed trees grew sparser and shorter. I didn't notice, however. With Masugu's bulk blocking the chill wind, and the stallion warming me, I was chattering on about how scary I had thought he was when I first saw him ride into the inn yard. "Of course," I said, "samurai are always sort of scary. That's why I'm glad my father stopped being one, because I wouldn't have wanted him to be scary."

After a moment of silence, Masugu leaned close to my ear, "Murasaki-*san*, do you know... why you father 'stopped being a samurai'?"

We were crossing a stream and I remember the slosh of hooves in water as I paused to answer. I knew what my father had told us: that he hadn't wanted to kill any more. But I shook my head.

The lieutenant gave a deep sigh. "I am not sure that I am the one to tell you this," he said, "but you should know. Your father was one of Lord Oda's warriors. One of his greatest. When I was a boy, I saw him fight. Kano Kazuo was famous for his skill with a sword, as well as for being a great poet and courtier. Oda Nabunaga ordered him on a mission—what it was, no one but Lord Oda knows, though it must have had something to do with the Imagawa—but he refused. The two samurai who were supposed to go with your father refused as well. So Lord Oda gave the three of them the choice: they could commit ritual suicide, or they could present themselves to Lord Imagawa as common servants. The other two warriors killed themselves rather than face such dishonor; your father became a poor scribe."

I was stunned. And yet it seemed oddly familiar and true. Mother never told me what happened to him, that day when he walked off to answer Lord Imagawa's summons. She never told me about any of it. To be honest, she hardly ever spoke of Father, unless she was sad or angry, and so Usako and I had learned never to mention him. Before Masugu had spoken it, I hadn't heard my father's name in two years. I had known that *Otō-san* was a samurai, known that he had seen battles, but the thought of him drawing his swords to fight, to kill... And the thought of what kind of mission could possibly have forced him to refuse...

"The other two," I asked, trying not to let my voice dissolve entirely, "the ones who killed themselves, who were they?"

"Yes," grunted Masugu-*san*, acknowledging that I had asked the proper question. "Hanichi Benjiro and Tarugu Makoto," he said gruffly. "Emi and Toumi's fathers."

I peered around Masugu to where the others were riding. Emi was, naturally, frowning. Toumi looked like a knife looking for a place to plant itself.

10—Dark Letter

We spent the night at a small Takeda fort guarding a rocky, barren place called, for some reason, Rice-Paddy Pass, which marked the border between Worth and Dark Letter Provinces. We were so high that there weren't any trees. I felt naked. The air was dry and cold, we were exhausted, and the soldiers manning the garrison were edgy, as if waiting for an attack, though how—or why—an army would march so far and high I couldn't imagine. Perhaps they were frightened of ogres.

The next morning, everybody—even Mieko—looked as grumpy as I felt.

Lady Chiyome shouted to rouse us. "Let's go! I want to be back at the Full Moon by mid-day so that I can take a real bath and eat real food."

As it turned out, the Full Moon was down in the valley below Rice-Paddy Pass. We began to descend, and for the first time in days I grasped the mane of Inazuma, Masugu's stallion.

"Easy," murmured Masugu—I think more for the horse's sake than mine. To me, he said, "I thought you liked heights?"

"Do," I answered through clenched teeth. It felt as if a stumble would be all that it would take to send the horse falling down into the valley, and us with it.

"Ah. Perhaps being on horseback makes it harder?"

I nodded, ashamed. Here, Masugu-*san* thought of me as a great samurai's daughter; how could I behave so disgracefully?

"No problem, Murasaki-*san*," he said, his kind voice cutting deeper than Toumi's sneering might have done. "We're going to be travelling pretty slowly. Do you think it would help if you were on foot?"

I nodded again, a bit less tremulously.

Masugu called out a halt, there at what felt like the roof of the world.

From the back of the line I heard Chiyome-*sama* bark, "What's the hold up? I'm sick of being squashed in this box like a ten-month pregnancy!"

"Murasaki-*san* has expressed the desire to travel on foot for a while, and I thought a few of the other passengers might enjoy the lovely walk."

As I slid back off of the horse onto the narrow mountain road just one other person took the opportunity to get back on solid ground with me: Toumi, who hated every moment of being on horseback.

She and I looked at each other, each unhappy with the other's company, but with no option. From above us, Mieko asked, "Would you like me to join you, Toumi, Risuko?"

We both shook our heads.

She peered at us, then nodded. "Please stay together. And please don't get separated from the rest of us."

"Yes, Mieko-*san*," Toumi and I said together.

As the horses began once more to walk, Toumi spat on the ground, then walked as quickly away from me as she could.

"Hey!" I called to her. "We're supposed to stay together!"

———

As we began to descend into the valley, Toumi and I played what, under better circumstances, would have been a game of something like Tag, in and around the horses. I was annoyed; it wasn't as if I wanted to be near her either, but Mieko-*san* had said...

After a while, I chased Toumi just for the pleasure of annoying her.

The road was making a long series of switchbacks down the steep mountainside. It meant that we had to walk quite a distance just to get a little further down the hill. We could see the road beneath us, winding back and forth, and I will admit, as lovely as the view was, the walk was getting a bit tedious.

At least we were back among the trees.

Just as the sun began to come up over the mountain behind us, Toumi stopped, staring down.

"What are you looking at?"

The Little Brothers rumbled by us; we were now the last in line.

"Why go back and forth?" Toumi muttered.

"Huh?"

She looked up at me as if she had forgotten I was there. "Going back and forth, it's stupid."

"The horses can't go straight down the hill."

"Well, I'm not a damned horse," Toumi snarled. "I'm just going to go straight down and meet up with the rest of them at the next switchback down." She started to step off the road.

"We're not supposed to!"

She turned around, one foot in the mulchy soil of the slope, the other still on the road. She grinned at me. "Scared?"

"No, but...!"

Not waiting any more, Toumi walked down off the road and into the bank of thick juniper.

"Come back!" I looked down at her, then the retreating backs of our party. *Well*, I thought, *Mieko* said *to stay together*. And so I plunged down the hill after Toumi.

In retrospect, what I *should* have done was to go and alert Mieko, Masugu, or the Little Brothers. But I didn't want to look like a coward or a telltale, and of course, the prospect of getting to climb won me over, even if it were just climbing down a rocky, scrub-clogged hillside.

I went barreling down after Toumi, sure that I would catch up with her before she reached the trees. But Toumi had longer legs than I, and she had been raised on the streets of the capital city, so that she could move very quickly.

The juniper there were much bigger than any I'd seen near home, easily three times a man's height, but they were still juniper, thick and tangled. As soon as we entered the trees, I lost sight of Toumi. I had to listen for the sound of her feet slipping down the slope, of breaking branches, and of her occasional swearing. "Hold up!" I called. "Wait for me! We'll get lost!"

"How can we get lost, *Mouse?* Just go downhill, or are you too frightened even to do that?"

That got me seeing red. *Scared?* I'd show her. I decided that from that point it was a race to the bottom—and I was going to win.

I could barely hear Toumi rustling through the trees over my own heavy breathing, but I knew that I was gaining on her, more comfortable in the grove's close quarters. I angled toward what looked like a clearing, hoping to get past her without her knowing. In my mind, I imagined sitting on the road, cleaning my nails as she stumbled out onto the switchback.

Caught up in my own exhilaration and my rage, I burst out into the clearing without looking at what I was running into—another mistake.

The clearing had been created by the fall of a large cedar. At one end, another cedar grew up from the old tree's rotted trunk, smaller than its parent but much taller than the tangled juniper that surrounded it. In its lower branches stood a man in a brown cloak peering down toward where the road was. At the cedar's base stood two other men, also in brown, with bows. Alerted by my noisy arrival, they were both staring at me. One of them raised his bow to shoot at me, and I tried to turn back up the hill, only to slip on the mulch of the fallen tree and tumble right at his feet.

At the same moment, a loud shout above me announced that Toumi had fallen into the clearing as well. With a thud and a grunt, she too fell to the ground, just where the other man could step over, grab her by the neck of her jacket, pull her up, and shove her against the cedar.

Trying to reach my feet, I stumbled against the man above me, sending his arrow flitting off harmlessly into the trees. Without a sound, the man clamped his hand over my mouth and pushed me against the rough bark of the cedar. I heard the hiss of a blade being drawn and screamed into the man's hand.

"Don't kill 'em yet," came a loud whisper from the man above. *"Even if we can't get anything off of this bunch, we can still sell these two."*

"You sure, boss?" The man's face was masked with a strip of cloth, so that I could only see his eyes squinting at me. "This one's awful scrawny."

"Shut up," hissed the man above. "They're probably reaching the switch-back soon. I need to get down to the look-out. Tie these two up. Gag 'em. Me and Sanjiro are going down by the road to signal the others. Shirogawa, you guard these runts and get the horses ready." With that, he leapt from the branch he was standing on down into the juniper behind us.

I heard a smack and a grunt, and felt a weight slam against my shoulder.

The man raised his knife, and I screamed again into his hand, but he was lifting it to Toumi's throat. She started to snarl at him, but stopped suddenly with a gulp as the blade bit into her flesh. "'Tie 'em up,' the man says," he muttered, followed by a string of words that I had never heard, not even after nearly seven days of traveling with soldiers. He leaned his body heavily against me, so that I couldn't move—I could barely breathe—yanked the cloth mask from his face, balled it up and shoved it in my mouth. Pushing back his leather helmet, he pulled off the greasy cap beneath and did the same to Toumi. When she tried to fight, he growled, "I'd be just as happy to kill you both, girl. We ain't here for no slaves. But if Tanaka says to keep you, I'll keep you. Now shut up and stay still."

Putting down his bow, but with his knife still at Toumi's throat, he pulled a length of thin cord from beneath his cloak and tied it quickly around first my wrists and then Toumi's. Squinting at us and then up at the tree, he spied the thick lower branches of the cedar. The cord went sailing over the branch and he caught it, then quickly pulled at it, so that our wrists were yanked in the air.

Toumi was standing on tiptoe; I, being shorter, was actually dangling by my wrists, which were burning as the cord cut into them.

"There," grunted the squinty man with satisfaction. "That ought to hold you two." Keeping the tension on our arms, he ran the cord over to one of the juniper trees and tied it off. Then he came back, picked up his bow, looked at us once more, and grimaced. "'Look after the horses,' right." He gave a nasty laugh. "Damn Tanaka to seven damned hells. Well, you squirts aren't going anywhere." He started toward the uphill edge of the clearing, and then turned. "Don't you get any ideas!" Almost without aiming he sent an arrow at us that missed my elbow by a hand's breadth.

As soon as he was gone, we started to try to get loose. I was desperately trying to scramble up the bark behind me to take the pressure off, but the more I struggled the tighter the cord was. My hands and wrists were on fire; I could feel blood dribbling down my arms.

I looked at Toumi, who was crying, for which I didn't blame her at all. Blinking at me, she tried to shove the gag out of her mouth. When that failed, she howled in frustration, but began lifting up with her chin and looking upward, as if she were trying to tell me to climb.

Climb? Climb what? I looked up; the branch wasn't that far overhead, but there was no way to climb to it—

Toumi kicked me, then lifted her chin again, first up, and then to the side. When I didn't respond, she growled and did it again. *CLIMB ME!*

Ah! I threw my legs around her waist as if she were herself a small pine and shimmied up. Immediately, the pressure on my wrists lessened, and I almost passed out from the relief, sliding back down so that cords began to bite back into my flesh.

Toumi growled, waking me to my purpose again, and, using my legs and—once I'd worked my way up just a bit—grabbing on to the cord itself, I climbed until the cord looped around my wrists fell away and I dropped to the ground.

The relief was so intense that for a second I couldn't stand, but Toumi started kicking dirt on me. I yanked the gag from my mouth. "I'll untie it from the other end. I can't cut it from—"

She shook her head emphatically, screaming through the rag stuffed in her mouth, then threw her legs up over my shoulders. Realizing what she was trying to do, I did my best to lift her until at last she was able to work her wrists free—releasing Toumi's full weight onto me. I collapsed to the ground beneath her.

We rolled apart, gasping for breath and shaking the blood and feeling back into our hands.

A shadow blocked the sun shining on my sweat-slick face, and I gasped, sure that the bandit had come back to kill us in spite of the ringleader Tanaka's orders.

"Well done, Risuko-*chan*, Toumi-*chan*," said a warm, hushed voice.

Mieko-*san* stood above us, her dagger in her hand, a twig in her hair the only other sign that the situation was at all unusual.

"But... but...!" spluttered Toumi. "I saw you riding away with the others!"

"Did you?" Mieko smiled mildly. "Come, girls. We must hurry."

"The man," I gasped, standing and brushing myself off. "The one who tied us up—"

"—is not likely to bother us."

"Really?" asked Toumi, eyes fierce, staring at Mieko's knife.

"I cut loose the horses," said Mieko, pursing her lips. "When I last saw him, he was trying to chase them down, and that should take some time."

"Oh," muttered Toumi.

"But we need to warn the others. They'll have just started back this way from the switchback. If we can warn them..." Mieko frowned. "But I don't want to risk exposing you to these bandits, or..." Her eyes swept around the clearing, ending on the cedar to which we'd been tied. Her eyes narrowed and she walked toward the tree, plucking the arrow that had nearly pierced my arm from the bark. She turned. "Risuko," she said, her voice suddenly low, "do you think it would be quicker for you to scurry through this bramble, or to climb over the top?"

I blinked. "Um. Through the canopy?"

She nodded and pointed to the right of the tree. "Go. Now. That way. Warn Masugu and the rest that there's an ambush."

Not waiting for another word, I sprinted to the edge of the clearing and clambered to the matted top of the juniper. Glancing back, I saw Mieko hauling Toumi into hiding in the brush.

The juniper branches were thick and springy. As I burst up through the top layer, I could hear the muted sound of our company. They had just turned at the switchback; squinting, I could just make out Masugu's tall stallion, where I should have been riding.

I set out at a sprint, running along one bouncy juniper limb, crossing to the next where they met. The branches were so thickly overlapping that, while the going was slower than it would have been on open ground, I was moving much faster than I would have through the underbrush below, and with a much clearer sense of where I was going. I zigged and zagged along the treetops for a few heartbeats...

When I heard a clatter behind me.

Glancing back I saw no one. I ran along a few more steps.

Another clatter. I turned around again. Nothing.

Then, from out of the trees downhill on the opposite side of the road, I saw a grey speck lancing toward me. Not pausing to think, I ducked.

The arrow hissed over my head like an angry snake.

I dropped down into the juniper.

I heard another arrow thud into a branch just ahead of me.

Crouching just below the top layer of branches, I tried to think. I needed to warn Masugu-*san* and the rest of the party. But I was too far away to shout, and if I tried to climb above the canopy again, the archers would be looking for me. I could try to make my way back on the ground, but the going would be slow, and—not going straight downhill, as I had before getting caught earlier—I would have a hard time keeping my sense of direction.

I could just hear the clatter of our party's hooves on the stony road, and knew that they would be in the bandits' range soon. Still, I had to be closer to Masugu and the rest than the bandits were. If only I could scout out a direct—

I gasped, stunned that it had taken me so long to remember. Placing my hands in front of my mouth—holding on to the branch with my knees, I let out three owl hoots—not caring what kind of owl this time, just making sure that they were as loud as I could make them.

I listened. The hoof beats continued.

Hoo! Hoo! Hooooo!

I thought I heard Masugu's voice, but it sounded as if the horses were still clopping toward the bandits' trap.

I breathed deep, squeezed hard with my knees, and hooted louder than any owl could have.

I heard the plitlieutenant's voice again, shouting this time. "Attack! We're under attack! Form up!"

Then there was yelling and shouting, and the clash of swords, and horses and men screaming, just as there had been at the Mt. Fuji Inn.

Only this time, I had absolutely no intention of sticking my head out where it might get shot.

11—The Full Moon

The battle, if that's what it was, didn't last very long.

Quickly, the sound diminished to almost nothing. There was still some shouting, but it was growing more and more distant.

I snuck carefully out of my hiding place and made my way downhill toward where I knew the road must be.

It was not quite the scene of carnage that had met us that morning when we had first met Masugu-*san* and his soldiers. There were three dead men I assumed were part of the bandit gang. They'd been piled by the side of the road. There was also one dead horse, and one of the lancers was growling in pain as one of his comrades pulled an arrow through his thigh.

Most of the rest of the Takeda soldiers were missing. Aside from the wounded man and his nurse, only Masugu was there. Lady Chiyome and Mieko were talking with him. Mieko held an arrow in her hand.

The Little Brothers stood guard while Aimaru, Emi, and Toumi were holding the horses. All three looked as if they were waiting for another attack.

"Ah, there's the little rodent!" said Chiyome-*sama*. "Come here, Risuko."

Uncertain, I slid down the bank to the road and walked, trembling, to my mistress. "Yes, Chiyome-*sama*?"

"Mieko here tells me that you're the one we have to thank for warning us before those ruffians attacked." The old woman squinted at me. "Is this true?"

Her expression made me feel very much as though I had done something wrong—though I had been feeling, as I thought about it, rather proud of myself. "Y-yes my lady. Mieko-*san* told me to."

She peered at me some more, smirked at first Mieko, and then Masugu, and walked toward where the Little Brothers were guarding her palanquin.

Blinking, I looked up at Masugu-*san* and Mieko-*san*. The lieutenant smiled at me. "Good job, Murasaki-*san*. I was just telling Lady Chiyome and Mieko that if they'd let you go, I'd find a job for you in the scouts today."

My cheeks burned at the compliment.

"And I was telling the lieutenant," said Mieko brightly—almost too brightly—"that you are very badly needed where you are going, and so that he would have to find his scout somewhere else."

"Um. Thank you," I said to both of them. *Badly needed?*

"Mieko," said Masugu-*san*, and seemed about to say something more, but didn't speak.

Mieko lifted her chin. "Masugu?"

After looking back and forth between them for an awkward moment, I was just about to excuse myself when Mieko sighed and held up the arrow for Masugu to look at. "Did you notice the fletching?" She ran a finger over the feathers, which were from a snowy owl—white, with brown spots.

He frowned. "You think this was an enemy raiding party? It's awfully far from their territory."

"I think," said Mieko with an impatient sigh, "that they probably weren't bandits."

———

Once Masugu's soldiers had returned from chasing the attackers—one more of the enemy dead, but the rest evaporated into the mountains—and once a bier was lit for the three dead men and the horse, we resumed our descent into the valley.

I did not mind riding in front of Masugu-*san* now.

We made our way through a narrow valley with muddy fields. The farmers came out to their fences and bowed to us as we passed.

We climbed a ridge that lay across the valley like a cat catching the afternoon sun. A low, gated village swelled out of hilltop ahead. Through the *tori* arch and the open gates I could see at least a dozen buildings, whitewashed so that they glowed in the sunlight. The Full Moon.

Mieko and her rider cantered up beside Masugu and me. "Welcome to the Full Moon," she whispered, smiling.

———

We passed through the huge red arch (and the heavy wooden gate behind it), entering a white gravel courtyard. In front of the largest of the buildings, which looked as big as the Temple of the Sun Buddha in Pineshore, stood a still line of figures: six or seven young women and a single man. The man and the three youngest women were dressed in blue like Emi, Toumi, and me. The older ones were all in the red and white attire of shrine maidens.

The two Little Brothers placed the palanquin on the ground with a quiet crunch, and then sprinted back to close the gate. The two youngest girls ran forward, knelt beside Chiyome-*sama*'s sedan, and slid open the door.

As Lady Chiyome stepped out, all of those assembled bowed deeply, touching their heads to the gravel in deepest respect. The old woman slid out of her box and stretched, grumbling.

As we all dismounted, she surveyed her troops, who rose to a kneeling posture. She gave a grunt that sounded almost satisfied, and called out to some of the women in *miko* dress, "Are the baths prepared?"

Two of the women nodded.

Chiyome-*sama* smiled grimly and spoke to the square-faced man in the line. "Kee Sun, see to the wounded boy and get some supper ready. I'm famished. Fuyudori," she called to the one blue-clad girl who had not opened her door; by her face, I'd have guessed she was at most three years or so my senior, but her hair was as white as a crane's tail. "These three are your new charges: Toumi, Risuko, and Emi. Get them stowed away. I want their training to start immediately."

With that, she strode forward toward one of the smaller buildings, one with steam rising from it that I took to be the bathhouse. Mieko and the other women seemed to be taking charge of the unloading of the pack horses. The soldiers began leading the warhorses away to an enormous stable just inside the gate.

Masugu-*san* ran from my side, pulling something from beneath his armor—a small cylinder—and whispered something to Lady Chiyome just as she was about to enter the bathhouse. She nodded at him, and then dismissed him with a wave. He walked back to supervise the care of the horses.

He went over to his wounded soldier, who was being helped by the older man in blue, calling, "No poppy juice, remember. I don't trust that stuff."

The man in blue growled back something that sounded like a confirmation, and led the wounded rider toward the big building.

Masugu nodded and turned.

I was about to ask him what he had been talking to Chiyome-*sama* about when I caught a glimpse of Fuyudori, the older girl who had been ordered to take charge of us. Her gaze had followed mine toward the lieutenant; she had a small, quivering smile. To be honest, it looked more like a grimace of anxiety than a grin.

As I considered her, I realized that this girl looked exactly as I'd always imagined a character in a fable my mother used to tell sister and me—the story of Long-Haired Girl who saves her town, but whose hair turns white in sorrow. Fuyudori was extraordinarily pretty, and the whiteness of her hair made her beauty all the more remarkable. She looked at the three of us, the uncertainty melting from her face, and in a sweet voice said, "Please close your mouths. It's not polite to stare."

As she led us away from the courtyard, I turned in search of Aimaru. He looked rather lost, following the Little Brothers as they unloaded the pack horses. I waved to him, but he didn't see me.

12—Novices

"My name is Fuyudori. I am the oldest of the initiates here, and so you may address me as Fuyudori-*san* or Fuyudori-*senpai*." We followed her steady stride toward the back of the compound. It was impossible not to watch the white, silken hair flowing behind her as she walked. "As the head initiate, I make sure that you know the rules and obey them. Any infraction is seen as a failure on my part; I do not accept failure easily. But I also like to think that I am here as an adviser and a friend."

In all honesty, my mind was still back at that morning's battle. I wasn't quite sure how we had ended up following this remarkable looking young woman around.

Toumi and Emi looked just as lost.

Following Fuyudori, we entered a small building that was just inside the rear wall, behind the bathhouse. There were two rooms. She led us to the one on the right, in which two bedrolls were leaned against one wall. "You will sleep with Mai and Shino, the two other initiates, in this room. As head initiate, I sleep over here." She pointed through the sliding door into another room, just as small (if not quite as neat), but with a single bed in it on a low platform.

We deposited our bedrolls next to those of the other girls—Emi and I on one side, and Toumi on the far, other side. It was almost reassuring to see that Toumi looked as uncertain as I was feeling.

"Fuyudori-*san*," Emi said, scowling as usual, "what's a... a novice?"

The older girl's mouth pursed in a tiny smile. "That's you, of course." She began to walk out of our new home, and we followed her. "Chiyome-*sama* likes to joke that we are nuns here, but it's not far from the truth. Just like novice nuns, you three will be given the most menial tasks, the most basic training. When you have earned the teachers' trust, you will be made initiates." She pulled dreamily at her sash, which unlike our blue ones was red, edged in white. "Once Lady Chiyome judges that you have completed your training, you will become a *kunoichi*. I am due to be given my robes after the New Year."

That word again. "What's a *kunoichi*?" I asked.

She turned and smiled sweetly at me. "You are the one Lady Chiyome called Risuko, yes?" I nodded. "You should treat your elders with respect. Ask permission before asking a question, Risuko-*chan*." *Squirrel-child*.

Next to me, Toumi gave a smirk—whether it was aimed at me or the older girl, I wasn't sure.

"I beg your pardon, Fuyudori-*senpai*," I said, "I'm sorry. Would Fuyudori-*senpai* do me the honor to answer my unworthy question?"

"Of course, Risuko-*chan*," she said.

"May I ask, what is a *kunoichi*?"

The white-haired girl smiled again, but this time the smile was more mischievous than sweet. "Yes, Risuko-*chan*, you may ask. However, I'm afraid that I'm not going to tell you." She turned and walked away.

Feeling tricked, I skittered after her.

"Nor will any of Lady Chiyome's other servants. If you are so interested, you'll just have to find out on your own. And before you ask, my hair is white because when I was a young girl, an attack on my village killed my family and all of the other inhabitants but me. I was rescued, and sent here, to learn everything that I could from Lady Chiyome and her servants about becoming a shrine maiden and, of course, training in the talents that make one a *kunoichi*. Keep up with me, please."

We trailed Fuyudori as she gave us a quick tour of the compound. She showed us the bathhouse—and told us that we were expected to bathe every evening. "The lady expects you to stay clean and healthy. Of course, as novices, you are expected to clean the baths out each night and to prepare them each morning for all of the inhabitants of the Full Moon," she said. Next to that was the older women's dormitory, which Fuyudori called the Nunnery. In the corner, between the gate and the women's dormitory was a small guesthouse. We saw Lieutenant Masugu moving his gear into it.

I was mostly noticing, honestly, that unlike our dormitory, the buildings at the front of the compound had decorative timbers that would make them easy to climb. Would they let me climb?

Past the gate were two low buildings: the stable and a teahouse where Fuyudori told us we would receive much of our instruction until we became initiates. Behind that was the men's dormitory, which was smaller than the women's, and which was called, we were told, the Bull Pen. We all started to giggle, until Fuyudori looked back at us very seriously and said, "As novices you are not to speak to any of the men—or boys—except at meals."

Emi's face twisted into an even deeper frown than usual, and she caught my eye. Were we both thinking of Aimaru? I gave the smallest shrug I could manage, and she nodded.

Fuyudori primly pointed out the main storehouse, and began to lead us back toward the big building where we had dismounted. "What's that place?" Toumi called out.

Fuyudori turned around with a mixed look of annoyance and amusement. Toumi gave a stiff bow. "Pardon me, Fuyudori-*senpai*."

"Yes—?"

"What's that building over there?" Toumi jerked a finger up toward a small building hidden behind a tall hemlock, up past the storehouse.

Fuyudori held her hand up in front of her face, but then regained her composure, though her ears were still pink. "I beg your pardon, Toumi-*chan*. I forgot about that one. That's called the Retreat. We go there during our moon time."

We all giggled nervously again, even Toumi.

Fuyudori looked us over. "You probably won't need to use it yet." With the smooth bearing she seemed to have studied from Mieko, Fuyudori walked toward the central building, and we all trailed behind her.

"This is the great hall," Fuyudori went on, smoothly. "Meals are served here in the morning, at midday and in the evening. Don't be late—Kee Sun doesn't wait. I will take you there now, to make sure you are on time."

Emi frowned and cleared her throat. "Excuse me, Fuyudori... Fuyudori-*san*. But what's a *kee sun?*"

The older girl let out a laugh like morning birdsong, and said, "Oh! Emi-*chan*, you are going to be such fun to have here. It's not a what, it's a who! Kee Sun is the cook. Mochizuki-*sama*, Lady Chiyome's late husband, brought him back from Korea; he said Japanese food was too boring for him, he'd never eat it again." Then she smiled and said brightly, "He'll be serving the pickled cabbage tonight—try it, it's delicious."

Next to me, Emi was looking at her sandals. I pulled at her sleeve, but she wouldn't look at me. "She wasn't laughing at you, Emi," I whispered.

She shrugged.

"Well, she was. But she was laughing at all of us. Come on," I said.

Still a little frightened of this new home, we scampered into the great hall behind Fuyudori and Toumi.

———

The interior of the large building was open and undecorated, except for a group of small statues in a shrine against the back wall. Three long, low tables were laid out in the shape of a horseshoe. The center table, which was toward the right-hand side of the hall, was on a slightly raised platform.

Toumi shuffled across the polished bamboo floor, muttering.

Fuyudori led us through a wide doorway opposite the tables into what was clearly a kitchen. Where the kitchen at the Mount Fuji Inn had been small and cluttered, however, this room was bright, spacious and as clean as a Buddhist temple. Indeed, a shrine to the Healing Buddha stood beneath a beam from which hung bunches of drying herbs.

At a cutting table just to the side of the fire pit, the blue-clad man we had glimpsed earlier stood with his back to us, his shoulders working and the woodpecker sound of his knife clacking away as he shredded some vegetable. This must be Kee Sun, I realized.

I was confused, however—I had thought we were coming in for dinner, and while the kitchen was full of the smell of the hot fire, spices and cabbage, there was nothing cooking.

The man turned and stared at Fuyudori, then at us. His face was broad and flat. A scar ran horizontally, from his right eyebrow into his scruffy beard below his left ear. As he looked us over, he ran his tongue over his lips. "Well, Ghostiegirl, what have yeh brought me for my supper today?"

His speech was perfectly clear yet incredibly difficult to understand at the same time, hard-edged and musical.

Fuyudori smiled politely. "Kee Sun, these three will be taking over kitchen duty from Shino and Mai. Emi. Toumi. Risuko." She pointed to each of us in turn.

As he smiled, Kee Sun's scar twisted too. "Never seen a scrawnier crew." He shook his head. "Least there're three of 'em."

He squinted at me, then at Toumi and Emi. "Gotta get better names for yeh all. I can never remember those silly Japanese handles." He scratched his chin and pointed at Emi. "Yeh're easy. Yeh'll be Smiley. Yeh," Kee Sun said to Toumi, "I think I'll call yeh... Falcon. And I won't trust yeh with any fish, either." He grinned at Toumi, who looked as if she had no idea what to do with this strange man.

Kee Sun rolled his eyes back to me. "Hmm... Much harder. Did Ghostie-girl here call yeh 'Squirrel?'"

I nodded.

He shook his head and ran his thumb along his scarred cheek. "I don't think so." Then he snapped his fingers and grinned. "Bright-eyes! That's yehr name, there, right enough!"

I bowed my head.

"So yeh'll all be working for me here, and out in the hall, cleanin', fetchin' from the storehouse, cleanin', fetchin' from the gardens, choppin', and cleanin' again. Understood?" He fixed us all with a glare until we had nodded that we indeed understood.

He looked to Fuyudori, who turned to address us.

"These duties are yours for as long as you are the youngest here," she said. "It is your honor to help Kee Sun as he sees fit in the kitchen, and to assist in serving the food. You will eat after the rest of us have finished."

I looked to the girls beside me. Toumi was fuming, as I might have guessed, no doubt angry at being forced to do such menial work. Emi, on the other hand, looked plainly confused. "Fuyudori-*san*," she began, and then stopped, chewing on her lip.

"What is it, Emi-*chan*?"

"Well," Emi continued, "didn't you say we weren't to speak to the men?"

None of us had any idea what Emi was talking about. Then she went on, "If we're not supposed to talk to men, how are we supposed to answer all his questions?"

Fuyudori goggled at Emi, and then looked to Kee Sun.

He smirked, put his hands on his hips, and said to Emi, "I don't count as a *man,* yeh see, Smiley. I'm a Korean. And besides," he said, a smirk twisting his scar, this time into a frightening mock grin, "as long as the grub is good, Lady Chiyome don't give a hoot what's goin' on in the kitchen."

For the first time since I had met her, Emi burst out into loud, belly-rumbling laughter.

Fuyudori's eyes went wide in surprise, but Kee Sun roared along with Emi, and, soon, so did I.

13—A Banquet

We began by fetching a large bag of rice from the storehouse. A pair of rats stared up at us when we entered, but Toumi growled at them while I swooshed the long stick that Kee Sun had given us to shoo them with, and they scattered. The bag was heavier than I was, and it took the three of us to drag it to the kitchen. Toumi muttered the whole way, and I would be lying if I said that Emi and I didn't join her once or twice.

Kee Sun kept us busy, hanging pots over the fire to steam the rice and soy beans in, lowering a battered metal grate to serve as a grill, fetching more charcoal. As the sunlight began to fade from the room, we lit candles in the kitchen and in the hall.

When we came back into Kee Sun's lair, we were overwhelmed by the thick scent of the strips of sizzling, black-marinated beef that were laid out over the fire.

I remember a few times when an old cow had died in the village, everyone coming together for a feast, roasting the poor, stringy old thing. There had not been even such a cow in a long time, however—not in our village.

And still, as good as that beef may have smelled and tasted, it was nothing to this. The air was rich with the scent, and we all stopped, our mouths watering.

"Don't stand there lookin' pretty like a bunch of *Kwan-um* statues!" snapped Kee Sun. "Grab the *kimchee* from that barrel, there, put it into these six serving bowls and get 'em out to the tables. Quick, quick!" he yelled, hands clapping.

The bowls were beautifully glazed, pale green like the ocean on a sunny day. Gingerly I picked one up and carried it over to the barrel. Balancing the bowl in one hand I tried to open the barrel-top.

"Both hands, both hands!" shouted Kee Sun over his shoulder, one hand flipping the strips of meat with long chopsticks, the other painting them with a black sauce. I couldn't tell whether he wanted me to hold the bowl with both hands, hold the wooden lid with both hands, or somehow to manage both two-handed, like some four-armed demon.

Toumi brushed past me, still muttering. "Stupid," she snapped, and for once I knew she wasn't talking about me. She picked up the lid, pulled out the ladle that was hanging on the inside of barrel, and began filling my bowl, which I held tightly in two hands. The *kimchee* was pickled cabbage, sharp-smelling and bright green and red.

I walked as quickly as I could without spilling any of the cabbage. By the time I had laid the first bowl at the head table and was coming back, Emi was shuffling out of the kitchen, her face a grimace of concentration.

As I walked back in to the kitchen, I saw Toumi starting to pick up a piece of the *kimchee* to taste.

"No!" shouted Kee Sun, slamming down his metal-tipped chopsticks so that the grate rang. "No one tastes in this kitchen except me, yeh hear!" A smile played briefly over his damp face. "That way if anyone dies, it'll be me, right?" He shook his head and turned back to the hissing grill. "I knew yeh'd be a falcon-girl, swoopin' in for the kill!" He demonstrated a hawk's dive with his chopsticks and chuckled, turning back to the fire.

The sky had now gone completely dark outside, and candlelight flashed in Toumi's eyes, bringing to mind an unsheathed blade looking for a place to bury itself.

We laid the tables with bowls of *kimchee* and boiled soy beans, mounds of rice, and bottles of rice wine from the pantry. Kee Sun barked out orders as he loaded three huge platters with the beef, the smell of which had now worked its way into our hair and our clothes, so that we were reminded of the delicious meal we could not yet eat even when we weren't in the kitchen. Then he grabbed an unused ladle, stepped over to the back door of the kitchen, and swung the spoon at an enormous, dented gong that was hanging outside the door.

From the hall came a great cheer, as the entire company—Lady Chiyome's household plus Lieutenant Masugu's soldiers—flooded in to the dining area. The smell of the dinner had drawn them like moths to a campfire.

Kee Sun fussed with the platters, placing a bunch of watercress at the end of each, then he turned to us, gravely, and said, "If any of yeh drops yehr platter, I'll skin yeh with the dullest, rustiest knife I've got, yeh hear?"

We all three nodded and said, "*Hai.*" Emi, though, began to titter, which caused Kee Sun's fierce look to soften.

As we carefully walked through the doorway, which Kee Sun held open for us, Toumi, Emi, and I were greeted with tumultuous cheers. Many of the men and women had clearly already helped themselves to the bottles of *sake*; most of them sported ruddy cheeks.

Chiyome-*sama* was seated in the middle of the head table, Mieko on her left and the other women arranged to that side. Just next to Mieko there was an unclaimed space with a bowl and a pair of old chopsticks. I couldn't imagine that someone hadn't heard the gong; who was missing? Mieko spooned some rice neatly into the latecomer's bowl.

Masugu-*san* sat to Lady Chiyome's right, with his troops beside him. The Little Brothers and Aimaru were at the bottom of the men's table. Aimaru smiled at me as I laid my platter at his table.

He seemed to be about to say something when I heard a loud voice from the other side of the hall call out, "Look at the new novices! They're so small! No wonder they call that one *Squirrel!*" The women's table exploded with laughter.

The voice had come from one of the blue-clad girls at the end of the table furthest from Lady Chiyome. *That must be Shino and Mai, the junior initiates,* I thought. Shino had a thick nose, as if someone had flattened it with a skillet. Mai's face was sharp, every angle. I knew in a flash that Kee Sun had probably called her Foxy-girlie or something along those lines. "*Squirrel,*" chuckled Mai again, and Shino snorted.

Fuyudori, our white-haired senior, was smiling, but coldly, I thought—disapprovingly.

Masugu-*san*'s voice rang out. "Murasaki-*san* is small, it's true. But the smallest squirrel will fight fiercely when provoked." He smiled across to the younger women. "I would think that the women of the Full Moon would know that to be true if anyone did."

Mai and Shino looked as though they had been slapped.

Mieko spoke, her voice low and pleasant, but her eyes flashing as she poured wine for Lady Chiyome—and for the missing guest. "It is most gratifying to learn that the men who visit the Full Moon have learned that lesson, too." She looked down toward where I was standing, but it was not to me that she was speaking.

"Ha!" laughed Lady Chiyome as she picked up a piece of meat with her chopsticks. "I said it would be entertaining having the two of them here!"

The older women, those dressed as *miko*, roared with laughter. Mieko smiled primly, while Masugu turned bright red.

I gave Aimaru a small wave and then sprinted back to kitchen with three empty rice wine bottles.

When I came back, Toumi had already resupplied the men's table, so I brought the *sake* to the women.

"Bring that here, Risuko!" called the youngest of the initiates. "Having fun serving at the tables?" she said, bright red circles marking her cheeks.

"You would know, Mai," said Fuyudori, "since you were serving here yourself at lunch."

Next to the white-haired girl, two of the older women chuckled.

"Least *I'm* not 'fraid of soldiers," slurred Shino.

Fuyudori's face blanched, until it was almost as white as her hair. "I am not afraid. But I have cause to be cautious." I thought of the story of how her hair had turned white—the attack on her village. "Do not we all?"

"Do not we all?" mimicked Mai. Shino snorted.

"Are those peas?" Fuyudori asked me, turning away from the two drunk girls.

"Uh. No."

She raised an eyebrow. "No, Risuko-*chan*?"

"No, no, thank you, uh, Fuyudori-*senpai*." A bead of sweat dripped into my mouth. "They're soy beans."

"Oh." Fuyudori's smile remained, but she looked a bit embarrassed, and I hate to say that her discomfort made me feel better.

I took an empty bowl from that end of the table and brought it back to refill it with *kimchee*.

As the meal went on and we brought out more and more *sake*, Lady Chiyome's band of women, her *kunoichi*, began teasing the soldiers across the way. I had seen some of the women in our village do that sort of thing, and the soldiers had teased right back, answering one rude joke with another.

Here, however, the men seemed almost too terrified to answer. And the quieter Masugu-*san*'s troops became, the rowdier the women got. As the meal finally wound down, the women began to make the sorts of indecent comments that would have gotten any Imagawa soldier slapped in our village. But these men took the comic abuse in silence.

As I began cleaning up at the men's table, I leaned over to Aimaru. "How are you doing?" I asked.

He shrugged. "Better now. I was hungry. But... oh, you haven't eaten yet, have you?"

I shook my head. Only the raucous conversation had kept my stomach's rumblings from being heard all over the hall through most of the meal.

"It's hard not being able to talk to anyone," he said. "It's not so different, here, from life at the temple, but even there I had friends I could talk to sometimes."

I smiled. "It's only until we become initiates."

"How do you do that?"

"No idea."

"Well," he said, grinning back, "let's make sure that happens soon."

As Emi, Toumi and I began to clear away the last of the empty platters, a deep bell rang from the back of the hall. All of the noise faded, like flames under rain.

The larger of the Little Brothers stood in front of the shrine. He had closed the doors and sealed them with a twist of white paper.

Mieko picked up the chopsticks at the empty spot beside her and thrust them into the bowl of rice, sticking straight up.

It was as if the whole building held its breath.

"Seven days ago," said Lady Chiyome, her voice just above a growl, "we lost one of our number. One of the *first* of our number. She fought bravely, and she fought well; it was all that she would have wished."

Some of the women grunted. A number looked as if they might be holding back tears. A few—Mieko among them—failed. The soldiers still looked uncomfortable, but they shared the solemn silence.

"Remember her," said Chiyome-*sama*, and I was shocked to hear her voice catch. "Remember her, and strive to honor the red and white robes that she wore so well."

The banquet ended then, as all of the Full Moon's guests and inhabitants left the hall, grave and quiet.

14 — Squirrel on the Roof

I was certain that Kee Sun wouldn't let us eat until after all of the cleaning was done. But as we brought the last of the dishes in from the hall, we found the cook smiling and gesturing to the small feast that he had laid out for us on the low cutting table: grilled beef, *kimchee*, soy beans, rice—even *sake*—was set out just as it had been for the banquet.

"Magnificent!" crowed Kee Sun. "Perfect! Not a drop spilled, and everything served hot! The three of you girlies made the last two look like the clowns that they are."

We sat, and that was almost as glorious as the tempting smells wafting up from the table. We picked up our chopsticks and started serving ourselves. Emi picked up a handful of edamame and began shelling the soy beans directly into her mouth. I had the beef right in front of me, and so I slid the succulent-looking meat into my bowl along with a serving of rice.

Toumi, who had been denied the *kimchee* earlier in the evening, grabbed a huge clump of the pickled cabbage with her chopsticks and plopped it into her bowl.

As I began to lift my first bite of beef to my mouth, I saw Kee Sun start to say something, then turn away with a smirk on his face.

The beef was unlike anything I'd ever tasted—tender, juicy, sweet and peppery. It was the best food I'd ever had. Just as I was swallowing that first bite and reaching for the next, Toumi sputtered loudly, *kimchee* flying out of her mouth. She let out a howl, and grabbed for the *sake*.

Before she could drink it, however, Kee Sun handed her a huge cup of water, which she drained in heavy, rapid gulps. "What are you trying to do, *kill us?*" she gasped.

Kee Sun smirked. "Well, you wanted it so much before dinner, I thought yeh knew it was spicy."

"*Spicy!*" yelled Toumi. "That's pickled fire!"

The scar on Kee Sun's face stretched and twisted as he rocked his head back and laughed. "Better get used to it, Falcon-girlie," he said, shoveling rice into Toumi's bowl. "'Cause the Old Lady loves my food, and the people here seem to also. Yeh Japanese and yehr food—yeh like everything sweet or as tasteless as the washing water." Toumi was still panting, as if trying to blow out a flame inside her mouth. "Balance! Everything in balance, yeh hear? Eat the rice, Falcon-girl—it will take away the fire," Kee Sun said.

"Mind," he added, "I think yeh're goin' t'need to stay away from hot foods anyway. Yeh got too much heat in yeh. Anybody could see that." He scratched his beard. "I think we're goin' to feed yeh up with some nice, cooling *yin* food."

Toumi gawked at him as if he were speaking in gibberish—which, in fairness, he was. Then she gave a disgusted snort, and began shoveling rice into her mouth.

The rest of the meal passed, uneventful and delicious. Emi and I even tried a little bit of the *kimchee*, which was very tasty and not really too hot to eat, especially if you knew what you were about to put into your mouth. It took Toumi a little while to get over her shock and discomfort and to trust the rest of the food, but hunger won out, and soon all three of us were groaning with contentment.

Kee Sun poured some of the rice wine into little *sake* cups and mixed ours with water. Then he poured a large mug-full for himself—undiluted of course. "Don't think I'm going to be able to feed you like this every night," he said. "But you certainly earned it." Then he lifted his mug. "*Wihayeo*," he said in Korean. "Cheers!"

We toasted him in response, sipping at our sweet wine, and feeling the warmth of it, so different from the heat of the spicy *kimchee*, spreading through our stomachs.

Even Emi was smiling as we finished cleaning the kitchen.

The night was clear, cold and bright. Shivering, we stumbled back to our room. An almost full moon was directly overhead, surrounded by a glowing circle of light. In the mountains, you can see so many more stars, and they are so bright that you feel as though you could climb right up the stars of the River of Heaven like a ladder.

As we went into the building, Fuyudori was sitting cross-legged on her bed, brushing her white hair. "You have done very well, for the first day," she said, with her sweet, mocking smile. "After you have gone and bathed, you should sleep. I will do my best to make sure that you are ready for helping Kee Sun serve breakfast."

We all groaned.

Her smile broadened. "Do not worry. Once you have finished your morning kitchen duty, you get to take a music lesson in the Tea House with Sachi-*san*."

"A music lesson?" asked Toumi.

"With Sachi-*san*?" I said. She was, I gathered, one of the older women. The *kunoichi*.

"Yes, Risuko-*chan*. With Sachi-*sensei*. Since she will be acting as your teacher, she should be addressed as such."

"But I would have thought Mieko..."

Fuyudori got her playful smile, the one that always let me know I wasn't going to get a straight answer. "Mieko-*san* has other subjects to teach. But none that you will need just at the moment. Nor would you would want a music lesson from Mieko-*sensei*, I think. Shino, Mai, and I will be joining you for the lesson. Won't that be lovely?"

The three of us looked at each other. It was clear that the other girls felt as I did: a music lesson didn't sound lovely at all—and the idea of having the three older girls join didn't make it any more appealing.

Fuyudori nodded, as if we had agreed with her. "Now off to the bathhouse with you," she ordered, and we shuffled silently next door. It was my favorite building at the Full Moon, so far—as big as our sleeping quarters, but bare inside except for the two large tubs. The smell of damp wood filled the air like steam.

The fires that heated the water had burned low, but the huge wooden tubs were still warm. We bathed in silence, fighting the urge to fall asleep in the tepid water. When we were clean, we trouped back to our dormitory.

Fuyudori was seated on her mat. "Be quiet as you go to bed," she said. "The others are already asleep."

"Not surprising given how much *sake* they were drinking..." muttered Emi, and then realized that Fuyudori was looking at her disapprovingly. "Fuyudori-*senpai*. Ma'am."

We tiptoed in and slid, exhausted, into our beds. As always, Emi was snoring within seconds of lying down.

I lay there, staring at the ceiling, listening to a squirrel scurry across the roof. *I wish I could be up there with you,* I thought. And then I, too, fell asleep.

15—The Music Lesson

When Fuyudori cheerfully woke us the next morning, none of us—Emi, Toumi, Mai, Shino, or myself—was very happy about it. My legs were sore from the combination of riding all day and then staying on my feet all evening. And that wasn't even counting scurrying through the juniper and gripping that branch with my knees while arrows hissed overhead.

One of the older girls, whined, "Why do we have to get up? They have kitchen duty."

"You have duties outside the kitchen, just as I have had for the past three years," Fuyudori said. She turned to me, Emi and Toumi. "Little ones, dress and get to the kitchen. You'll have your music lesson later today."

When we arrived back at the kitchen, Kee Sun was looking quite unhappy. His hair was sticking out like a dog's that has been rolling in pinesap.

We got through breakfast—reheated rice and platters of scrambled egg.

Several of the women weren't given egg—they were fed bean curd. One such, much to her annoyance, was Toumi.

"Told yeh! Too hot! Meat is the last thing a temper like yehr's needs. No, none for a Falcon-girl!" Kee Sun laughed, and made sure that not a bit of animal flesh—not even egg or fish—passed through her lips. "Too *yang*," he muttered, and plopped a serving of the bland, white bean curd into Toumi's bowl. I could see that she thought about refusing, but like all of us, she knew what hunger truly felt like, and so, a glower of extreme distaste on her face, she ate the bean curd. All of it.

Once we had eaten, it was time to clean. Then, once the kitchen was back to normal, which didn't take anywhere nearly as long as it had after the feast the night before, we went to our first lesson in becoming a *miko*.

Music, Fuyudori had said; I assumed it would be learning to beat the drums and the bells that they always play at the forest shrine at home, or perhaps a flute. That didn't sound terribly difficult—or terribly interesting.

Toumi, Emi and I wandered meekly down toward the Tea House. Fuyudori, Mai and Shino were already there, sitting demurely behind a set of stringed instruments—two big *kotos* and a hand-held *samisen*.

Sachi smiled at us as we entered, cleaning out a long *shakuhachi* flute with a rag on a stick. "Men like watching me do this, for some reason."

We sat nervously in a corner, close neither to the other three girls nor to our teacher. For once, even Toumi seemed more nervous than angry.

Then Sachi raised the flute to her lips and played.

My mother played the flute—*Otō-san* had loved to hear her play it—and she had tried to teach me to play. However, I had never been able to get the shape of the lips right, so I had never managed to produce much more than scratchy wind sounds. The *shakuhachi* is a simple instrument—a hollow length of bamboo with five holes for your fingers—but the sound that Sachi produced was anything but simple. It was loss and longing, and it was beautiful.

She finished playing, and yet the music filled the silence. Lowering the flute from her lips, Sachi smirked. "Not bad."

All of us—novices and initiates alike—laughed.

She turned to me, Emi, and Toumi and held up her instrument. "Any of you play?"

All of us looked down. After what I had just heard, I could barely say that my mother *played*. I certainly wasn't going to claim my own feeble attempts for music.

"Hmm. Well, what's your name—Emi? You've got the lips for it."

Next to me, Emi cringed.

"Sorry," Sachi said, "I'm getting ahead of myself. I'm always doing that." She snorted, and took a breath. "I'm supposed to welcome our newcomers. My... teacher welcomed some of us our first day here." With her flute she gestured at the three initiates. "I heard her give *these* girls here the same talk when they arrived. So I'll try to do it justice."

Taking a deep, slow breath, Sachi raised a hand to her chest, the open palm facing out. "Welcome, ladies, to the beginning of your formal training here at the Full Moon. Lady Chiyome began this school in order to ensure that our nation's old ways were never forgotten, but also to put to use the talents of young women such as yourselves, whose abilities might otherwise be wasted in the sheer struggle to survive the troubled times in which we live."

Fuyudori, whose face seemed almost always to be set in a polite smile, scowled.

"Everything that you do here at the Full Moon is intended to prepare you for your new life. In particular, the lessons you learn with me and with the other *kunoichi* will offer you an opportunity to learn skills that you will need in the years to come." Sachi paused, and I shivered. She seemed to be calling up the spirit of Kuniko, who I realized must have been the teacher that Sachi had mentioned. She looked at us one at a time. It may have been her intention to see whether we had any questions, but it felt as it were Kuniko looking through Sachi's eyes, testing us. I don't know what the others were thinking, but I was absolutely certain that I was failing.

"A shrine maiden has many duties," Sachi continued in the same low, expressionless voice. "You will learn to dance, to lead some of the important rituals, to prepare shrines for festivals. And you must also learn to sing in praise of the gods."

She held up the *shakuhachi*, and suddenly Sachi grinned and her true spirit broke through again. "You'll also learn to play instruments. Making music during the rites will be one of your most important duties as a *miko*. And, like I said, men love a woman with good fingering. Now," she said, "any questions?"

Sachi was, as I have said, a much better musician than my mother. I must admit, too, that she was a much better teacher. By the end of the first lesson, Emi had produced a few warbling notes from the flute, and I had managed to get something resembling a musical tone from the *samisen*, much to the annoyance of Mai, who was working with me. Sachi managed to bring music out of each of us as *Okā-san*, wonderful as she was, could never do.

However, I am quite sure my mother never told anywhere nearly as many dirty jokes.

———

By the time Sachi waved us farewell, the sun was high and the gravel in the courtyard was so bright that it hurt our eyes.

Masugu-*san* was standing next to Lady Chiyome and several of the older *miko*. The nine lancers who had ridden our party to the Full Moon were lined up before their commander and our mistress.

The horsemen all had stoic expressions on their faces, but they didn't appear to regret leaving at all. They seemed almost glad to be departing this community of women for their army camp. Masugu himself looked less than happy that he was staying with us, though I found that I was very happy that he would. He was one of the only adults there who I felt treated me just as who I was.

"Give my greetings to Captain Yamagata at the Highfield garrison," he said. I noticed for the first time how different the lieutenant's voice was when he spoke to the men as their commander. This voice was hard and sharp-edged, not at all like the warm voice he used when he was talking to them at dinner—or when he was talking with me. Masugu-*san* gave a crisp salute, barked out an order, and the horses wheeled to their right and broke into an immediate gallop out of the gate. The Little Brothers closed the gate as the last charger passed through.

Before the swirls of dust had even settled, Chiyome-*sama* and her ladies turned and withdrew into the great hall. Fuyudori, Mai, and Shino joined them—though Fuyudori seemed to be emphatically *not looking* at Lieutenant Masugu in that funny way that older girls have. As if he would notice.

I thought she didn't like soldiers, I mused.

As I began to shuffle behind Emi and Toumi toward the kitchen to begin helping with the midday meal, I felt a tap on my shoulder. Turning, I saw Masugu-*san*; he had touched me with the cylinder I had seen him with the day before. It was a metal tube, I realized, capped at both ends. A letter case, such as I had seen my father use when sending or receiving work from the castle. It was sealed, I noticed, not with the four diamonds of the Takeda, but with a crest of three wide ginger leaves in a circle.

"How are you, Murasaki-*san?*" he asked, his open face bent in a smile. "Are you finding your place here?"

I began to answer him, but then saw Toumi standing by the kitchen door, watching me. Unsure what to do, I looked down.

"Not supposed to talk to me?" Masugu-*san* sighed, and lowered his voice. "Ah, well. Listen, I just wanted to thank you for yesterday. You saved lives. Perhaps mine. And..." He lowered his voice to a whisper. "I wanted to say, what I told you about your father? About the other girls?"

Still looking at the gravel, I gave a small nod.

"Don't take it too seriously. I think I may have been over-reacting. The other girls probably know nothing about it. It's best if you don't mention anything. Understand?"

Again I nodded. Toumi was still waiting.

"Listen," he continued, "I know you're only supposed to talk to us at dinner time. But if you need help, I'll be very happy to do anything I can."

Still looking down so that Toumi wouldn't see my lips move, I said, "Thank you, Masugu-*san*."

"It is my pleasure, Murasaki-*san*," he said, a grin in his voice. He strode away in the direction of the storehouse, whistling and tapping the scroll on his shoulder.

As I began to shuffle over to toward the kitchen door, I sniffed, sensing a sour wind coming over the mountain. Snow was coming soon.

Toumi was smiling as I reached the door. "I saw you talking to him."

"Are you going to tell?" I asked, trying to look unconcerned.

"No, no, I can't bother with something as puny as that." She leaned close and whispered into my ear. "I haven't forgotten, Kano Mouse. One day, in front of Lady Chiyome and all the rest, I will show them all who you really are."

Smiling predatorily, she turned and went into the kitchen.

I followed.

16—Blades

As I entered Kee Sun's kitchen, I kept my face down so as not to catch Toumi's eye, or Emi's. I didn't want either of them to see that I was upset. I took a stack of bowls and began to walk toward the dining hall to get ready for the mid-day meal, but Kee Sun stopped me. "No, girlie," he chortled, his scar twisting, "Not to go in there this morning. Yeh don't go in there while Lady Chiyome is running her ladies through their paces unless yeh want yehr head handed back to yeh in one of those bowls."

I looked at him blankly.

"There's classes yeh three aren't welcome to join till yeh're *initiated*," he said with something like a smirk, "so we get ready in here and then run like wood demons to serve out the meal once they're done. Now, set yehr little squirrel fingers to work."

Toumi was sidling over toward the door, her face empty even of its usual anger.

Kee Sun didn't even have to look up to stop her. "What they're doing in there," the cook said with a look halfway between a grin and a scowl, "is not for little girlies, yeh hear me? Now, yeh two, there, yehr gonna help Bright-eyes, here."

Toumi bristled, and Emi frowned. But then, Emi always seemed to be frowning.

"What exactly are we doing, Kee Sun-*san*?" I asked.

Now the cook grinned—and it was definitely a grin this time. "Well, Bright-eyes," he said, "are yeh any good with a blade?"

"A knife?" I asked.

Toumi suddenly looked much more interested in the conversation. Emi was still frowning.

"Think yeh're up to attacking these long beans?" He gestured to a mound of long, thin bean pods.

"Beans?" Toumi spat.

"Beans," said Kee Sun, his scar bending as his smile broadened. "I want yeh girlies to take this pile of beans, reduce its resistance, chop it into submission."

Now Toumi could only snort.

"You ever handle a blade, Falcon-girlie?"

Her narrow eyes flickered.

"Come over here, all three of you," he said, pointing to the cutting table, "and learn."

Now, I wasn't going to tell them that *Oka-san* had taught me how to chop vegetables, that I'd learned how to handle her long, lovingly sharpened kitchen knife years earlier, that I'd even started teaching my sister to use it. I didn't want Toumi resenting me any more than she already did.

When Kee Sun brought out three gleaming curved blades, each no longer than my hand, even I didn't need to pretend to gasp. The steel was polished to a high gleam. The edges were un-nicked and fine. *Otō-san*'s swords never looked more beautiful or more deadly.

Toumi reached out to grab one of the knives by the back of the blade.

"Don't yeh ever let me see yeh treat a good blade that way!" barked Kee Sun. He plucked the knife from Toumi's fingers and flourished the blade across a bamboo beam from which some herbs were drying. At first, the bamboo seemed unscarred, but suddenly it collapsed, neatly cut in two, spilling the herbs onto the table. "Yeh treat a knife with respect, yeh hear me?" He handed the knife back to a properly stunned Toumi, handle first.

Chastened, Emi and I carefully picked up our knives by the handles.

It wasn't until much later that I wondered: if he had wanted us to take the blades by the handles in the first place, why had he put them down in front of us tip-first?

He then showed us—much as Mother had done, much as I had tried to do with Usako—how to rock the blade across what you're trying to cut, using your other hand to control the food, careful to keep your fingers away from the blade. Soon, we were slicing away as he prepared the rest of the mid-day meal, occasionally giving us pointers on keeping the size uniform, on keeping from tiring too quickly.

It was soon obvious that Toumi was desperate that her pile be the largest of the three. I knew I could cut faster than she could, but, since I didn't want her angry with me, I quietly shunted every third or fourth bunch of sliced beans into Emi's pile, since she was working methodically, obviously concerned to have the sharp blade so close to her fingers.

Every once in a while, we heard a dull thud or bang coming through the grate near the ceiling, which opened to the great hall. With the sharp blades in our hands, however, even these odd noises seemed less urgent than paying attention to what we were doing.

When the long beans were finally gone, Kee Sun sauntered over from where he had been preparing a huge pot of chicken stock. "Everyone got yehr fingers?" he asked. We all held out our hands. "Hmmm. No blood, no sliced nails? I think I'll keep yeh all in the kitchen for quite a while!" He appraised the three piles. "Well done, Smiley! Yeh were working quickly!" When Emi and Toumi stared down at the piles, both perplexed that Emi's pile should be larger than Toumi's, Kee Sun winked at me.

———

At lunch that day, Mieko once again set out a bowl of rice beside her, and once again, plunged Kuniko's chopsticks into them. She would continue to do this for the next seven weeks. It quickly became less eerie, more normal, which, as I think back on it now, is the whole point: repeating the ritual so that the person's death seems real. Natural.

After, we were sent to clean out the baths. Mai and Shino taught us about draining them, rinsing them, and refilling them from the huge cistern where all of the compound's water was stored. Shino told us—or rather, she told Toumi, since neither she nor Mai seemed at all interested in talking to me or to Emi—that the reservoir was filled by a spring, which was why the Full Moon had been built where it was, since even if the manor were surrounded, the defenders would never run out of water.

Once the baths were refilled, we lit a fire under the hot tub so that it would be ready for use that evening.

———

Our days quickly fell in to a pattern. Every morning we had breakfast duty, followed by a lesson of some sort—singing, dancing, playing instruments. Very few dealt directly with rituals. I assumed those would be taught to us when we had earned the initiate's red-and-white sash.

The lessons were always led by one or more of the older women, who came and went often enough that we barely got to know their names. I do remember one named Mitsuki whose voice sounded like the scurrying of a mouse through dry leaves, leading us through an unbelievably boring morning learning how to walk in a lady-like fashion.

One of the oddest and most frustrating exercises was carrying rocks. Each of us was given a waist-high pile of stones that we were to carry from one side of the courtyard to the other. The cold stones would leave our fingers raw and bloody. The next day, we would carry the stones back—in sun, rain, or snow.

Not surprisingly, I was always the last to finish.

We were almost always accompanied at these lessons by Mai and Shino—whom Emi had taken to calling the Horseradish Sisters—and by Fuyudori. The white-haired girl's gentle encouragement often seemed crueler than the other two girls' open derision.

Soon, the Horseradishes began taking Toumi under their wings, whispering to her whenever we were together. They always had something nasty to whisper to Toumi just when the teacher was occupied elsewhere. Once, while we were working on music, Sachi and Fuyudori were both trying to teach Emi how to arch her hands properly, and Shino, who was just behind me, whispered that Emi was more stupid than the flute, and perhaps it should try to play her. Toumi snickered, and so did Mai. But when Sachi turned to see what was so funny, they went right back to their playing.

Mai seemed to accept Toumi reluctantly, so long as she kept her place, and so long as Toumi was willing to make fun of me and Emi. In this, Toumi needed no encouragement.

Frequently, one or two of the older women would join us in our studies, though I think it was more to gauge just what dunces the three of us were than actually to work on their own skills, which were considerable.

Mieko never appeared at these sessions, however. During this time, I rarely saw her. Often, at dinner, I caught her and Lieutenant Masugu both following me with their eyes. Once they spotted each other, however, they spent the rest of the meal focusing on the bowls before them.

After morning lessons, we helped with the mid-day meal, cleaned and refilled the baths, and helped with the evening meal. Then off to the baths, off to bed... and ready to start all over again the next morning.

17—Moon Time

The routine was almost reassuring: lessons, work, Toumi growling—all of it flowed from one day to the next like a line of ducks swimming up-river. Even the rock-carrying became routine. Occasionally, one or two figures in *miko*'s robes wandered in through the front gate; just as often, one or more of the women would leave after the morning meal. Yet the little community remained very much the same.

The odd sounds from the great hall were different every day, and always infuriatingly fascinating: sometimes grunts, sometimes shouting, and once what sounded like breaking wood. But we weren't allowed to look, and so this too became part of the pattern.

One day, when the great hall was unusually silent, we were sorting dried mushrooms by color. Kee Sun was very particular about the mix of colors and flavors in all of the food that we prepared. Once we were well into the boring work, he informed us that he had to "go visit the King," a phrase we never understood, and never wanted to. However, we knew that he would be gone some time. When he had gone, Emi's sharp elbow bounced against my ribs.

"Ow!"

Without looking up, she elbowed me again.

"What?"

She sighed. I looked around. Toumi was pointing up to the grate near the ceiling.

Oh! I mouthed. I didn't need to be told what to do. Springing up into the rafters from which herbs and pots hung, I tiptoed along the beam that came into the wall right below the ventilation grate. I felt exhilaration, not at doing something we weren't supposed to do, but just to be up above the ground for the first time since we arrived at the Full Moon.

As I approached the grate, I ducked down so that I wouldn't be seen.

A low murmur of voices echoed from the great hall. I carefully raised my head so that I could just see into the big room.

The tables were pushed back. A battered suit of armor was propped up against the men's table. In front of it, the women were standing in a circle around Mieko, who seemed to be...

She was taking out hairpins. At least, that's what it looked like. She held the two objects, which appeared to be short, flat chopsticks, and then inserted them back into the neat bun on the back of her head. The other women took out their own hairpins and copied her.

Perplexed, I made my way back down to the kitchen. Something about what Mieko had been showing the others looked familiar, but I couldn't think what.

"Well?" Emi and Toumi both asked as soon as my feet hit the stone floor. I told them what I'd seen.

"That's boring," said Emi, her everlasting frown deepening. Toumi and I both nodded, and had just gotten back to sorting our mushrooms when Kee Sun returned. "Isn't this fun!" he chuckled.

We didn't bother nodding at him, but settled back into the pattern of our day.

———

A few weeks after we arrived at the Full Moon, however, the routine suddenly broke.

One morning, we prepared breakfast as usual, but when we brought the meal in to the great hall, there were just nine *kunoichi* at the table along with Lady Chiyome and the men. Four of the older women were missing, as were all three initiates. When I returned, perplexed, to the kitchen with the left over food, Kee Sun scowled at me. "Did yeh spit in my good food, Bright-eyes?"

"No!" I said, staring down at the half-full bowls. Toumi sniggered as she scrubbed the rice-pot clean, preparing it for the mid-day meal.

Emi came in behind me, frowning even more deeply than usual. Her bowls were just as full as mine. "Why would they all leave without eating?" she asked.

"Leave?" Kee Sun said, scratching at his neck.

"Well," Emi said, "Fuyudori and the other initiates weren't at breakfast, and some of the other women were gone. Why would they have gone... doing... whatever they do, without eating?"

Kee Sun scowled at her, and back at me. Then he did something I'd never seen him do: his ears, his cheeks, his forehead and the neck below his beard turned a bright, cherry red. He swore in what I assumed was Korean, his voice higher than usual, and stabbed his knife into the table. "Should have known! Yeh lot comin' threw me off so's I lost count!"

Emi and I exchanged a look; even Toumi was looking as if Kee Sun had suddenly sprouted horns and a furry tail.

Seeing us all looking confused, Kee Sun cleared his throat and growled. "Well, don't just stand there letting the food get cold!" He thrust a scarred finger toward the door. "Bring it to the Retreat, d'yeh hear? Bright-eyes, Smiley—now! Get!"

I remembered the building, of course, but I couldn't understand what he meant—that building was always empty. "The...?"

Leaving his knife wobbling in the wood, he reached up and grabbed lids for the bowls that we were carrying. "GET!"

We took the lids, we slammed them on the bowls, and we got. As we scooted past the well, Emi suddenly slammed to a stop. "Oh!"

I turned and looked at her. "What?"

"The Retreat!" She stared back at me, eyes owl-wide. "It's where the women go during their moon time!"

"Moon...? Oh!" We both looked back down at the bowls in our hands. "Oh."

We started to walk toward the rear corner of the compound, back behind the huge hemlock tree, when Emi halted again.

"What?" I whispered.

"All at once?"

I stared at her.

"Well, I mean," Emi sputtered, "would they all have, you know, started their... time, at the same... time?"

I shrugged at Emi, she shrugged back at me, and we continued on our way—not quite as quickly now.

When we approached the Retreat, I noticed that there was smoke curling from the covered chimney. I put my serving bowl down on the threshold and knocked.

"What?" snapped a sharp voice from inside.

"F-food," stammered Emi.

"Leave it," answered another voice. This was a voice that I'd always heard pitched low and kindly; Mieko's voice didn't sound particularly kindly now. "Leave it on the stoop."

"Yes," Emi and I said. She lay her bowls beside mine, and we scooted quickly back to the kitchen.

Toumi was still scrubbing at the huge rice pot, but she wasn't smirking any more—her face looked the thin grey of spring snow and she didn't look up at all when we came in.

"Might as well get used to it," grumbled Kee Sun. "By this evening they'll all be in there but yeh lot and the lady." He wrenched the knife free from the table, only to stab it in again so hard that the metal of the blade sang with the impact. "Blah!" he muttered. "Women!"

———

Kee Sun was right. By the time that our lessons were over, three more of the women had gone to the Retreat. As we brought the food to the cabin for the mid-day meal, I could only think that it must be awfully crowded in there.

And they didn't sound as if they were in a terribly good mood.

By the time we served that evening's meal, only Lady Chiyome, Lieutenant Masugu, the Little Brothers and Aimaru were seated at the three-sided table. Aimaru looked exceedingly uncomfortable when we served him.

Emi seemed as if she were about to ask him something, but Chiyome-*sama* broke in first, her face twisted in a wicked smirk. "It is so lovely to be in the company of men, from time to time. Don't you agree, Lieutenant?"

Masugu-*san* shrugged. "Certainly, my lady—a soldier learns to enjoy the companionship of his fellows. Yet I must admit that I am pleased still to enjoy the beauteous company of ladies." He lifted his *sake* cup, first to Lady Chiyome, and then to Emi and me.

I found heat rising up my neck to my ears.

"Flatterer," said Lady Chiyome, still smirking, as I backed away, trying to hide my shame at my shame.

———

The women remained in the Retreat for four more days, during which time our lessons were suspended; our teachers were all gone, and we had all the duties of Lady Chiyome's women to attend to.

I'd never been so tired, nor so happy to go back to working in the kitchen. At least there it was always warm.

On the fourth night, as we were settling into our beds, Emi poked me. When I yelped, she shushed me. "Toumi!" she whispered.

"What? Why aren't you already asleep?"

"Wanted to tell you something." She looked over at Toumi, who had fallen into her bedroll and begun her high-pitched saw of a snore. "I talked to Aimaru today, when I was fetching water for the baths," she whispered.

"Aimaru?" I mumbled. I'd hardly seen him in days.

"Shh!" she hissed. "At the well."

"Some of us were working."

"I was working." It was hard to tell in the dark, but her face seemed to get darker. "He said that Masugu-*san* told him that women who lived close together over a long period would begin to enter their moon time together."

I leaned up on one elbow. "Really?"

"Yes." Emi nodded. "I guess Lord Imagawa has a whole flock of daughters. Masugu-*san* lived with them for a while as a kid. He learned to avoid the women's quarters during their, you know, time, because he could count on a less than a friendly welcome."

"Oh."

"Good night, Murasaki."

"Good night, Emi," I answered, but as always, she was already asleep.

Mieko and the rest slowly returned from their seclusion over the next few days in twos and fours as if nothing had happened.

———

One night soon after, as Emi, Toumi and I stumbled out of the kitchen, we realized that it was finally snowing again. But it wasn't the wet, hard snow we got on the coast, near home; these mountain flakes were big as a fingernail, light, and almost dry. The three of us stared up at the white sky. I tried to catch a flake on my tongue—and soon the three of us were spinning around, arms outstretched and mouths open, trying to catch the tumbling flakes on any part of our bodies. Giggling, we careened around in front of the bathhouse.

Then I slammed into Toumi. The habitual sneer pulled Toumi's features back out of shape, and she stumbled in to take a bath. Emi laid a hand on my shoulder, and then followed her.

I remained outside in the fast-falling snow and began to cry. For just a moment I had forgotten flat-nosed Shino, and sharp-nosed Mai; I'd forgotten the isolation of this place, forgotten to mourn my shamed father, my banishment from home, the hole that Mother and Usako used to fill. I had forgotten it all in a blanket of white. But for just a fleeting moment...

I did not hear anyone walking—the snow was already muffling the sound of feet on the gravel—so when a heavy hand came down on my shoulder, I let out a squeak and leapt in the air.

"What's the matter, Murasaki-*san*?" asked Lieutenant Masugu.

I found myself weeping against his chest.

Masugu-*san* sighed, patting me stiffly on the back. "Murasaki-*san*," he said, "you are here for a reason. I am sorry that you had to leave your mother and your sister and your childhood behind. Your mother wouldn't have let you go for nothing—and I don't just mean money. And Chiyome-*sama* wouldn't have paid so high a price for you without a very good reason." He held my shoulders and looked down into my face; his own was grim. "Think of what your father would have done, what he would have wanted you to do. Lady Chiyome wants to give you a chance to redeem your family honor."

I stood there, sniveling, not knowing what to say. With a sad smile and a pat to my shoulder, he turned and began to walk away.

I had almost reached the warmth of the bathhouse when he called back to me.

"Murasaki-*san*!" I turned back toward him in the darkening snowfall. "You haven't been to visit me, have you?"

Perplexed, I shook my head.

"I wondered," he said. "Someone has been in my room. But it wasn't you?" When I shook my head again, he held up his hand and wished me good night.

18—A Fly

"If you come with me quietly, Risuko-*chan*," Fuyudori said in very hushed tones, waking me from a dreamless sleep, "I can show you something worth watching." She pulled down my covers, giving me no choice in the matter.

Yawning and shivering, I threw on a winter coat and sandals. Fuyudori placed her finger over my lips, looking down at Emi and Toumi, who were still sleeping.

It always felt as if it were the middle of the night when Fuyudori woke us. But as we made our way out of the relative warmth of our dormitory, there was not even a hint of a winter dawn in the night sky. The snow had stopped and the sky cleared. The stars blazed down on us, big as snowflakes themselves.

I followed Fuyudori out across the undisturbed snow blanketing the courtyard. Dark and moonless as the night was, even the white of the snow seemed dim and grey.

Fuyudori pulled me relentlessly toward the great hall, but before we arrived, I finally woke enough to stop, digging my heels in. "What's going on?" I asked.

The older girl blinked at me, a rare scowl of annoyance cracking her usually calm mask. "Chiyome-*sama* and Masugu-*san* are arguing—arguing about *you*," she muttered in as low a voice as she could manage. "I thought you might want to hear—that it might be to your benefit. But if you don't want—"

"No," I said, shaking my head stiffly. "I... I want to know."

Her face fell back into its familiar blank smile, and I followed meekly where she led. To my surprise, we did not go to the front door, nor toward the kitchen entrance. Instead, we went to the side of the hall where there was no door, over toward the storehouse. Dry as that mountain snow was, my feet were beginning to feel chilled and damp as we slogged along.

We arrived at the northern wall of the great hall, ten paces or so from the enormous hemlock that I had been aching to climb since our arrival. The wall of the main building was blank except for some half-timbered beams and a single window just below the roofline. A flickering light on the eaves showed that the window was open.

I felt Fuyudori's breath in my ear. It tickled. Very softly, she whispered, "That's Chiyome-*sama*'s private chamber. I heard them yelling at each other before they stormed up there. It was your name they were yelling."

I could make out a low rumble from above, but no words. "We're supposed to climb up and spy at Lady Chiyome's window?" I hissed, before her hand clamped down over my mouth.

"Not *we*, Risuko-*chan*. I cannot make a climb like that. I doubt if any of the women here could. I have been told, however, that you are an excellent climber. Besides, one of us needs to stay down here to keep watch." Her hand still on my mouth, she moved in front of me. Though her white hair glowed in the starlight, her eyes were dark as coal, and lightless, and the hard line of her chin let me know just how determined she was. "This is for your own good, Risuko-*chan*. We need to know if you are in trouble. If you are in trouble, it will reflect on me. Please."

I considered. I did want to know what Lady Chiyome and the lieutenant were saying. And I ached to climb again, but if I was caught...

Fuyudori's eyes pleaded with me.

I nodded.

Her face relaxed. "Thank you, Risuko. You won't regret this. I will hide beneath this fir tree."

"Hemlock," I yawned.

She frowned up at the lowering bows as if just noticing the short, bristly needles, totally unlike the long, silver needles of a fir. "Yes. *Hemlock*. If someone is coming I will give you a signal like a wood owl's hoot." This at least she quietly managed to imitate—more or less.

I shrugged and pressed a foot into the bark of the tree.

"No," whispered Fuyudori, grabbing my shoulder. "Not the tree—the *hemlock*. It's too far, you won't be able to hear."

We both looked over to the great hall's icy wall. I gulped.

"Well," Fuyudori sighed in her kindest, cruelest voice, "perhaps it is too difficult...."

Before she finished the sentence I had stridden over to the wall and begun my ascent.

It was, perhaps, wrong of me to enjoy doing something so dangerous and so obviously likely to anger my patron. But digging my fingers into the narrow, icy half-timbered beams provided enough of a challenge that my breath began to pull. When I reached the first horizontal beam, I looked down to see Fuyudori staring up at me, her mouth and eyes perfect circles of astonishment. I allowed myself to grin as I continued on up.

The last section of the climb was extremely difficult. The only handholds were two beams that ran straight up to either side of the small window. I had to press with all of my strength against either side with my toes and thumbs, scooting up slowly. The wood was cold and I had to move carefully so as not to slip, and the plaster rubbed roughly against my cheek and stomach. It was the hardest climbing I had ever done. The muscles on the outsides of my legs and arms, my shoulders and my hips ached and began to quiver from the strain.

Just as I was sure that my strength would give out, dropping me to a certain broken bone or three, my forehead hit something.

It was the window ledge. I had made it.

Looping one set of fingers and then the other over the outer sides of the ledge—I didn't want my fingers to be visible from inside—I could at last use my fingers and the insides of my arms to hold me up, allowing the thumbs and outsides a well-earned rest.

As my heartbeat stopped racing and I caught my breath, I could hear Lieutenant Masugu's low voice rumbling from the room. "I will stake my honor on it, lady, it wasn't her."

Lady Chiyome's voice managed to be even colder than usual. "You'll risk so much on such a little creature? One whose family honor is hardly equal to yours?"

There was silence in the room, and my heart sped right back up again as I suddenly realized that the family she was insulting was mine.

When it came, Masugu-*san*'s voice was quiet but as sharp as a falcon's cry. "It wasn't Murasaki. She saved our lives."

"Hmmm." Unfazed, she clucked her tongue. "Well, unless you think the spirits have been playing games, then someone was in your chamber, Masugu."

He grunted. "I think the spirits must have better things to do than to move my papers around. The Little Brothers tells me there are signs of the raiders still being in the valley."

"Perhaps. Perhaps not. Even so, do not let your affection for the girl blind you to what she is," the old woman said, her voice as cold as her ledge.

Masugu muttered something that I could not hear.

My shoulders were beginning to quake with the effort of keeping myself in place, and yet I could hardly move. I needed to know what it was that they suspected me of. Looking down, I saw Fuyudori skulking at the base of the tree, her white hair like snow, gleaming in the starlight; she looked even more ghost-like than ever.

"In any case, Chiyome-*sama*," Masugu-*san* said, "it wasn't found. It's still safely hidden away in the chimney."

"Good," Lady Chiyome grumbled. "Lord Takeda's plans depend upon it being delivered, Lieutenant. Don't forget that. As tedious as this service may be, my young friend, stuck among all of these young ladies, it is nonetheless essential, yes?"

"Yes, lady," Masugu answered, though he didn't sound terribly happy.

"Now get back to your room, Masugu, and let an old woman get her sleep."

"Yes, lady," he said, and I heard his steady footsteps going down the stairs.

Before I was able to begin my descent, however, I heard Chiyome-*sama* speak once more. "Come in, Risuko. You'll catch your death hanging outside of windows like that."

19—In the Web

My shaking arms suddenly went still, as if instantly turned to ice. Looking down, I saw that Fuyudori had disappeared. I was trapped and alone.

"Do hurry, Risuko-*chan*," said Lady Chiyome in that quiet voice that still managed to sound quite piercing. "I don't want to have to call Kee Sun to haul you in. He might slip and drop you, and that would be the most awful mess."

Arms trembling, my back screaming with the effort and the cold, I pulled myself up, one elbow at a time, peeking over the sill into Chiyome-*sama*'s chamber.

It was smaller than I would have expected. Most of the space was dominated by a large, black bed that amounted to a small room of its own—a tall box almost like a huge palanquin, self-contained as Chiyome-*sama* herself, and almost enclosed, with a chair and a desk built into the entry. The space remaining was taken up by *tatami* mats, in the middle of which stood a small kneeling desk; she was seated cross-legged behind it. Before her on the desk stood a number of small, brightly colored shapes.

"Good evening, my little squirrel," said Lady Chiyome, smirking sourly. "It is so lovely of you to join me. And by such an unusual route. Extraordinary. Not even Mieko in her prime could have undertaken such a climb unaided. I am most impressed."

I collapsed to my knees, staring down at the *tatami*, utterly bewildered. "Thank you, Chiyome-*sama*."

"Hmm. You were unaided, I suppose? No mechanical assistance? No one helping you?"

I thought of Fuyudori, who had urged me to climb, and then disappeared. "Nobody helping me," I said.

She rested a finger to her nose, and then grunted. "Yes," she said. "Most impressive." Squaring her shoulders, she peered at me. "Tell me, Risuko, what did you hear?"

"N-nothing, lady," I spluttered.

"Do not lie to me, girl. You were beneath the window ledge well before Masugu left."

I knew better, but I could not help staring at the old woman. "*How*—?"

She favored me with a wicked grin. "Little girls shouldn't be too curious. Now tell me, Risuko, what did you hear?"

My stomach, which had been clenched tight, suddenly felt as though Kee Sun had force-fed me lead. "I..."

She waited, unblinking.

I took a deep breath. "You were speaking with Masugu-*san* about me. About whether I could be trusted. About whether I'd done... something. I couldn't figure out what though. He said something about spirits in his rooms?"

She grunted again. "And were you playing the fox spirit earlier tonight, Risuko-*chan*?"

I blinked in confusion.

"Where you the *kitsune* haunting Masugu-*san*'s chamber? Someone has been playing games there."

"No, Chiyome-*sama*!" I said, shocked. "Absolutely not!"

We sat there, staring at each other, until I thought I might choke or that my beating heart might explode out of my chest. Finally, the old woman gave a half nod and said, "Perhaps not. Perhaps not." She twirled one of the colored shapes on her desk between her fingers—I saw that they were pebbles of various sizes, painted in bright colors and distributed over a large, creased piece of paper that had been webbed with squiggly lines and cramped calligraphy. At the top was written *Land of the Rising Sun*. The wicked smile reappeared. "Do you know what this is, my little squirrel?"

I was about to shake my head, when the lines and shapes that marked the paper suddenly seemed to come unclouded and I recognized them. "It's a map. Of Japan?"

My patron clapped her hands together, clearly pleased. "Ah, well, done, my dear. Your father didn't waste your childhood entirely. Can you find our location upon the map?"

Scowling with concentration, I looked down and found my family's home province, Serenity—toward the eastern edge at the top. It had many red stones to the northern, left-hand edge, as many of blue at the southern edge and one large green stone in the middle, just where I knew my family's home to be. I touched the pebble briefly, and then followed the blue line that marked the Weatherbank River's flow down to Pineshore, and the heavy dashed line that showed the Eastern Sea Road, the great coastal highway up which we had marched—had it been only weeks before? It felt as if that journey had belonged to another lifetime.

Tracing our path through Quick River and Worth Provinces (a sea of red stones, small and large) and into the mountains, I found the southern end of Dark Letter Province; here there were more red pebbles, one at what looked like the Rice Paddy Pass garrison, and one very small one over the tiny mark of a full moon. Clustered around the stone were a number of sharp, metal spikes—pins, such as my mother had sometimes used to use when she was mending our clothes. The top of each was painted red and white. "Here," I said, pointing.

"Well done, my little navigator. And what would you guess these are?" She touched a dry finger to one of a large number of white stones that stood near the Imperial City.

The painted pebbles were scattered around the map in clusters; the largest number where white, red and blue, with a number of other colors sprinkled here and there. The red-and-white pins were distributed in ones and twos across the provinces, seemingly at random, always near a pebble.

The stones weren't towns—those were painted directly onto the map, their names labeled in a cramped, neat hand. They could represent rice or gold, but it seemed odd that so many of the stones were gathered around the center of Honshu Island, the main island of our nation; I knew that other parts of the country produced food and wealth.

Knowing that Lady Chiyome hated it when I stuck my tongue out, I bit it as I continued to scowl down at the map. "Are they... ?" I did not want to appear to be stupid. "Are they armies, Chiyome-*sama*?"

A look of pleased surprise rushed over her face, and I felt relief rush through me. "What makes you say that, my squirrel?"

"Well," I said, "It looks like a multicolored game of Go, like *Otō-san* used to play with old Ichihiro from the castle." Peering back up at her, I asked, "Is this a game?"

The old woman loosed her wheezing, mirthless laugh. "Yes! Yes, indeed, it is a game—a very complicated and deadly one." She touched the one green pebble where it stood near our home. "Do you see this green marker?"

I nodded.

"Does it look familiar, child?"

I blinked. The large green stone surrounded by smaller stones of blue and red. "The picture I drew for you. That I saw Lord Imagawa and the soldier looking at."

"Indeed. That told me that a large battle was coming, though Masugu and his friends brought it to us rather more quickly than I expected. This green piece represents the remaining force of the Imagawa—a considerable army, but a shadow of the power that they used to wield."

"Then the red... The red are the forces of the Takeda?" I reasoned.

"Well done," the old woman said, though the praise was fainter in her tone than in the words. Pointing just north of the tiny stone that marked our own little army, she said, "This stone represents the garrison at Highfield, where Masugu's riders are serving, guarding our territories from the forces of the Uesugi." A group of yellow stones stood further to the northwest.

Pointing down the river from the red and yellow markers around Highfield, she said very quietly, "And there is Midriver Island."

Her hand swept southeast, toward the provinces directly below Serenity Province. A group of blue stones sprawled throughout this region. "These are the forces of the Matsudaira; they used to be loyal to the Imagawa, but the arrogance of that old clan drove them to ally themselves elsewhere. Currently they are loosely allied both with Lord Takeda and with the current shogun, Lord Oda. These are his armies." Her hand passed over the sea of white in the center of the map. "What do you think each of these armies wishes to do?"

Again I frowned—there were a number of ways of answering that question, depending on how you looked at it. "Um, to defend their provinces?"

She waved a dismissive hand, "Of course, of course. But do you think it is good for Japan, this sea of warring colors?"

Trusting that I knew how she wished me to respond, I shook my head.

"No, it is not!" she barked, as forcibly as I had ever heard her. "Our nation has been at war with itself for almost a hundred years. Since the Kamakura shoguns were overthrown, warlords up and down the nation have strived to unite all of Japan under one banner, to become shogun, and to bring law and peace back to our blessed islands. Yet no one lord has been strong enough to defeat the others, and so there has been a constant game of changing allegiances, of treachery, and bloodshed, each lord aiming to protect his own clan's best interests. It *must* end."

"And Lord Takeda can stop it?"

She grunted and gave a grim nod. "He is the greatest general of the major powers—noble and strong of mind, unbeatable on the battlefield, lacking Lord Oda's inconstancy, his fascination with gimmicks and foreign oddities. Once the Imagawa are gone, Lord Takeda will be the strongest force left, save for Lord Oda and his armies. When the other lords unite beneath the four-diamond Takeda banner, the Oda will have to relinquish the capital city to us, and Takeda Shingen will rule a united Japan as the emperor's *shōgun*."

Why was she telling me all of this? I certainly couldn't have told you at the time. I think in part it was a test—to see if I could follow what she was talking about. In part, too, I think that it was a subject close to whatever served the old woman for a heart. It was a topic about which she had clearly thought long and deeply.

Eventually, she took and released a deep breath. Indicating the white pebbles with one elegant, wrinkled hand, she asked, "And what do you know about Oda-*sama*, young Kano?"

I thought of the conversations that I'd had with Masugu-*san* on the long ride to the Full Moon. I couldn't tell her everything—both because I couldn't stand to admit how little I knew, and because I wasn't sure that the lieutenant was supposed to tell me and I didn't want to get him into trouble. "I... I know that my father served for a time as a samurai beneath him."

Chiyome-*sama* narrowed her eyes. "And do you know why your father left his service? Not everyone does, you know."

"I..." I looked up into her shrewd face. "I know that my father, Emi's and Toumi's were sent on a mission that they refused. That is all I know."

"Then you know more than I thought you did. Do you know anything about this mission?" When I shook my head, she daintily straightened up the stones around the capital. She quietly waited until I was once again feeling on the edge of bursting. "Ask yourself, Risuko-*chan*, what your father valued more than anything. More even than his own honor."

"I..." She was asking such an impossible question, yet I did not know how to refuse or to avoid her gaze. "Family," I whispered.

"Yes," she said. "Then ask yourself what mission Lord Oda could have given to so honorable a man as your father that he would have refused."

My eyes must have given some sense of the horror that swept over me at that moment, because Lady Chiyome laughed. "No, silly girl, he wasn't ordered to kill *you*. Why would Oda-*sama* have bothered?"

"Then...?"

A wry smile twisted her still-powdered face. "Such a bright girl as yourself, you should be able to work it out."

"I... I can't imagine, Chiyome-*sama*." I stared down at the board. "Lady? What are these, these red and white pins?"

Her smile broadened. "I expect you to work that out on your own as well, Risuko. Now I'm tired of idle prattle. Leave me, girl."

Uncertain, I stood and began to stumble back toward the window.

Her rough, dry laugh burst forth again, stopping me. "No, no! The stairs, stupid child! Once you've been caught, you might as well take advantage of the easiest route of escape." Her face still bore all of the signs of amusement, though her eyes were mirthless. "Do shutter the window, however. It is getting chilly."

With a nod of my head, I pulled the shutters closed.

"And, my squirrel?" the old woman muttered as I began to withdraw toward the stairs. I froze, afraid of what she might have to add. She smirked at me thoughtfully. "When next you decide to listen at windows on a frosty night, do remember that the steam from your breath rises. Place yourself to the side."

Stunned again, I mumbled a quick, "Yes, Chiyome-*sama*," and tiptoed down the stairs and back to my quarters as quickly as my wobbly legs could carry me.

20—Smelly Work

When I arrived back at our cabin, Fuyudori was standing just inside of the door looking pinched and pale in the dim light of the entryway. "What took you so long?"

"I could ask you the same thing. Where did *you* disappear to?" I snapped, much to my own surprise.

She seemed as shocked as I was at my outburst. "I... Lieutenant Masugu came out and walked right toward where I was standing. I gave the signal, but then I had to hide behind the Retreat. When I came back, you were gone. I assumed that, since he had already left, you must have climbed back down, but you've been gone so long, I was beginning to be worried."

I looked up into her face and realized suddenly that she was lying to me. Not in a large way, but for some reason she wasn't telling me the entire truth. I decided to return the favor. "I reached the top, but it was quiet. I listened to see if anything was going on, but when I didn't hear anything, I went up to the roof and climbed down from there. It's not easy climbing down a slick wall in the middle of winter, you know."

Her eyes narrowed, but she nodded and said, "Well, it's a good thing you didn't fall. Sleep well, Risuko-*chan*."

The next morning, Toumi looked quite pleased with herself, watching Fuyudori, Lady Chiyome and Masugu-*san*, and making nasty comments to me about finally getting my payback. She had clearly told on me—whether about talking with the lieutenant or sneaking out at night, I couldn't be certain. I waited for punishment to fall.

No one mentioned anything.

Through the days that followed I found myself looking over my shoulder, sure that *someone* was going to take me to task for my activities that night, though Lady Chiyome certainly hadn't seemed terribly upset.

It became clear that I wasn't going to get in any trouble. And it was entertaining watching Toumi's frustration grow.

A few nights later, as the other girls lay in their bedrolls, huddling against the cold and snoring, I woke Emi and told her about everything that had happened—everything but the bit about our fathers. She blinked at me, scowling. Then she broke into a rare grin. "Serves Fuyudori right, making you do her dirty work for her," she whispered. "And I bet that's why Toumi's been sniffing around like a dog waiting for a rice cake to fall."

I nodded. "But no one seems to be itching to punish me."

"That must be awful for poor Toumi," tittered Emi, before rolling over and going back to sleep. I finally managed to follow her not long after, but didn't sleep soundly.

Toumi remained in a foul mood for days.

Somehow, though I was amused, I wasn't relieved.

———

One afternoon, as we shuffled into Kee Sun's kitchen to take up our evening duties, we were presented with a new challenge. Once again, each of us had a knife, laid with ritual precision across the bottom of a cutting board. Where we had always had piles of vegetables or butchered meats, however, each of us was presented with a trio of slaughtered chickens.

Emi made a face, and Toumi grumbled, but I knew how to start at least—this much mother had taught us, on days when we were fortunate enough to catch a bird, or one of Irochi-*san*'s hens was no good for eggs any more: I began plucking the feathers from the flesh.

"There yeh go, girlies!" laughed Kee Sun. "Bright-eyes's got the idea! Can't eat feathers, now can yeh?"

We stripped our carcasses—Toumi never stopped grumbling, nor did her expression lose any of its edge. Emi, however, was so engrossed in the unpleasant, difficult job that her usual scowl faded. Her face seemed as blank and neutral as a Jizo-bosatsu's statue.

Once we had each stripped the carcasses of their feathers—the mess now filled baskets at our feet—Kee Sun called out happily, "Well, it's about time, girlies! Now you're going to learn the proper use of a blade."

With glee, he proceeded to instruct us in the technique for gutting, cleaning, skinning, and butchering a chicken.

I won't pretend that Emi and I didn't throw up.

Toumi did too. Twice.

So it was that we—orphaned samurai girls not yet in our first woman-hood—began to become master butchers. Over the next days, after our lessons in music, dance or calligraphy, we learned with great effort to reduce the bounteous meat, poultry and fish that graced Lady Chiyome's dining table to edible portions. Chickens first, then ducks and geese; trout and boney carp; pigs, which were much heavier, obviously, and required us to work together; I took great care to keep an eye out for Toumi's blade on those occasions.

It was smelly, disgusting work, but soon enough the odors became as familiar as the scent of pine I so associate with my childhood home.

———

The amount of food that we prepared—that we and Chiyome-*sama*'s other servants consumed—was overwhelming. We ate three full meals a day, with some sort of meat served at least once a day, and often twice. Frequently, we were able to serve fresh vegetables as well—huge *daikon* radishes or soy beans that Kee Sun had carefully packed up in the storerooms by the Bull Pen, or that were brought up the muddy, icy road to the Full Moon by exceedingly respectful farmers.

I had peered in the windows at Lord Imagawa's castle often enough to know that, except for the occasional banquet, even they didn't eat anywhere nearly as richly as Lady Chiyome and her household—even Lord Imagawa himself and the fancy ladies mostly ate rice and occasionally some bits of fish and poultry. It looked like much nicer rice and much finer flesh than what we were used to down in the village, and I know they'd occasionally buy one of old Naru's pigs to slaughter, but I doubt they were eating meat anywhere nearly as often as the inhabitants of Lady Chiyome's compound.

When I asked Kee Sun about that, he just smirked. "Lady's orders," he said. "She says to feed yeh like my lord used to feed his troops before battle, and that's the way yeh're gonna be fed. Right, Smiley?" He threw the knuck-lebone of the pig we were cutting up at Emi, who looked up, blinking, and caught it on the fly. "It certainly agrees with the lot of yeh!"

It was true. I was much less skinny than I had been when I met the others. Though the constant work kept the new muscle that was beginning to cling to my bones from ever growing soft, my ribs no longer stuck out of my chest like maple boughs in winter. Even Toumi had fleshed out a bit, so that it no longer looked as if you would cut your hand if you were to touch her. Not that I was ever tempted to touch her.

Though at first it seemed as if Emi had changed the least—her face still in a perpetual frown, her hands and feet still bigger than her arms and legs could seem to carry—I realized that the hand that had caught that bone was now well clear of the sleeve of the jacket that she wore. Looking down at her feet, I realized that the cuffs of the pants didn't reach anywhere near her ankles.

Carefully placing the knuckle in the offal bucket, Emi looked at me—looked down at me—and scowled. She didn't seem to know how to react to her growth. I certainly didn't know either.

———

After every meal, we brought the unusable bits out to the rubbish pit out the back entrance of the Full Moon. As much as the pit itself stank, giving off steam even on the coldest days, I loved being out near the woods. Outside of the little world of the compound.

One day, as Emi and I were coming back from dumping fish bones and scales in the pit, Emi stopped, her nose twitching. "Do you smell smoke?"

Frowning I nodded. "Could be from the kitchen."

Emi shook her head. "Wind's blowing the other way." She pointed up at the the Full Moon's wall, where the smoke from the kitchen fire was clearly blowing away from us. "Farmer?"

"Don't think so. They're all too far away. Someone must be in the woods." We both peered at the groves that choked either side of the ridge. The smoke certainly wasn't coming down the cliff behind us.

We looked at each other.

"I don't suppose," Emi said, "that you could...?" She pointed at the thick woods that hemmed the Full Moon in on either side of the ridge.

Nodding, I said, "Tell Kee Sun I'm, um, 'visiting the King' or whatever—I'll be right back."

The trees were tangled oak and bay that weren't easy to climb through, yet didn't provide a much cover in the winter. I clambered carefully toward the faint smell of smoke—but stopped when I heard the faint whicker of a horse and a voice: a man's voice. And then another, fainter in the wind, but higher. A woman. *Who?*

Before I could get any closer, however, I heard Kee Sun's voice calling my name. Quietly cursing, I made my way back to the back entrance.

"Bring me any acorns, did yeh, Bright-eyes?" The cook's arms were crossed and a scarred eyebrow raised.

Chastened, I followed him back to the kitchen.

———

After days spent up to our elbows in fins and feathers and intestines, we entered the kitchen the next morning to find the entire space between the cooking fire and the pantry taken up with the carcass of a cow. Groaning at the size of the beast, we looked to Kee Sun for instruction.

The cook, who was sitting atop the barrel that held the brewing rice wine, simply laughed his peculiar laugh and gestured to the worktable. Knives were laid out as usual, gleaming.

Toumi started to complain, but Emi shook her head. "No point," she said, her voice matching her glum face for once. Squaring her shoulders, she walked to the cutting table and picked up the largest knife I had ever seen.

Nervously, I looked over at Toumi. She seemed as overwhelmed as I felt, but when she saw me peering at her, she narrowed her eyes, grabbed a sword-sized cleaver and a thin blade for skinning, and strode over to where Emi was already starting the process of reducing the animal to food.

I looked at Kee Sun and he looked back, unflinching. His face was blank and his eyes empty of their usual humor. Gulping quickly through my mouth so that I wouldn't have to smell the animal, I picked up my knives and went to help out.

And so that is how we spent the entire day, for Kee Sun told us with great glee that we would be spared from our usual lessons—as if that were a favor. He made breakfast and lunch, whistling and singing.

Whatever lesson Mieko was teaching to the women in the great hall that day had them all howling with laughter, which didn't brighten our moods in the kitchen. We worked away, butchering that enormous creature, carefully skinning it and laying aside the hide for tanning, cleaning the carcass, dividing it into workable portions, removing all of the edible bits—there are edible parts of a cow that you wouldn't even want to begin to think about—and delivering them to Kee Sun in neat, evenly cut cubes and leaf-wrapped packages, all by the time that Kee Sun had begun to chop the vegetables and clean the rice for that evening's meal. We were covered in blood, and the stench there in the kitchen was awful, but I think we all felt a certain amount of pride at having completed the gruesome chore.

"Well done!" he called, and once again we received a portion of rice wine with our meal after everyone else had eaten.

I enjoyed the meal. All but the beef. I couldn't eat the beef.

21—Lessons in Dance

The day after we butchered the cow, we began a new set of morning lessons. As we cleared up the kitchen, Mai, who never entered the kitchen if she could help it, poked her head through the door and informed us that, for the first time, we would be taught by Mieko-*san*.

As she withdrew, Kee Sun asked whether Mai had actually walked into the kitchen before delivering her message. When Toumi snarled that no, she hadn't—making it clear that no one in their right mind would enter Kee Sun's domain willingly—the cook gave a nod and a grunt, saying, "That's good. 'Cause I told her if she ever stepped a foot in here again, I'd cut it off."

It was always a bit difficult to know whether he was joking or not. To be honest, I was never quite able to work that out.

Nonetheless, I was excited by Mai's news; I had hoped that we would be able to study with Mieko, not only because she was kind and lovely but because the other women in Chiyome-*sama*'s service seemed to respect her so. Even the boisterous ones listened quietly when she spoke.

As we finished cleaning up the kitchen and preparing it for the next meal, we all speculated in excited whispers. "Maybe we'll learn Chinese for poetry and such," Emi said.

Toumi snorted. "I just want her to teach us about knives."

I remembered Mieko calmly wiping her blade as the bodies of her two attackers bled onto the floor of the Mount Fuji Inn beside her. Returning it calmly to its sheath.

Instead of leading us down to the teahouse as usual for our lesson that morning, Fuyudori walked us very solemnly to the stables of all places. As we entered the low building, we saw that the central space had been swept clean and the stalls on one side removed, leaving a large and open area that had been covered in *tatami* mats. Masugu-*san* had apparently taken his horse out for a morning ride so that the remaining stalls were empty, the spare saddles and other gear were all stored away, and a small charcoal stove had been lit, so that the usually drafty room was warm. Clad in a *miko's* red and white robes, Mieko knelt on a mat in the center of the room, head bowed, looking quite at peace—much as she had on that awful morning at the Mount Fuji Inn.

All of the inhabitants of the Full Moon knelt around her, facing her—all but Masugu-*san*, Kee Sun, and Lady Chiyome herself, of course; like the lieutenant and the cook, the lady was absent.

Toumi's joke had infected my imagination. I felt a quiver of anxious anticipation. Was Mieko going to teach us how she had defended herself from those two soldiers? Would she be teaching us yet another use for the knives with which Kee Sun had made us so proficient?

No harm, Murasaki, I heard *Otō-san* saying. *Harm begets only harm. No fight; no blame.* I tried to cleanse from my mind the image of lovely, graceful Mieko wiping the blood from her knife with as much poise as a samurai cleaning his *katana*.

And yet, in some secret part of me, I did not care what our father had taught us about how our actions affect us in this life and those to come.

Kneeling to the straw with the others, I shivered and lowered my eyes, waiting for Mieko to speak.

After a long, still silence, she addressed us in her musical, quiet voice. "Many of you have already approached this lesson. Our three novices and the young brother, however, have not, and we are fortunate that this is so: we shall be pursuing an art in which all of us are forever novices, and studying it again with a novice's unsullied eyes is the best way to continue to grow in it. I will, therefore, begin at the beginning."

Without saying another word, Mieko stood in that smooth, unfolding motion that always struck me as so breathtakingly impossible—as if the ground had lowered from her, rather than that Mieko had expended any effort to stand. She planted her feet at shoulder width and reached down without looking, pulling her red skirt up between her legs, tucking it into her sash as if she were one of the old grandmothers of the village getting ready to go and harvest rice.

The rest of the women—as well as the men—stood, none as smoothly as Mieko, but nearly all without a sound.

Beside me, Toumi was already springing to her feet, and Emi and I scrambled to join her. We, at least, had no robes to deal with and so we were able to fall into the oddly masculine stance at the same time as the rest of the women.

Mieko looked at me—at us—and smiled. It seemed a very sad smile, and yet it filled me with a funny tickle of pleasure that she had smiled at me. At us.

Her hands lifted slowly, so that it looked as if she were holding a ball immediately in front of her belly, and just as slowly she began to sway toward one foot and lift her hands above her head. "The Two Fields," she whispered.

The whole group mirrored her actions, and Emi and I tried to follow. Toumi jerked herself so that she reached Mieko's final position before we did; I could see a smile on her lips too, and I was sure again that I was its cause, but this smile did not fill me with pleasure.

When we had caught up to her, Mieko remained still for a breath, and then shifted to the opposite foot, stepping to the side on it and extending that invisible ball held in her hands over her head. "The Bamboo Bud."

We all mirrored Mieko, stepping to one side and bringing that invisible ball above our heads.

Next, Mieko stepped toward us, lifting what had been her trailing leg, and then bringing it and her hands down. "The Key to Heaven."

Again we followed; again Toumi made sure to finish before us.

Her smirk ceased to bother me soon enough, however. First, it became clear that moving quickly was not the point—the more Toumi rushed, the more Mieko seemed to slow down, flowing from one movement to the next so that you could not tell where one movement ended and the next began.

Second, my mind was fully occupied. Between the movements themselves, which became slowly more challenging, though always as slow and flowing as if in a dream, and the fact that there seemed no point to what we were doing, I had no room in my head to think of Toumi at all.

Dance. It was a dance. We had learned other dances at the Full Moon—dances that I recognized as going along with some of the ceremonies and songs that we were learning. Yet this dance was so slow and so unlike any that I had ever seen that I was bewildered.

I was bewildered too because as much as it didn't seem like any dance that I had ever seen, nonetheless, after a time of following the ice-slow flow of arms and legs, I began to feel as if I knew the movements—as if I could anticipate them before Mieko began to lead us into the next step, the next sweep of the arms, the next gentle lunge.

As the lesson went on, I found that, no matter how quickly Toumi raced, I had always anticipated the movement that Mieko was about to show us, and reached the next shape before Toumi could.

Was I simply growing accustomed to this peculiar dance? In the moment I could only have told you that I felt as if I were remembering it from another lifetime, which made me think of *Otō-san*, and that it gave me a deep feeling of peace.

As we moved, I found myself remembering the couple whose voices I'd heard outside in the woods. Masugu-*san*, perhaps? And who else?

After a time, Mieko returned us to the first position—*The Two Fields*, feet wide, hands before our bellies. "Again," she said, and lead us back into the flowing pattern of movements that felt as comfortable to me as walking or as climbing a tree.

————

She led the whole company through the dance eight more times, so that after a while even Emi and Toumi were beginning to move with the rest of us, rather than looking to see what the next movement might be. In the end, Mieko stood for a moment in the beginning posture, but instead of saying "Again" and continuing, she brought her feet together, placed her hands on the fronts of her thighs, and bowed. We all bowed with her, as if we were her mirror. It was a startling feeling—that some twenty people were moving, not as individuals, but as a single being. We straightened and stood.

There was no sound but the hiss of the wood burning in the little stove.

Without a word, Mieko left, followed by the Little Brothers, with Aimaru trailing behind them, blinking.

The rest of us stayed to return the stable to its normal, cluttered state. We had just finished when Masugu-*san* rode in, his horse sweaty and covered in mud, his eyes bright as I had not seen them in weeks.

————

As soon as we left the stable, Toumi snarled, "What kind of idiotic nonsense was that?"

Mai and Shino pulled her aside, whispering urgently—clearly trying to help Toumi avoid one of the older women overhearing—but they needn't have bothered. One of the older *kunoichi* made a sour face and clicked her tongue before turning toward the great hall. Looking like a dog that's just been hit, Toumi ran toward her least favorite spot in the Full Moon, the kitchen.

"Well," whispered Emi as we followed in Toumi's wake, "I guess she could have found a more polite way to ask, but I have to say I'm just as confused. You knew the moves. Do you know what that was about?"

I shook my head. "I don't even know that I really knew the dance, or whatever it was. It just felt... as if I just knew what she meant us to do."

Emi stopped and looked at me, frowning. Of course, Emi was always frowning, so it wasn't easy to know what she was thinking. "You've really never seen that."

"No. At least, I don't think so."

Emi nodded, but as we both walked up toward Kee Sun's domain, her frown hadn't lessened at all.

22—Feather Soup

The following day, after the midday meal, Emi and I were taking the remains of a dozen chickens out through the gate in the back of the compound wall to the rubbish pit when we heard a sharp hiss from behind our dormitory. She and I blinked at each other, dull and incapable of thought after the long ordeal of plucking and butchering the birds.

"Emi! Murasaki!" It was Aimaru's voice, whispering as loudly as he could manage.

Blinking at each other again, Emi and I scanned the compound. It was not snowing—it hadn't in over a week—but it was bitterly cold as only those mountains can be, and everyone seemed to be indoors, shutters closed. I led the way back to where Aimaru was hiding.

Our friend was wearing what looked to be every piece of clothing he could pull on—he could barely bend his arms to gesture.

"You look silly," Emi said, her scowl lightening slightly. He looked like a rag doll.

"Very funny," he said, and Emi and I choked on our laughter, unable to cover our mouths since our hands held baskets full of bones, feathers, intestines and beaks.

"Look, I've been waiting out here forever since the end of the meal. It's cold!"

We laughed again. It wasn't very kind of us, but after all of the dismal and odd things that we had been doing, it felt good to laugh.

"We apologize, Aimaru-*san*," I said finally with a giggle, bowing as deeply as I could without spilling the chicken offal onto his feet.

"Fine! Fine! I've wanted to talk to you two for days! But if you're having such a lovely time, clearly you don't need to talk to me," Aimaru grumbled, and I tried to settle myself as much as I could. Emi was scowling so fiercely that I was certain that she was biting her cheeks. He peered into our baskets. "What are you doing?"

"Well," I grumbled, "now that we've butchered these lovely chicken carcasses so that you can have some stew tonight, we're taking the bits that even Kee Sun can't figure out how to make edible out to the offal pit."

Aimaru frowned—the expression seemed wrong on his face.

"Would you like some feather soup, Aimaru?" Emi asked. "I'm sure Murasaki and I could whip some up for you in no time."

He snorted, the frown gone again. "Not just now, thank you."

Emi scowled—at least, I think she did—and said, "What a shame. I was looking forward to seeing if you really would eat anything."

Sighing, Aimaru said, "Close enough. The Little Brothers have me working and training so hard, I'm ready for the mid-day meal before the sun has cleared the horizon."

"What are you doing?" I asked.

"Oh, working with a spear and on my strength. It's mostly pretty boring."

I giggled. "Really?"

He shrugged as much as he could in all of that clothing. "We do hours of meditation, just like when I was at the monastery. They have been taking me out on their rounds, though."

"Rounds?" I asked.

"Yes, the Little Brothers serve as Lady Mochizuki's bailiffs, making sure that her farmers are all well, and collecting..." Suddenly, Aimaru grew thoughtful, his brows contracting toward the center of his usually smooth face.

"What are the villagers like?" I had hardly thought about the outside world in weeks, except as a map covered with pebbles and pins; it seemed odd to think that there were farmers and tanners and scribes down in the valley, living very much as my family had always done in the shadow of the Imagawa castle. "What do they think of Lady Chiyome?"

"Fine. Very respectful." He was staring down at the guts and feather in our baskets.

"You didn't change you mind about the soup, did you?" Emi asked. She held the basket up as if to let him smell.

"No," Aimaru said, no smirk at all this time. "No, I was thinking. You've been butchering chickens?"

"Yes," I said. "We just told you. And pigs. And the cow the other day. That was horrible."

"Yes," he said, but I couldn't tell what he was agreeing with. "The thing is, the farmers usually butcher the animals before presenting them to us. I hadn't even thought about why they were presenting them to us unprepared."

"Well," I said, shrugging, "it could be the storms?"

"Butchering is indoor work," Emi muttered, "and not exactly cold. I'd think we'd want the meat separated from the offal as soon after the animal was slaughtered as possible."

"I suppose," I said, though I knew that they were right. "Maybe it's just Kee Sun?"

"Maybe," answered Emi, wrinkling her nose.

After a moment of silence in which all three of us stared into the nauseating stuff in the baskets, I asked, "Why would they care so much about *us* doing the butchering?"

Another moment of silence followed.

"Perhaps they want to train us as cooks," Emi said, chewing on her lip.

Aimaru shook his head. "Murasaki, Chiyome-*sama* told you that she wanted you to be a... what was it? A...?"

"A *kunoichi*."

"Yes. Isn't that what the older women are?"

"Yes," Emi said firmly.

"Huh." He patted his stiff, padded arms against his body to warm himself.

Another silence followed, this one even longer. I tried to imagine Mieko-*san* plucking, gutting or boning a chicken. I couldn't.

"It was nice to see you yesterday morning at the dance lesson," said Emi.

Aimaru nodded and shuffled his feet. "That's why I wanted to talk with you. I thought we were just going to clear out the stable. I had no idea we were going to join you...."

Emi scowled at him; it seemed almost a relief to watch her face return to its normal expression. "So you don't have any idea what the point of that lesson was?"

"None!" he answered, eyes wide. "Is that what you've been learning?"

We both shook our heads. Emi grumbled, "Oh, no. We've been learning to play bad music and pour cold tea."

"That sounds... interesting," he said, looking perplexed again.

I laughed. "Hardly. And it isn't as bad as Emi is making it sound—at least it's better than skinning cows and plucking chickens."

Aimaru favored us with a smile. "Well, I suppose that's true. Though at least, in the kitchen, you get to stay warm!"

Emi and I joined his smile, but she shivered, and I became aware of the chill.

At last I sighed. "We need to get back. Tonight's *mizutaki* won't cook itself, yeh know!" I said in something vaguely like Kee Sun's sharp-edged accent.

That broke the spell. They both laughed.

Emi and I began walking toward the gate to the offal pit and Aimaru stomped straight-legged and straight-armed toward the stables. Before we'd gone more than a step or two, Emi laughed her strange laugh. "Look!" She was staring down at the patch of snow where we'd been standing. "It's the Chinese character for *goat!*" she giggled.

There in the white, trampled snow the blood dripping from one of the baskets had drawn what did indeed like a Chinese *kanji* character. All I could seem to see, however, was the blood.

———

After we had emptied the baskets, Emi and I were on our way back to the compound when we both heard a noise.

"What was that?" Emi's brows pursed.

I listened, but heard nothing but the sound of the wind swirling through the tangled woods. "A... a horse? Maybe?" I was thinking of the voices I'd heard when I'd climbed through the oaks. *Masugu? And... Mieko?*

"Emi-*chan*! Risuko-*chan*! You should not be out here speaking to this *boy!*" Fuyudori seemed to have appeared out of nowhere just inside the Full Moon's rear gate. Her white hair disappeared into the snow, which was falling again, and her cheeks glowed red.

"Yes, Fuyudori-*senpai*! Sorry, Fuyudori-*senpai*!" Emi and I both spluttered, hurrying back inside under her glare.

———

Late that night, as Toumi, Mai and Shino all began to snore in a sort of odd, grating musical chord, Emi and I whispered quietly about Mieko's lessons—and about Aimaru's questions concerning our work in the kitchen.

"Do you think they have anything to do with each other?" whispered Emi, looking thoughtfully at the thin door to Fuyudori's room.

"I can't imagine what," I answered. Stifling a yawn, I whispered, "Maybe you should ask Aimaru."

Her eyes got round and she looked at the door again. "We're not supposed to talk to boys," she answered loudly. Then she turned over. "Good night, Murasaki." As always, she was asleep before I had even finished answering.

As I tried to follow her, I remembered the sound we had heard outside the gate. Had it been a horse? Had it been Inazuma, Masugu-*san*'s charger? I drifted off to the image of black hair and white snow.

23—Poppies in Winter

Evidently, Emi did not sleep as well as usual. When we three walked into the kitchen the next morning, Kee Sun looked at her and scowled. "Smiley, yeh look like the demons have been chasing yeh."

Emi frowned her most ferocious frown, and her neck turned pink. "I... could not sleep."

"And yeh, there, Falcon-girlie?" the cook asked Toumi, who was slumped against the big wooden cutting table.

"Stomach ache," muttered Toumi, though I couldn't think why the previous day's work would upset anyone's stomach—thankfully, it had just been chickens, not a pig or another cow.

Kee Sun grunted, and then gestured toward me with his cleaver. "Well, at least Bright-eyes here looks like she's had a good night. But since I don't want none of yeh slicing off any of those fingers o' yehrs belonging to the lady, perhaps we'll be starting on something I was going to teach yeh later."

He finished filleting a carp in four smooth, swift passes of his thin boning knife, wiped the blade, placing it carefully on cutting table, and then walked over to the beam where dozens of herbs hung, dried and drying. He ran his fingers almost reverently along their tips, and then looked at us, crossing his arms. "In Korea, we call this *Hanyak*. Medicine. Plants, yeh know, can make our food taste good—basil and ginger and garlic and pepper and the like. But they can do more than just that."

He pointed up again. "Ginseng. Mugwort. Wormwood. Corydalis." He waved his hand at what I now realized where not just cooking herbs but hundreds of different plants. Leaves. Fruits. Roots. Dried mushrooms. "Herbs. Yeh little beggars know about the five elements? The two forces?"

We all nodded, but I could tell that neither of the others felt any more sure of her knowledge than I did.

"Right. Yeh know how we're always careful to balance the flavors, the colors in meals? Sour, bitter, sweet, hot, salty? Green, red, yellow, white, brown?"

Now we nodded more certainly; he'd been drilling that into us for weeks. The evening meal the night before had included green negi onions, red smoked trout, yellow squash, white *daikon* radish and brown mushrooms. Of course, in Kee Sun's opinion, which he shared with us during the preparations for every meal, the Japanese taste in food ran far too much to brown and sweet.

"Well, it's not just 'cause it tastes good or looks good. We're all of us made up of five elements—fire, wood, earth, metal and water. Each o' them matches up with a color and to a flavor—so wood is green and sour, and fire is red and hot, and so on. And each of them elements has two sides—light and dark, or, if yeh'd rather, hot and cold. Female, male."

I remembered *Otō-san* telling me about the same things once as he was drawing a sketch of the cherry blossoms on the tree outside of our house.

"*Yin* and *yang*," said Emi.

"There yeh are. Those're the Chinese names for 'em. So we're all made up of these, and just like a good soup has just the right balance of broth and meat and this and that, so're we. We need balance. So we have to eat in balance—sour, bitter, sweet, hot, salty. Green, red, yellow, white, brown. Understand?"

We nodded again.

"Well," he continued, "each o' these plants here has the power to move that balance." He looked back up at his herbs, and pointing at one we knew well—his huge clump of dried basil leaves. "Basil—that's sweet and green and pungent; it has the power of building up the warm energy in the bits of yeh that are made up of earth. And if yeh're feelin' rheumy and sniffly—if yeh're runnin' cold and wet—that's important. But if yeh already got too much heat and too much earth, well, then, too much basil's gonna be bad for yeh, see?"

Once more we nodded; even Toumi seemed interested.

"There's different bits of yehr bodies that need more or less of different elements, or more *yin*, or more *yang*. Well, each o' these herbs affects different parts o' yehr body. And people are what they eat, yeh know. So a good cook is like a healer; gotta make sure folks get all as they need." He crossed his arms again, scowling in a manner that I had come to recognize was his way of letting us know what he was about to say was important. "Thing is, each of these herbs can help keep a body healthy, if they're used one way—or they can make a body sick if they're used another. Sick. Or worse."

Toumi snorted. When Kee Sun scowled at her even more deeply, she snapped, "Well, come on! You're trying to tell us that *basil* can be a poison?"

The cook chuckled, but his eyes were still serious. "It'd take a powerful lot of basil to make a body sick. But sure—it'd work well enough. Give enough basil to a woman who's newly pregnant and she'll lose her child—and whether she wants the babe or not'll decide whether she thinks it's poison or healing."

Now Toumi scowled back, her arms folded as his were. But she remained silent.

"So," said Kee Sun. "Herbs. Now, Smiley-girlie, do yeh recognize this one here?" He pointed up to a clump of dried flowers that reminded me of the sea urchin shells my sister Usako had tried to collect once at the beach. The paper-thin grey shells had disintegrated in her fingers no matter how careful she was, and so she had disintegrated into tears. Thinking of her tears, looking at the dried flowers made me think....

Mouth turned down even further than usual, Emi shook her head.

"Any of yeh?"

I cocked my head. "Are those... poppies?"

Kee Sun raised a scarred brow. "And how'd yeh know that, Squirrel-girlie?"

I remembered the sound of my sister's arm cracking like a dry twig when she'd fallen, trying just the one time to follow me up into the trees, and I shivered. The sound of her cries. "They grow on the hill below the castle, in our village. We'd pick a couple of plants every spring. My mother used to get the seeds for baking, and the juice for brewing tea when we were hurt."

He grinned. "There yeh go. I keep it around for bad pain, just the same. And for when some of the girlies go nights without sleepin'."

Emi cleared her throat. "Isn't poppy juice... dangerous?"

Kee Sun gave a brisk nod. "Ayup. I told yeh—the difference 'twixt a healin' herb and a poison is how much yeh use, and when yeh use it. The lieutenant, he *hates* poppy juice; thinks it feeds the demons. But this here is the best medicine there is for pain, and also for not sleepin', 'specially for young ladies at... certain times. Slows the heart. Slows the bowels. Slows everythin'. Gives a body dreams...." He shuddered dramatically. "Well. We got the dried pods, here, for the seeds and for making tea, but I also squeeze the juice when they're green, which is even stronger; I've got it all ready." He pointed to one of the line of small clay bottles he occasionally used to cook from. "Make a tea with a bit o' mint, and a drop or maybe two o' that poppy juice—just a drop or two, *no more*—and I promise yeh'll be off in dreamland. Yeh'll sleep as sound as a bear in winter. And yeh'll wake less grumpy."

Even Emi smiled at that. "What's the mint for?"

"Good for the bowels. But mostly? Makes it taste better," said Kee Sun with a wink, and Emi laughed for the first time in what felt like days. "Now, takin' too much of this stuff can make a body terrible sick. Can kill. And takin' it too often is a good way to get yehrself possessed by a demon, and no doubt: it'll take yehr soul till there's nothin' left in yehr body and yeh wither away like last autumn's rice stalks. It'll kill yeh with dreams. It'll kill yeh slow, and it's not a nice death—that's a fact."

We all stood there listening, eyes open wide.

"So, I'll brew yeh a bit if it gets real bad, Smiley, but 'till then..." He pointed up to a net hanging beside the poppies. "Know what these are, Bright-eyes?" When I didn't respond, he raised an eyebrow to the others, but they shook their heads. He took down the net and showed us the fingernail-sized bits it contained: they were button-shaped and golden brown, like flattened rabbit pellets, and I felt sure that I'd seen our mother buying them off of the herbalist who came through every summer. "Well, this one yeh'll all get to know better. Corydalis root. Puts a body t'sleep and takes away aches—not as good as poppy juice, mind, but good enough, and the sleep yeh fall into ain't as like to last a lifetime. It's a favorite of some of the older girlies, if yeh catch my drift. And to help the lady sleep sometimes when she can't."

"Really?" asked Emi, scowling; I was probably scowling too, since it hadn't occurred to me that Lady Chiyome slept at all, or that she would want to. Somehow, taking a sleeping draft seemed... human.

"Ayup." Kee Sun grunted. Then he smiled again. "But I don't want yeh coming in here usin' knives when yeh haven't slept well, so I'll show yeh girlies how to make a good tea with this"—he let a handful of the corydalis fall through his fingers—"that'll give even a crabby old man like me a good night's sleep."

———

Later that day, we went out to the stable for another lesson with Mieko-*san*.

As we arrived, the women were still moving the equipment out of our way. one of the women barked, "Hey! Where are all of the blankets?"

"Blankets?" asked Toumi.

"Yeah. We usually move all of the saddle blankets, but they're not here."

Pointing to the far wall, Fuyudori answered brightly, "See! They're over here, already out of the way. Perhaps Masugu-*san* moved them."

Emi muttered, voice low so that even standing beside her I could hardly hear, "Or maybe it's our fox spirit again."

Before I could begin to wonder what she meant, Mieko stood silently and led us through her dreamlike dance once again. Once again, I had the odd, disturbing sense that I knew the movements. Perhaps I had danced it as a child. Perhaps I had danced it in a previous life. Perhaps I was simply imagining it.

Now that they were sure that they knew where they were going, my limbs wanted to go faster, but Mieko-*san*'s steady, flowing movements lulled me into following at her pace.

My hands. My hands felt... empty.

And the air was full of the metallic scent of snow.

———

True winter closed in that night. A blizzard turned the whole world into a huge sheet of blank paper, and didn't let up.

After several days of being snowbound, we all began to feel jumpy. We were only outside long enough to scurry from one building to another.

At meals, the women became quieter for a time, but soon some of them began to grumble—though not so loudly that Lady Chiyome could hear. "It can stay like this for weeks at a time, up here in the mountains," muttered one of the women into her soup one night. "We won't be going out on any trips any time soon."

A broad-shouldered *kunoichi* who had come in just before the blizzard answered, "Trust me, you're not missing anything out there."

As the rest of us became gloomier and gloomier, only two people seemed to be merry. The first was Lady Chiyome, who said that the valley needed a good snow, and who always seemed most cheerful when others were miserable.

The other was snow-haired Fuyudori, who seemed to be in her element. At lessons, she chirped and laughed. At meals, she sat near Masugu-*san* and flirted shamelessly.

Mieko-*san* didn't seem to find anything about the proceedings at all amusing. She glowered in the opposite direction—at Kuniko's nightly memorial bowl of rice. At me. At the wall.

Masugu-*san* sat like a stone statue of himself. Then again, he hadn't been able to take his horse out. He was never happy when he couldn't ride.

24—Visitors

The snow did not relent for days. Every morning, Emi, Toumi and I had to break the ice that had formed atop the well in order to fill the tubs. As the snow kept piling up, Emi pointed out that we could use the drifts that had fallen in the courtyard overnight. Not only was this easier than trudging all of the way to the back of the estate where the well was, but it had the benefit of clearing the snow from the area immediately around the bathhouse, which made walking to and from the kitchen easier.

Though we never discussed it, we began to stay in the bathhouse longer and longer, letting the heat of the fires and the warming baths thaw us.

Having to trudge out into the cold again each day just as the baths began to heat up was unbearably hard. That we were able to flee to the warmth of Kee Sun's kitchen was at least a small blessing.

Kee Sun continued to teach us about herbs. And each night, after we had finished cleaning out the tubs for the day, Emi went to the kitchens to pick up a pot of corydalis tea that the cook had prepared; he had already brewed one for Lady Chiyome, he said, so one more was no trouble, if it meant that Emi came to work in the mornings with a smile on her face. I think that he was joking.

The tea certainly helped Emi sleep. Sometimes it seemed as if she went through the rest of the next day barely awake.

———

After five steady days, the blizzard let up. Emi, Toumi and I were in the teahouse that morning with the older girls, writing out one of the Buddha's sermons. Even when we warmed the ink stones at the small fire, it took a great deal of rubbing to get the ink sticks to mix smoothly with the water, and even then the ink was thick as honey from the cold, full of clumps that left splotches on the page. Mai just laughed when Emi's attempt to write the Chinese character for *bliss* came out looking more like—as Mai said—"a kid's drawing of a cow turd."

Suddenly, the screened walls of the teahouse glowed brightly, as for the first time in days something like bright sun broke through the overcast. We all stumbled to the door—though the clouds were still heavy and it was still cold. "Go!" said our teacher, sighing. "I want to read some more of what the Buddha had to say about cow plops."

We looked up, all of us, as if the mottled grey overhead were the bright blue of a summer's day. "Hey, Risuko," laughed Shino, "you're supposed to be such a great climber—think you can get up into the big tree and see if the rest of the world is still there?" She pointed up at the huge hemlock that grew beside the great hall.

"No!" Emi gasped. "The tree is covered with ice! That would be dangerous."

"Well," sneered Mai, "I guess she isn't such a great climber after all."

Not waiting to hear any more—happy simply to get away from them all, if only for a moment—I leapt at the trunk of the huge hemlock. Though the bark was covered with glistening frost, it was rough and wrinkled, and the crevices were ice-free—perfect for climbing. I scampered up to the first branches in no time at all. Looking back down, I was pleased to see all of the other girls blinking up at me.

Fuyudori's gaze connected with mine, and I knew with pleasure that she was thinking of a much more difficult climb that I had once made.

"Well," grumbled Mai, whose sneer couldn't quite cover her shock, "what can you see?"

I looked out over the wall. There was nothing but white. The downpour had stopped, and the clouds had lifted enough that I could see feathers of snow lofted from the ground by the soft, chill breeze. But all beyond the wall was blank and white—mountains, valley, sky. It was as if the rest of the world had been wiped away, as if nothing beyond the Full Moon still existed. "Nothing," I said, hoarsely. "I can't see anything at all."

"So much for squirrels having sharp eyes," muttered Mai, and Shino and Toumi laughed.

"Wait!" I called, as a pair of dark shapes began to push up over the invisible line of the ridge. "Riders!"

"You're joking!" laughed Shino again, while Mai said, "Impossible."

Emi frowned up at me, about to say something, but Fuyudori beat her to it, chirping, "It must be the Lieutenant. He left with Aimaru-*chan* and the Little Brothers this morning to check on the farms in the valley."

"I don't think so," I called down. "It's two horses. And they're riding hard." Even in the white-on-white landscape, and even though the grey chargers seemed to be making no sound, I could see the snow flying as they galloped, the riders leaning forward.

"Flags?" called our *sensei* from the teahouse. I could see the ink stains on her clenched fingers.

I suddenly felt cold. "Um. None. White cloaks?"

Before I had finished speaking, the teacher began to beat a rapid alarm on the small gong at the entrance to the teahouse. "Stay up there, Risuko!" she shouted, and then began to run toward the stables.

Women burst from the great hall and from the Nunnery, some in their *miko* garb, and others in light trousers and jackets.

The two horsemen charged on along the ridge; they were half of the way toward the front gate. I thought I could hear their hooves tearing at the snowy ground, but perhaps it was the sound of the women's feet or my beating heart.

"What is it?" called Mieko.

"Riders!" shouted Fuyudori, who was wringing her hands beneath me.

One of the *kunoichi* sprinted out of the storeroom with two long glaives, one of which she tossed to our Chinese teacher, who caught it smoothly with one hand.

Behind the two white-cloaked riders, a third now appeared, his horse much larger than theirs, charging like a bolt of black lightning. On his helmet he wore a stag's antlers. "Masugu-*san*!" I shouted. "He's chasing them!"

The first two thundered toward the Full Moon, the steam from their nostrils clearly visible now. Were they going to try to jump the wall?

The two spear-bearing women had somehow made their way to the roofs of the guesthouse and of the stable, the long blades of their glaives flashing in the winter morning sun.

"They're splitting!" I called, as one rider veered toward the east wall of the compound while the other flew west.

"Raiders?" barked Lady Chiyome from the front door of the great hall.

"Can't tell!" one woman shouted from the wall. "Can't see any insignia!"

I thought of the men who had captured me and Toumi that morning on the switchbacks. Enemy raiders. Bandits.

The two riders rounded the front corners of the compound at almost exactly the same time.

Where did they mean to go? The woods to either side of the Full Moon were thick and tangled, and behind the compound the ridge quickly gave way to a sheer granite mountain slope.

Masugu was clearly closing on the rider to the west, who I could see was looking for a way through the impassable woods, his head moving left and right even as his horse charged straight ahead.

I heard a sharp slap below me. Fuyudori had her hand to her pale face. "Snap out of it!" Sachi shouted, her expression empty of its usual laughter.

Like a peal of summer birdsong, metal met metal. Over the wall to the west, I could just see Masugu's sword crash against the white-cloaked stranger's. The impact seemed to knock the stranger back in his saddle, but he managed to stay on his mount.

"What's happening?" shrieked Fuyudori.

I climbed higher, hoping to see better, dreading what I would see.

Masugu's momentum had carried him past the other horseman. He wheeled his stallion and came at the other man, his *katana* raised high.

A flash of movement to my left drew my eye. The other horseman had rounded the rear of the compound and was charging at Masugu's back.

"Masugu-*san*!" I screamed. "Behind you!"

I looked back to the lieutenant in time to see the opponent he was facing fall from his saddle, a shower of red rain falling with him. Masugu wheeled to meet the second horseman, raising his blood-slick sword defensively.

A long black bolt suddenly erupted from the charging rider's throat, and he was thrown backward from his saddle, a look of shock on his face.

It was Shirogawa, the man who had trussed me and Toumi up from the tree like pigs to be butchered.

Masugu turned his stallion, looked at me, and then at the Full Moon's wall.

We both saw a figure standing atop the storeroom holding a bow taller than she was, leaning forward as if still watching the arrow's flight. It was Mieko, her face as calm as ever.

———

By the time I made my way down, the women had all climbed off the rooftops as well. I could see that they had used the timbers that decorated most of the buildings near the gate to climb, and it occurred to me that, unlike the great hall's, those walls were *meant* to be easy to climb, so that Mochizuki's inhabitants could defend its walls—though not from the rear of the compound. Not that any enemy would ever attack from the sheer granite slopes behind us, nor the dense woods to either side. And I couldn't imagine that old Lord Mochizuki had intended the walls to be defended by a bunch of young women in shrine maidens' garb.

Fuyudori stood alone beneath the tree, her face as pale as her hair. Toumi trailed two older women, gazing with undisguised hunger at the long glaives in the *kunoichis'* hands.

Emi looked at the gate, biting her lower lip.

"I'm sure Aimaru and the Little Brothers are all right," I whispered.

She shook her head, but before I could ask what she meant, Lady Chiyome burst out of the great hall. "Don't just stand there! Open the gate!"

Mieko sprinted past her mistress, moving more quickly than I had ever seen her do, and the rest of us followed her. It took eight of us to do what the Little Brothers did with so little effort, but we managed to get the gate open just as Lieutenant Masugu led his horse through the tall red *tori* arch.

"Masugu-*san*!" I shouted, and found that Fuyudori had shouted with me.

The lieutenant removed his helmet, his expression grim.

"Who were they? How did you find them? Why were they here?" Fuyudori continued, her voice shrill. "Are you all right?"

"Enemy raiders," said Lady Chiyome, sweeping Fuyudori aside.

Masugu shook his head and shrugged, his armored shoulders lifting like broken ice in a river. "No. The same feathers on their arrows, but no insignia on the armor or on the horses. And the enemy—cavalry, scouts, even raiders—they always use chestnut mounts, not greys. Though the greys are harder to see in the snow, it's true." He shrugged, then looked at the circle of women around him. He shook his head again. "Villagers said they'd seen strangers sneaking around. We spotted them as we reached the bottom of the hill. I couldn't think of a good reason for them to be on the road up here, so I called. As soon as I did, well, they ran for it, and then I *knew* they were up to no good. I followed and..." He held up his hands as if to say, *And here we are.*

"You fought well, Masugu-*san*," I said. I said it quietly—not meaning to say it out loud at all—but he heard it.

He smiled grimly. "Not much of a fight. Me on the bigger horse, more heavily armed. And you to watch my back. Thank you for the warning, Murasaki-*san*."

Feeling the heat rise to my face, I mumbled, "You're welcome."

His grin warmed, and then he turned to Mieko, who was still holding her bow. "Nice shot, Mieko-*san*."

"Yes," she answered.

In the silence that followed her flat statement, Masugu turned and patted his horse. "Well, I need to get Inazuma here back into his stall and brushed down, don't I, boy? It's been a while since he had a chance to ride hard like that."

The circle of women parted to let him lead his horse to the stable, looking for all the world as if he had just come back from a vigorous morning's ride, and not from a fight to the death. Not as if he had just killed.

In my mind's eye, I could see the spray of blood as he struck down the first rider. *But they would have killed him,* a voice said in my head—a voice that sounded very much like Lady Chiyome's. *And who warned him, after all?*

"Enough gawking at the pretty soldier and his pretty horse," Chiyome-*sama*'s actual voice barked. "Kee Sun and the Little Brothers will dispose of the ruffians later. For now, close the—"

"Chiyome-*sama*," said Emi, pointing out through the open gate, "pardon your humble servant's interruption, but the Little Brothers and Aimaru are coming."

We all stared out into the bright, white landscape, where three more figures were in fact cresting the rise. Or rather, two figures, and another who looked like a walking wall.

"But what in the name of the gods are they carrying?" snorted Toumi.

25—To Roost

Even from a distance, I could see that they were all red-cheeked from the cold and from the climb up from the valley. None of them seemed to be injured, which made me release a breath I hadn't realized that I was holding.

Though the shortest of the three, Aimaro looked twice as wide. As they approached, we could see that he carried a load of open boxes that were hung from a pole across his shoulders. Cages. There were birds inside—chickens.

"Oh, good," said Sachi, "the morning's entertainment isn't over."

Some of the older women laughed, the tension leaking from the assembly like water from a punctured tarp.

We stood there in two files as they entered. Aimaru looked to the chickens, who were complaining in their confinement, and then to Emi and to me, as if to say, *Now what?*

I shrugged. Emi frowned down at the snow-muffled gravel.

Chiyome-*sama* gave her own mirthless chuckle. "Welcome back, gentlemen! Masugu has gotten rid of the rascals he was chasing, so we know about that. What's the rest of the news from the valley?"

The elder of the Little Brothers nodded deferentially. "We checked with most of the farms here in the center of the valley. All of them survived the blizzard intact, though a few animals wandered off into the snow."

"Their bodies will probably be found once the spring thaws come," added the younger Little Brother, "so not too much was lost."

The elder pursed his lips, and the younger lapsed back into their habitual silence.

Aimaru cleared his throat. "Masugu-*san* rode up as far as where the valley narrows. He said that he heard tell of some fighting down by the garrison."

Chiyome-*sama* grunted. "There is always fighting down by the garrison."

"It must be all of those soldiers," said Mieko. If it had been anyone but she, I'd have sworn it was a joke. The other women chuckled, but they stopped when Chiyome-*sama* glared at them.

The older Little Brother said, "Masugu-*san* was told that the garrison had caught and killed several more of the band of raiders that we met on the way in."

After pursing her lips for a moment, Lady Chiyome nodded at the Little Brother, and then walked toward Aimaru. "I like my food fresh," she said, pointing to the caged chickens, "but I must say, I generally prefer not to eat it live."

"Er, no, my lady," answered Aimaru. "The farmer said that he'd been told not to slaughter them."

"Told?" said Lady Chiyome, voice raised but grinning. Aimaru looked as if he might faint. "What an odd thing to tell the man. Who would do such a thing?"

Again a giggle passed among the women; this time Chiyome did not stop it.

Aimaru gulped. "I... I do not know, my lady."

I could see Emi across from me, still frowning down at the ground. Her lips were moving silently.

Lady Chiyome gave her dry, rasping chuckle. "Well, I suppose someone will have to slaughter the things. Novices."

"Yes, Chiyome-*sama*," we all three said together, far more in concert than we ever managed to be in Sachi-*sensei*'s music lessons.

"Relieve this young gentlemen of his burden and get these chickens ready for Kee Sun."

"But—?" I found myself saying. After that morning, after watching the battle, after watching two men die, I couldn't imagine plucking chickens.

"Do it. *Now.*"

"Yes, Chiyome-*sama*," I said. Emi and Toumi echoed me. We all approached Aimaru; he seemed as if he were about to say something, but I shook my head. Emi and Toumi picked the pole up over his shoulders and we began to walk back toward the kitchen.

"Oh, no," said Lady Chiyome. "Kee Sun is very superstitious about never slaughtering anything in the kitchen. He always insists that it be killed outside. Something to do with the animals' spirits cursing the food or some such silliness."

I looked at the other two girls. Toumi was grimly not looking at me—or at anyone else, I think. Her lips were pressed together so hard they were white.

Emi nodded for a moment and then turned back to Lady Chiyome. "Should we slaughter them out here, my lady?"

"An excellent idea," said Chiyome. "Certainly no chance of some angry chicken spirit haunting the kitchens from here."

"Yes, my lady," said Emi, her mouth bending downward.

I looked into the closest of the cages, which was just below Emi's fingers. The hen was glaring at me with reptilian, golden eyes. I thought of the blood that I had already seen that day. My stomach churned.

"Do it, girls." Lady Chiyome continued to smile. Her expression did not help. "Have you never killed a chicken before?"

Once again we all answered with one thin voice. "No, my lady."

"Well, then," she said with another chuckle, "this should be entertaining."

The women around us all laughed—even the initiates. Suddenly all eyes were on the three of us, standing there in the snowy courtyard, gawking uncertainly at a dozen chickens in cages.

I don't know about the other two, but I couldn't tear my eyes away from that chicken's gaze.

With a snarl, Toumi dropped her end of the pole, setting the stack of suspended cages on the ground. She reached out and flicked the latch to the top cage.

"Toumi, no—!" I said, but she was too quick—she flung open the door to the cage and went to reach in.

What I'd been trying to say, as any girl not raised on city streets would know, was that quick as Toumi's hands might have been, a chicken that senses escape is even quicker. It gave Toumi's reaching palm a vicious peck with its beak, and when Toumi flinched back it exploded into the air, an irate fury of feathers and useless wings.

I grabbed for it, but caught nothing but a couple of loose feathers.

The assembled women—and even, I think, the Little Brothers—all burst into raucous laughter as the hen, newly liberated, decided to make the most of its newfound freedom and half-flew, half-scurried away from us and toward the stable.

I ran after it, trying not to think what I was going to do with it if I caught it. Emi trotted off to my right; at first I couldn't think what she was doing, but then I realized she was trying to keep the bird from moving toward the still-open gate or the storerooms.

Our audience was calling out what sounded like what was meant to be encouragement. "Don't let it get you! Vicious beasts, chickens!"

I wanted to climb to the top of the hemlock tree and hide.

Instead I kept on after the chicken, gaining on it. Trying not to think of Masugu riding down the white-cloaked rider. I lunged, trying to grab it by its tail, but it swerved away to the left.

"The great hall," panted Emi, and I could see that she meant that we should herd it toward the largest building in the compound, where it would have the hardest time escaping us. We sprinted after it, me to one side of the creature and Emi to the other.

The chicken squawked madly as it tried to stay away from us, but eventually it ran out of room—the great hall loomed before it, blocking any flight in that direction, and Emi and I stood like hunting dogs, cutting off any escape back toward the courtyard. *Poor chicken,* I found myself thinking. *If only you could fly.* Mad eyes glared at us as it sought a fresh chance at freedom.

Emi lunged, trying to grab the hen by its head—trying to keep from getting pecked as Toumi had—but of course that left it free to scratch with its feet, scoring Emi's grasping fingers. Before the bird could get away, I pulled off the winter jacket that I was wearing and threw it over the bird, dropping my weight on top of it so that it couldn't escape once more.

A cheer went up among the watching crowd. "Well wrestled, Risuko!" shouted one of the women, and the rest hooted and cackled.

I lay there panting. The bird was struggling beneath me, trying to find its way out of the jacket. I looked up at Emi, who was sucking at the cuts on her fingers. She didn't seem to have any suggestions for what to do next. Picking up the bundle, holding it tightly, I looked for someone to give it to. It fought in my grasp, and its head poked out through the neck of the jacket, desperately looking for something to peck at.

They all stood there, grinning and laughing, even the men.

I stared down at the chicken, which was squawking again, loudly and furiously. *This could be the soul of someone I know,* I thought. At that moment, Toumi stepped up, grabbed the bird's head, and twisted it so that the neck gave a dull snap.

I dropped it; the chicken's body struggled for a few moments, trying even then to run out from under the jacket, though its neck hung limp.

I backed away until I slammed into the wall of the great hall. I turned, and emptied my stomach against the stone foundation.

As I stood there, retching, I felt a hand touch my shoulder. Turning, I saw that Mieko was holding out a handkerchief. I took it and wiped my face.

I tried to hand it back to her, but she stood there, her face still. "All that lives dies," she said. "All that lives, lives on the living."

I gawked at her. Mieko-*san* smiled sadly, and walked away.

———

Once we had killed the remainder of the birds, we brought them to Kee Sun, who informed us that they should be prepared for him to grill them. As we cleaned the chickens, my hands trembled, and my gorge rose and rose again.

I had been plucking and butchering chickens for long enough that I hardly noticed the mess or the smell. Why was this any different? The other animals had been just as dead.

And yet their deaths had been somehow distant. Another person's actions, another person's dream.

Perhaps it was watching those two men die. The blood. The shocked expressions.

I looked up, swallowing back the bitter taste of my own discomfort.

Toumi was standing, still as the table against which she was leaning. Her face was white. She saw me looking at her, clenched her jaw, and went back to dismembering the carcass.

I glanced over at Emi. She had been watching too. Her forehead was shiny with sweat. She nodded, and we both went back to cutting up the meat for that evening's meal.

Kee Sun announced that he was going "to visit the King," and wandered out into the snow, which had begun falling heavily once again. No sooner had the door closed behind him than Toumi turned to me and pointed up.

For once I didn't feel like climbing, but when Emi too pointed up toward the grate, I sighed and scampered up into the rafters. I had no sooner started to tiptoe my way toward the grate, however, when I heard a howl of anger from the hall, and I leapt back down. Feeling as if I must have been caught, I tensed, ready to climb again.

The howl sounded again, and Emi and Toumi were both staring at the door to the hall, their mouths open.

"Get everyone, in here! RIGHT NOW!" shouted Chiyome-*sama*.

A muffled voice answered her, but she didn't wait for it to finish before bellowing, "I DON'T CARE! Someone get the three little wretches in here, and Mieko, stop simpering at me and tell the boys to get in here *at once!*"

The three of us stood frozen, gawping at each other.

"Did you let someone see you, Mouse?" hissed Toumi.

I shook my head desperately.

One of the women slid open the door. "Follow me," she said to us all. "Your mistress commands it."

Gulping, we followed.

The great hall had been transformed. The three long tables were pushed back to the wall opposite the front door. Beneath the shrine, where Lady Chiyome usually sat, stood a suit of battered bamboo armor stuffed with straw. From the chest protruded several slender blades.

Chiyome-*sama* stood, arms knotted before her, halfway down the stairs from her apartment. She looked a very small thundercloud, and I didn't want to be the first one struck by lightning.

The older women looked just as nervous as I felt, all staring down at the floor, their loose hair hiding their faces.

As soon as a blast of cold air announced the arrival of Masugu, Aimaru, and the Little Brothers, Lady Chiyome barked, "So."

She scanned the assembled crowd until her eyes met mine. "So," she repeated, "someone has been visiting my room. Visiting my room and *looking through my belongings.*"

Silence answered her. I couldn't help but hold her gaze.

"You are *not* welcome there," she continued. "None of you. I will see to it that these gentlemen make your lives very, *very* unpleasant before they make it very, very *short.*" At last her gaze released me. I began to breathe again. "Do you understand me, girls?"

"Yes, Chiyome-*sama*," we all mumbled.

"WHAT?"

"YES, CHIYOME-*sama*!" we all shouted together.

"You three!" she called to us. "Don't just stand there. Get dinner ready!"

With that, she stormed back up the stairs, and we scurried back to the kitchen.

Kee Sun was back, wandering along the storage shelves, muttering in Korean.

Still stunned, we watching him until he suddenly yelled something, and then turned to us, his cleaver in his hand. "None of yeh lot went and stole a bottle of the *sake*, now did yeh?" It sounded perhaps as if he might be joking. However, he growled the question again: "Did yeh?"

We shook our heads and, twitching, returned to our work. What would one of us do with a bottle of wine?

26—Climbing the Walls

The cook was in an even fouler mood than usual, because one of the jars of rice wine had gone missing. He made it very clear that he suspected one of us.

Emi had gone all but silent, though she would occasionally look my way, her perpetual frown lightening in a way that seemed to suggest a greeting.

The blizzard descended again, and it felt like as much of an attack as the charge of the two horsemen. More of an attack.

The other inhabitants of the Full Moon were clearly feeling the oppression of the weather as keenly as I was. Where the dining hall was usually alive with raucous conversation, only two people were talking there at all: Lady Chiyome and Fuyudori. Lady Chiyome was telling an elaborate joke at my expense—something about how most squirrels were supposed to hibernate during the winter, but some poor, silly ones clearly liked climbing icy trees instead.

The only person who laughed was Fuyudori. She had managed to seat herself on one side of Masugu-*san*, where the elder of the Little Brothers usually sat. She tittered into her hand, her flashing eyes fastened to the lieutenant's face. "Of course," she said, "the wolf hunts all through the winter," and tittered again.

I had no idea what she was talking about, nor—judging from his expression—did Masugu.

Mieko-*san* understood something. She slammed down the cup of *sake* that I had just refilled for her, splashing the rice wine onto the black lacquered table and into dead Kuniko's rice. Then she stood, her usually pale face dark. She rose with a jerk. "Good evening, my lady," she said, bowing stiffly to Chiyome-*sama*. "Gentlemen." She bowed to the Little Brothers and to Aimaru, who blinked back.

Turning in a flash of red-and-white silk, she strode out of the room.

Mopping up the spilled *sake* and picking up the abandoned plate, I glanced toward Lady Chiyome, who was smirking at the lieutenant. He shook his head like a wet dog, and then he too stood and bowed to Lady Chiyome. "I believe that I should also retire for the night if I am to get out tomorrow morning for a patrol."

Then he too left the hall.

Lady Chiyome gave her odd, dry chuckle and glanced sidelong at Fuyudori, who was beaming as if she had done something very clever. What it might have been I still couldn't guess.

Then, with a cluck of her tongue, Lady Chiyome returned to her meal. The rest of the remaining party silently followed her example.

I picked up the nearly untouched plates to either side of Chiyome-*sama's* and brought them back to the kitchen.

When I returned with two nearly full plates, Kee Sun slammed his cleaver down into the table. "What're those worthless lumps complaining about now!"

"Mieko-*san* and Masugu-*san*... are... not feeling well," I said. "They retired early."

"Retired early," sneered Toumi.

"I think they were unhappy with each other." Emi had come in from the main hall after me.

"For a change," muttered Toumi.

Kee Sun yanked his knife free, gave us a sour look, and then slammed the blade back into the table. Pointing to me he snapped, "Rubbish. Out."

"*Hai*, Kee Sun-*san*." I grabbed the basket and strode toward the door.

"Robes!" barked Kee Sun, but I was already through the door.

"I will be right back, Kee Sun-*san*." The fact of the matter is that I was happy to be away from everyone—not to have to think about who was talking about me, who was watching me, or who was trying to ignore me. The night was cold and the snow was barely falling—tiny flakes appearing out of the dark sky around me as swarming moths around a torch.

Squirrels should be hibernating? I thought, stomping toward the door that led through the back wall to the rubbish pit. *Ha!*

As I put down the steaming basket of bones and burnt rice to unbar the small rear gate, I heard a bang in the darkness—not from the great hall, but from the direction of the Retreat.

I have no memory of making the decision to climb the wall in order to creep across to the other side of the compound and investigate. It was more as if the decision made me. I found myself atop the thick wall, stepping carefully between sharp spikes of bamboo, wondering what it was that I thought

I was going to see, and what I could possibly say to whoever had made the sound if they caught me. The faint light of the great hall—spilling from the shuttered doors and windows of the opposite side—caused the ice and snow on the wall top to glisten very slightly, or I would have had no idea where to put my feet.

A sound wafted through the falling snow, muffled and indistinct—a voice. Two? The same as the ones I'd heard in the woods?

I made my way along the wall, lifting my feet carefully over the spikes and loose pebbles. The snow flurried, dancing in the wind, and I lost sight of the great hall, so that the whole world seemed to be bounded by snow: just the top of that wall and me.

I heard the sound again, closer but still ahead of me. It was definitely two voices, but they were still too muffled for me to understand what they were saying, or even to know for certain to whom they belonged. Then the wind whipped across my face and I had to move forward even more cautiously, feeling my way with my hands.

At the edge of the bubble of flake-filled air that bounded my vision, I made out two looming shapes: one to the right—a roof, the Retreat—and ahead of me the corner of the compound wall.

I stopped. The voices couldn't have come from outside of the compound, could they?

"You know, there are a hundred and eight ways that I could kill you." The voice was colder than the air that bit at my face and hands, and so clear that I stumbled and nearly fell off of the wall.

"You killed me five years ago," said another, sadder voice. "I don't think any of the other hundred and seven could have been any more effective."

I looked to my right: the Retreat's stone chimney with its wooden cover stood within touching distance; the voices were floating up like smoke from inside the small building. My heart stopped racing.

"Please," said the first voice, and now it sounded as if the voice, which had been as keen as a knife's blade, had crumbled like shattered ice. "Please. I had no wish—"

It was Mieko. And I knew, before hearing the other speaker answer, that it was Masugu.

"Of course you didn't. You did what you had to do. Your duty. As you do in all things. As do I."

I listened intently, but the chimney conveyed nothing more but silence.

———

When I stumbled, shivering, back into the kitchen, Kee Sun was in the midst of pulling on his winter coat. "Where were yeh, idiot-girl! I was thinking yeh'd turned into an icicle out in that storm!"

"G-got t-turned around out in the s-s-snow." I put the empty basket down. Emi and Toumi were both gone—cleaning out the baths, no doubt. I should have left immediately to help them, but the kitchen fire was warm and I was wet and chilled to the bone; I couldn't move.

"Going out without yehr robes. Fah!" The cook frowned at me, and grunted. "They're already well on their way to draining the tubs. If I count it right... Well, it'd probably be a good night to give Smiley-girlie a pot 'o that mint-and-poppy tea. Why don't yeh stay here and brew her up a pot." He tossed me a huge towel, which I wrapped gratefully around me as I stumbled over to the area where the herbs were stored.

I blinked up at the shelf beneath the Buddha shrine on which the oils were stored; where the small clay bottle had been that Kee Sun had shown us the morning when he started teaching us about herbs, there was an empty space. There were bottles on either side of the space, but they were clearly marked in his blocky hand: oil of chrysanthemum, oil of mint, oil of clove, oil of pine... "Kee Sun-s-*san*," I asked, teeth still chattering. "D-do you want me c-cut up some of the dried poppies to make the t-tea? The b-bottle of p-poppy juice is g-gone."

"WHAT?" he bellowed, stomping over to where I was standing and rifling through the bottles and jars. He spat a torrent of what I was fairly certain was Korean and assumed to be quite profane; he searched on the shelf again, and then on the floor below. Finally, he glowered at me. "Yeh didn't take that *too*, did yeh, Bright-eyes?"

27—Killing Dance

We had to brew Emi's sleeping tea with corydalis root instead of poppy; the poppy had gone missing. Kee Sun snarled in frustration. It wouldn't work as well.

By the time I arrived to deliver the tea, Emi and Toumi had in fact finished draining the baths and were back in our room getting ready for sleep. The others were, as usual, already snoring in their bedrolls. Fuyudori, of course, had her own chamber, which I had never resented more than that night.

"Here is your tea," I said, holding the small pot out to Emi.

She shook her head. "No, thank you. I'm so tired, to be honest, I really don't think I need it."

Biting back my frustration at having wasted my labor, I turned to bring the pot back to the kitchen. Toumi stood in my way, her arms folded. "Where have you been, Mouse-*chan*? Peeking at the Lieutenant so you could sigh some more?"

No, I kept myself from saying, *I was eavesdropping on him having an argument with* Mieko-sensei, *you vulture*. Instead, I repeated the lie that I had told Kee Sun: "I got lost in the snow after I dumped the rubbish. The wind turned me around and I couldn't find the door. And then I had to chop up corydalis for this tea, because someone took the poppy juice. Did you decide to have some poppy with the *sake*, Toumi?"

I'd hoped to get some kind of a reaction out of her, but she gawked at me in confusion. "Why would I want a bunch of poppy juice? I sleep fine."

"Who knows? Excuse me: I need to return this pot."

As I left the dormitory, I saw through the thickening snowfall a shadow moving toward the front gate. Not wanting to run into Masugu-*san* or Mieko-*sensei*, I fairly ran to the kitchen. By the time I had gotten back to our dormitory, Toumi had joined the others in snoring. I assumed that

Emi too was asleep, since she could fall asleep as quickly as a drop of water freezing on an icicle.

I hung my clothes on the rail by the tiny stove that kept our room more or less warm. Shivering, without even the meager heat of a tepid bath to cut the deep chill, I crawled into my bedroll, prepared to lie there, teeth chattering, no one's company but my own until the darkness took me.

As I pulled the bedding up to my nose, I heard Emi's voice. "Murasaki?"

"Yes?"

"Did you really get lost? On the way to the trash pit?"

"Why?"

"Well, it isn't that far. And you always seem to know where you are."

"Not always," I muttered. And a part of me wanted to leave it there. "But... not exactly. I kind of overheard something, and so I kind of had to stay out."

"Stay out?" I could hear her shifting in her bedding, turning toward me. "There was someone outside of the Full Moon? On a night like this?"

"Um, no, not exactly. More like I heard them and I climbed up, and..."

"Oh. That makes sense." We lay there, silent for a moment. "Who was it?"

"I... It was kind of private. I think." I was feeling very uncomfortable; on the one hand, I really wanted to talk with Emi about what I had overheard. I needed help understanding just what it was that they'd been talking about. "I..."

"Well," Emi said, very slowly, "you don't have to tell me, if you don't want to."

"It's not that. I..."

We lay there in silence for a while longer.

"I suppose," Emi mused, "that it must have been the lieutenant and Mieko."

I turned toward her, gawking into the darkness. "How did you know that?"

On Emi's far side, Toumi muttered, "Honest, officer, I didn't take the radish!"

Emi and I giggled as we hadn't done in days. She moved her bedding onto my mat. "You're shivering," she whispered.

"I didn't get to take a bath. And it is cold outside."

"True." She moved closer to me, pulling me close with one arm; even through our bedding, her warmth washed over me.

"Thanks."

"Welcome," Emi sighed. "So, it was Masugu-*san* and Mieko-*san*?"

"Yes. I think they were having a fight."

"They've been having a fight since before we got here."

That was true enough. "But I think he said she'd tried to kill him." And I told her what I had overheard.

"And then they just stopped talking?" Emi asked, when I was finished.

"Yes. I thought it was strange. And I was worried that they would come out and see me, so I hid for a while, but they didn't. They stayed in the Retreat."

"The Retreat?"

"Yes."

"That's a funny place for them to fight. Funny place for him to be at all."

"That's what I thought," I said, though I hadn't thought it in so many words.

"Hmm," Emi said, and then she began to snore.

———

I dreamed that night: a vivid dream, a dream that felt as if it had been sneaking up on me for days.

Father was standing out in the snow, his sword in his hands, doing the exercises that he used to do every morning: a swift, flowing dance of space and steel. "Do no harm, Murasaki," he said, slicing the air as he moved from foot to foot.

"But *Otō-san*...!" I cried.

"No harm," he said as he danced on, cutting at the air. Only now, the snowflakes began to bleed as he cut them. *Battle of white and scarlet...*

"*Otō-san*, what can I do?" I wept in the dream, my tears freezing to my cheeks.

"Dance," he said, his face still and calm, his blade whistling through the air. Blood flew from the tip of the sword, painting characters of death and disaster across the white ground.

Dancing.

Mieko, wiping the blood from her knife, the two dead Imagawa soldiers dead on the *tatami* before her.

Father dancing, just like Mieko, the steps and moves that my body knew as if it had taken them before. With a blade in his hands, however, Father moved with a predator's speed rather than Mieko's dreamlike grace, and it seemed as if the dance was whole. Its hidden purpose was clear. It was a killing dance.

"A *kunoichi* is a very special kind of woman indeed," Father growled as he moved; the voice was not his but Lady Chiyome's.

I wept in the dream, and I have no doubt that I was weeping in my bed, but Father danced on, and the smell of blood filled my nostrils, sharp and metallic as the smell of the falling snow.

28—Broken Dishes

The next morning I woke with the scent of blood still fresh in my nose. It made me want to throw up.

As I sat up, trying to calm my stomach, I noticed that Emi was gone, her bedding too. I scrambled over to Toumi, who was still sound asleep, her thumb lodged in her mouth.

"Where's Emi?" I growled. "What have you done with her?"

Toumi coughed and pushed back at me, but I didn't let go. "Wha?"

"Where is Emi?" I found my fingers knotted in her shirt.

She blinked blankly.

"Emi. What did you do?"

"Do?" She pushed back at me again, but I held tight. "Do? Retreat. Went to the damn Retreat."

I tumbled backward. "The... Retreat?"

Toumi wiped the heel of her hand across her face. "Moon time. Her 'n' Mai. Middle of the damn night. Cleared her bedding and off t'the damn Retreat."

"The Retreat?" I sat back on my heels.

She pushed back at me once more, harder this time, and I let go. "Retreat. Retreat. Yes! Now, let's go."

———

I was anxious that Toumi would take advantage of Emi's absence to torture me even more than she normally did. I needn't have worried. She was just as surly as ever—if not more so—but since there were only two of us and just as much work to be done, she seemed mostly intent on getting the baths ready so that we could get to the kitchens.

We began piling the previous night's snow into the tubs. I felt as if I could indeed smell blood in the metallic snow-scent.

As we worked—filling the tubs, lighting the fires—I could hear Toumi grumbling about bean curd, but even so, she seemed in a hurry to eat some of the previous night's leftover rice—and, if Kee Sun wasn't watching, some of the chicken that he would never let her have.

I couldn't imagine eating chicken—or any flesh—ever again.

And of course, Kee Sun was watching. He always was. "Get that out of yehr beak, yeh!" he snapped when Toumi tried to sneak a piece of the meat that he was warming on a skewer over the fire. He slapped the back of her head with his fingers and she opened her mouth in surprise, sending the stolen bit of chicken flying into the flames. "Bean curd is what yeh need, and yeh know it. Chicken's too hot for yehr liver. That there is for Bright-eyes here."

Toumi glared at me. I suppose it might have affected me more if I had slept somewhat better and if I hadn't already been certain that she hated me.

As we prepared the morning meal, it was Kee Sun's eyes I felt on me, not Toumi's. As we waiting for that morning's rice to finish, he said, "Yeh're both awful quiet without yehr smiley friend. What yeh eat, Bright-eyes, that's got yeh looking like yeh swallowed yehr tongue?"

"Nothing, Kee Sun-san," I answered. "I had... a bad dream."

"Oh?" He peered at me, eyes dark.

I would have loved to talk to him—to someone—about the nightmare that had haunted me, but I did not feel ready somehow. I merely nodded.

"Hmm. And yeh, Falcon-girlie? Yeh been sneaking kimchee?"

"Like I'd want that stuff." Toumi's face twisted in disgust. Then she turned away and muttered, "Like I'd get away with it."

"Oh, I have no doubt yehr capable, Falcon-girlie. That's why I'm watchin' yeh so close, see?" Kee Sun chuckled, though I couldn't tell what the joke might be. "You have bad dreams too?"

"No," said Toumi through tight lips. "Stomach ache."

"Ay!" groaned Kee Sun and slapped his palm against his forehead. "Just do me and Bright-eyes here a favor, will yeh, and wait till after the evening meal?"

"Wait?" asked Toumi. "Wait for what?"

But Kee Sun just waved a hand at us both dismissively and banged the gong to let all of the Full Moon's inhabitants know that the morning meal was ready to be served.

As everyone filed in to the hall, I could see that many of the women were already absent; clearly, they had gone to join Mai and Emi in the Retreat.

I felt twin tremors of curiosity and concern about my friend wash through me as Toumi and I served out the meal.

Fuyudori was sitting silently, which was a relief, since her flirtations with the Lieutenant had begun to annoy everyone. Thankfully, Masugu himself wasn't present. Perhaps he was taking his horse out for a morning ride, as he had said he would. The Little Brothers and Aimaru were gone as well—most likely engaged in morning meditation and exercise, as they often were.

Like Fuyudori, most of the remaining handful of women still left were glum and silent.

Mieko-*san* certainly seemed pleased, smiling as I had not seen her do since we had arrived at the Full Moon. Whether it was Fuyudori's silence or Masugu's absence that had cheered her up or whether her good mood was due to something else entirely I couldn't tell, but Lady Chiyome noticed as well.

"Stop grinning, Mieko," the old lady snapped. "You're ruining my appetite."

"This humble servant apologizes, lady," said Mieko, bowing her head demurely. The smile disappeared from her face, but somehow she managed to look just as pleased.

As I began to bring several empty platters back to the kitchen, Toumi squawked, and the tray that she was carrying clattered to the ground. She stood, knees bent and pressed together, looking as if she were trying hard not to make water.

The table closest to her burst into laughter—the first that I had heard in the hall in days. "Come on," brayed Sachi, who had returned from what she'd called *a hunting trip* the night before. "Let's get you to the Retreat."

"Retreat?" Toumi said the word with the same bewildered tone that I had that morning. Still bent over, covering her lap with her hands, she didn't move; her eyes were perfect circles of shock, and her ears burned red.

"Yes, the Retreat. It looks as if all of that bean curd that Kee Sun's been feeding you has actually done you some good. Come on, I might as well go too. You'll have lots of company there. No. Not through the kitchen. Kee Sun would have to wash the whole place down," Sachi giggled, grabbing Toumi's elbow and leading her through the main doors.

Moon time, I realized. Toumi too had reached her first moon time. I was going to be alone.

"Pick up the girl's tray," barked Lady Chiyome to the girls nearest to her. "Help the squirrel here bring our food before you disappear too."

It was a mark of the authority and fear in which all of the women held Chiyome-*sama* that they didn't even hesitate in following her order.

As I started back toward the kitchen to refill the serving platters, the door to the hall opened again. Aimaru poked his snow-covered head in and peered around.

As he began to leave again, Lady Chiyome snapped, "Well, boy? What is it? Why have you let a draft in and turned our tea to ice?"

"Pardon, my lady," Aimaru said, eyes downcast. "I was looking for the lieutenant. I saddled his horse as he asked last night for us to do—usually he's up before we are, so I thought he must be in here."

"Probably sleeping in," the lady growled, and for some reason flashed an angry glance at Mieko, who was sipping her tea, the very portrait of studied innocence. "Go wake him!"

"Yes, my lady," Aimaru said, bowing through the barely-open door.

"And shut the door!" Chiyome-*sama* yelled. "It's freezing in here!"

Wisely, Aimaru closed the door rather than answer again.

Kee Sun, whom I had almost never seen outside of his kitchen, met me outside of its entrance and exchanged my empty platters for a steaming metal tea pot. "For the lady," he whispered, and disappeared back into his domain.

I scurried up to the head table and refilled Chiyome-*sama*'s cup. She put both hands around the cup and grunted, "Leave the pot." It seemed as if that were the best response I could hope for.

As I turned to Mieko-*san*, who seemed to have finished the rather large helping that I had given her, the door flew open again.

Lady Chiyome took a deep breath, ready to shout at whoever had, once again, let in the cold, but the two Little Brothers had entered at a dead run, closing the door behind them. Their swords were drawn.

Even Lady Chiyome didn't seem to have anything to say about that.

The smaller of the pair ran to take up a place behind her, looming menacingly there with his sword. I instinctively scampered out of the way to give the larger one room as he moved directly in front of her and knelt.

"Lieutenant Masugu has been poisoned," he said.

The low rumble of his voice seemed to wash over the hall like an enormous ocean wave. All of the women leapt to their feet. "Masugu!" shouted Fuyudori and started to run toward the door.

"STOP!" yelled Lady Chiyome. It hardly mattered whether the order was aimed at Fuyudori, who was poised to sprint to the door, or at the smaller of the Little Brothers, who had begun to move to intercept her, his sword raised high: all motion in the hall stopped.

Chiyome-*sama* stood, her arms extended, her face a mirror of the dismay that had clutched me.

Mieko stood as still as a snake before it strikes. Her face was a neutral, lovely mask as always, but there was a fierce concentration in her eyes that I had seen once before: at the Mount Fuji Inn.

Lady Chiyome lowered her arms, which I noticed were shaking. "How do you know he was poisoned?"

The Little Brother before her turned again and knelt, even as the other took up a position just inside of the door. "He is unconscious. His pulse is very slow. There was a jar of rice wine by his bed, and it smelled of poppy juice."

"Poppy juice?" snapped Mieko-*san*, and Lady Chiyome turned toward her, her face twisted both with shock and annoyance that her usually deferential maid was suddenly so outspoken. "He hates it. He won't allow his soldiers to use it, even in the greatest pain. He would never touch it knowingly."

Lady Chiyome held up a shaking hand once more to reestablish the proper order of things. "Is this so?"

"Yes, my lady," both Little Brothers answered.

A sob broke out at the far end of the room. Fuyudori was standing, her fist shoved into her mouth, tears flowing down her face.

"Stop it, girl!" Chiyome-*sama* snarled. "I think the meal is over. Shino. Take this worthless, white-haired idiot off to the Retreat. If it isn't her moon time or yours, it will be soon enough."

"But—!" Fuyudori sobbed.

Lady Chiyome had had enough. "GO! NOW!"

Fuyudori's mouth snapped shut and her eyes flew open. She followed a fuming Shino out of the hall.

"And the rest of you stay where you are. All of you!"

Everyone in the hall was absolutely still.

"AND WHERE DO YOU THINK YOU'RE GOING?" roared Chiyome-*sama*.

I flushed with fear, thinking perhaps that I was the one at whom she was yelling. I hadn't moved a muscle, of course. I was terrified that someone could have tried to poison Masugu-*san*—someone from our own community.

Mieko however was standing with her hand ready to open the door. I was standing right next to where she had been seated and yet I hadn't seen her rise or move. It was as if she had simply appeared on the other side of the hall. I saw the Little Brothers both flinch, telling me that she'd managed to move without their noticing either.

Mieko gave a simple, almost military bow. "This humble servant was anticipating her mistress's always-wise command."

Lady Chiyome's rheumy eyes narrowed, but she didn't say anything.

The maid, looking anything but humble, straightened. "I know more about poison than anyone at the Full Moon. I am the person best suited to treating Takeda-*sama*'s representative."

Without looking away from Mieko, Chiyome muttered to the Little Brother still kneeling before her, "Is the boy there?"

"Yes, my lady."

"Go with my *humble servant* there. Send the boy back. Make sure nothing happens."

The Little Brother touched his head to the floor of the hall.

Grunting, Chiyome-*sama* leaned forward onto her elbows, glaring at Mieko. "Don't do anything stupid, girl."

Mieko bowed again, less stiffly, and fairly ran through the door as soon as the Little Brother reached her.

I know more about poisons....

"Risuko!" shouted Lady Chiyome.

I found that my own feet had begun to lead me to the door. I knew that I couldn't let Mieko alone with Masugu-*san*, not when she'd already threatened to kill him. For a samurai to die by poison was a dreadful waste. For Masugu-*san* to die...

Blinking, I turned back toward the mistress of the Full Moon, knelt and bowed deeply, my forehead touching the tray full of dirty bowls.

"Go tell Kee Sun what has happened to the lieutenant. Tell him to... *assist* that presumptuous chit in treating Masugu. Tell him that you may assist him, if he needs."

Leaping to my feet, I started to run to the kitchen, stopped and tried to turn, bow and start running again, and tripped, sending the tray and bowls flying. Several of them shattered.

When I started to try to pick them up, Chiyome-*sama* roared. "Forget the dishes, idiot. GO!" As I flew through the door, I heard her growl, "The rest of us are going to stay right here."

29—Proper Duty

"Mugwort!" growled Kee Sun, pulling out a bag full of tiny herb pellets. "*Mogusa!* The old folks burn these on your back every year, right?"

"Yes," I said. My hands were shaking. I only hoped that the Little Brothers were watching Mieko closely. "On New Year's Day. One pellet—"

"—for every year, yes, yes." He took a deep breath. "Light these and hold them against the bottoms of his feet, hear? Till he wakes up. Raise blisters if yeh have to. Don't stop till he wakes."

"Yes, Kee Sun."

He grabbed a pot of pickled ginger. "And wave this under her nose."

"Her nose?"

"*His* nose! His nose." He looked as if he were about to throw the clay pot at me. "Don't sass me, girlie."

"No, Kee Sun-*san*." I took the ginger and held both herbs to my belly.

"Go." He turned back to the stove, where he had a pot of water starting to boil. "I'll be there as soon as the tonic is ready."

"Yes, Kee Sun-*san*."

"*Go!*"

I went. My mind was full with the previous night's dream—about my father's sword exercises, which were the same as Mieko's slow dance—and with the argument that I had overheard, and with sound of the bodies of the two Imagawa soldiers thumping to the *tatami*—and I knew in my heart that Mieko was a killer. As lovely and graceful as she might seem, and as kind to me as she had been, she was trained to take life; I could not let her take Masugu-*san*'s.

The snow had stopped and the clouds broken; the morning was clear and still and very cold. I ran across the snow-covered courtyard holding the ginger and the mugwort as gently as I could in my trembling fingers.

The older of the Little Brothers stood at the entrance to the guesthouse like one of the statues of the thunder-hurlers at the entrance to the temple of the Buddha at Pineshore. His feet were set wide and his hand was on his sword hilt. Though his face was impassive, he was watching me fiercely.

"I b-brought the herbs for M-masugu-*san*." When he didn't move aside, I added, "From Kee Sun-*san*."

Though his expression didn't soften in the slightest, he stepped aside and slid the door open for me.

Inside, the guesthouse was a mess. Screens had been tipped over, *tatami* mats rolled up and replaced carelessly, and a vase lay in the middle of the floor. I began to pick it up, but realized that my hands were already full, and that I had more urgent work than to neaten the lieutenant's rooms.

The other Little Brother stood at the entrance to the bedchamber, a scowl of distaste on his usually warm face. I heard a groan from the other room and then a quiet, high-pitched curse. "Hiding things! I told you," snarled a hard-edged voice that I had to convince myself could possibly be Mieko's. "Play games with the *kunoichi* and you're going to get hurt. *I told you!*"

I wanted to rush forward, to try to help Masugu, but fear rooted my feet in the floor.

The lieutenant gave another wordless groan, and Mieko shouted, "You had to drink it all! Idiot!" And a missile—a *sake* bottle—flew through the doorway and shattered against the wall by the Little Brother's head. For the first time since I met him, he actually flinched.

Now my feet tore themselves free; I ran into the room, the medicines still clutched to my belly, ready to defend Masugu.

The lieutenant lay on his side on his bedroll, his eyes open but unfocused, his face slack and shiny with sweat. Mieko too was sweaty, but where his face was pale, hers was unusually flushed. Her hair, which was usually so neatly arranged, flew wildly around her head. She looked like a bear. An angry mother bear.

She punched his shoulder with a force that surprised me and he groaned. She growled and shook him, muttering, "Idiot! Nothing to throw up. You had to drink it all last night, didn't you? *Baka-yarō!*" Mieko gave Masugu another shake and then slapped his back.

I must have gasped, because she looked up, and when she saw me, her face hardened. "You."

"I won't let him die," I squeaked.

Slowly her eyes widened. "What have you got there?"

I walked and knelt opposite her, in front of Masugu, trying to let her know that I was going to protect him. "Ginger. And mugwort."

"From Kee Sun?"

I nodded.

"No tonic?"

"He's making it now. He said the ginseng needed to be fresh."

Now her eyes narrowed. "Give me the ginger."

In spite of my mistrust, I gave it to her. As she opened the lid, I looked down at Masugu's face. His eyes looked warm yet somehow inhuman; it took me a moment to realize that it was because the pupils had all but disappeared.

She sniffed at the pickled ginger, and then pulled out a slice and nibbled at the smallest portion. She nodded, her face settling back into the calm, focused mask that I was used to. "Give me the ginger," she said. "You can burn the pellets—against his feet, I think."

"I..." I pulled both herbs back to my chest. I don't know what I envisioned—that she was somehow going to use the ginger to finish poisoning him? "I... don't know how to burn the *mogusa*. I might hurt him."

"You could hardly hurt him any more than he already has been." When I remained frozen with the herbs held tight to me, she huffed, but held out her hand again. "Then give me the mugwort."

I did. I could think of no excuse not to.

She yanked a long straw from the *tatami* and lit it from the small brazier that warmed the room. "If you're going to be helpful, crush some of the ginger under his nose."

I did this too, squeezing a slice between my thumb and finger. His nostrils twitched at the fragrant scent, though the rest of his face continued to sag.

The bitter odor of burning mugwort clashed with the sweet heat of the ginger. I looked down to Masugu's feet, where Mieko knelt, that fierce concentration still on her face: a she-wolf, now, rather than a bruin. In her long, elegant fingers, she held one of the smoldering pellets against the lieutenant's bare instep. Her eyes flicked up. "Don't cram it into his nose. He needs to breathe."

Glancing down, I realized that I had in fact pushed the ginger into his nostril while my attention had strayed. "Oh. Sorry. Sorry, lieutenant." I cleared the airway and got a fresh piece of ginger from the pot.

She grunted, lit another pellet of mogusa, and held it against Masugu's foot. This time, he actually gave a small wince. "So," she said, "did you find what you were looking for?"

"Find—?" I began, but at that moment, the lieutenant groaned, and his eyes, which had been open but misty, focused up at my face.

"'ko?" he murmured, and then his face, which had been as lax as that of a dead man's, twisted into a flabby grin.

"*Ko?*" I asked. I couldn't think why he would call me by my nickname; he was always so careful to call me *Murasaki*.

"'ko-ko," he burbled, and his fingers reached up to stroke my cheek. They were cool. Out of the corner of my eye, I could see Mieko stiffen. "Ma'me?"

"What?" I blinked down at him in confusion; on the one hand, he was awake, which was good, but on the other, he as behaving so...

"Ma'me!" he repeated, and his face twisted in a babyish pout. His fingers closed on my chin. Mieko's eyes widened. Big, round tears rolled across Masugu's nose. "Ma'r'me! Mar'me, 'ko-ko!"

"Ma—?" I sat there, unable to move. "Marry you?"

"He doesn't mean you," whispered Mieko, her voice deathly low. "He thinks he's talking to me."

"Kill me 'gain," sobbed Masugu. Then his eyes rolled back into his head, his hand fell limp from my chin and he drifted back into the open-eyed sleep that I'd first seen him in.

Kill me again. What did he mean?

"Don't let him fall unconscious again!" barked Mieko, but she was crying—tears of guilt no doubt, at his accusation.

"You!" I snarled, the ginger forgotten in my hands. "He wouldn't want to marry you! He knows you tried to kill him!"

Mieko sat back on her heels, apparently surprised by the vehemence of my attack. "What are you talking about?"

"He knows you're the one who poisoned him, who... destroyed his rooms, and—!"

"Me!" Mieko let out an angry growl of a laugh. She dropped the pellet—it had apparently burned her fingers in her inattention—and had to smother it with the sleeve of her robes to keep the straw *tatami* from catching light. "He knows that I would never hurt him. You were the one—"

"I heard him!" I was suddenly standing, my feet wide. "Last night! In the Retreat! He said that you'd tried to kill him five years ago. I heard him."

She stared up at me. "You heard—?" I expected her to become angry again, but her expression bowed downward into sadness. She shook her head, lighting another pellet and applying it to the lieutenant's feet. "Oh, Risuko. I thought that I had heard someone moving about outside. This idiot told me that I was imagining things, but I knew.... You are one of us after all, aren't you? You gave him too much of the poppy, and you made a mess out his rooms, but you are a *kunoichi* after all."

"NO!" I howled, rage coursing through my body. If I had had a sword then.... Well, I would have used it, in spite of everything. No harm. "No! I'm not a killer like you! Lady Chiyome talks about *kunoichi* being 'a special kind of woman,' but that's all you are, all of you! You're murderers! Assassins! I couldn't be one of you. Not ever!"

Mieko's sad gaze never broke from mine. "Yet you drugged Masugu's wine. He could still die from that, you know—and though it is me that he wants to marry, he is quite fond of you."

"Drugged?" I spluttered. "I never! You—!"

"And why?" sighed Mieko. "Just so that you could ransack his rooms. What a waste."

"That was your work, not mine." My fists clench around the clay pot and the ginger. "Remember, I know that you were the person he accused of trying to kill him!"

"Five years ago," sighed Mieko, the sadness spilling over into tears, "he asked me to marry him. And I—"

"She refused," said Chiyome-*sama* from the door behind me, "knowing her proper duty."

Mieko and I both gasped and turned. Our mistress favored us with her usual smirk of sour amusement and walked toward us. Kee Sun trailed at her shoulder, scowling.

"Congratulations, Risuko," said Lady Chiyome. "You have earned an initiate's sash." Her face. "The question, I suppose, is whether we shall have to use it to hang you as a traitor."

30—Battle of White & Scarlet

"I am no traitor!" I shouted, and then dropped to my knees and bowed. The ginger spilled onto the mat. "Mieko was the one who—!"

"No," said Chiyome-*sama*. "While I suppose that Mieko might have gone against her own sentiments and drugged Masugu there to search his rooms, she would never have done it so sloppily." I looked up in surprise. Lady Chiyome was staring at Mieko, who was bowing beside me. "And of course, if she had wanted him dead, he would have died. No doubt without any of us being any the wiser."

Chiyome-*sama* sniffed and looked back down at me. "This was done by an amateur. A child." She gestured around the jumbled room in disgust. "None of my *kunoichi* would have made such a mess of such a simple job. Least of all my Mieko."

I turned to accuse the maid, but she had gone silently back to burning pellets of mugwort against the soles of Masugu's feet. Kee Sun was lifting the tonic to the lieutenant's lips, forcing the liquid down; Masugu seemed to be gagging on it.

"Risuko. Look at me." Chiyome-*sama*'s sharp tone pulled me back around. "I visited the ladies in the Retreat just now. Fuyudori and Mai tell me that you were wandering about late last night—and they seldom agree that the sun has risen. I learn now that you used your delightful talents to spy on the lieutenant and Mieko."

I tried to speak, but fear bound me, squeezing my throat, my chest, my bowels. I tried to plead with her with my eyes, but her face was empty of any humor at all and I could only look away. Behind her, a scroll hung askew from the door screen.

"Perhaps," Lady Chiyome said, her voice low and cold, "you chose to visit Masugu's rooms while he was gone? Perhaps you brought the drugged wine along in case he returned before you were done? Kee Sun tells me you've been learning about herbs; of course, he swears to me that you're far too deft to have used a whole bottle of poppy juice at once."

The inscription on the scroll was a familiar one:

Soldiers falling fast

Battle of white and scarlet

Blossoms on the ground

The calligraphy too was familiar. It was my father's.

"Who are you spying for, girl?" asked the old woman. "The Imagawa? They're finished."

The scroll was, in fact, identical to the one hanging inside of the door at my home, except that instead of a picture of cherry blossoms, the bottom of the parchment was taken up with a carefully rendered circle—the full moon that is the Mochizuki crest.

Father. A brush poised like a knife. I was just learning to write myself, and I loved to watch him practicing his calligraphy and his drawing. He sat in our yard, staring at the bare cherry tree, a length of rice paper on his scribe's lap-desk. I tried to imitate with a stick in the dirt Father's beautiful handwriting, the beautiful blossoms. As he wrote out the poem for what felt like the hundredth time and began to draw the cascade of flowers, I asked him why he was drawing cherry blossoms in the autumn. He thought about that for a moment, put down his brush, and said, "The blossoms fall just once each winter, yet in our memories, they fall every day."

"SQUIRREL!" snapped Lady Chiyome. "What on earth are you staring at?"

Without even looking back at her, as I should have, I pointed and gasped, "Where did you get my father's poem?"

Lady Chiyome blinked at me and then at the huge scroll. When she looked back at me, her furious expression had been replaced by a more familiar one: shrewd calculation. "Your father's?"

"Of course!" I blurted. "I know it by heart! I would recognize that handwriting anywhere! I swear that is my father's poem!"

"I know," she said. "He gave it to me."

Masugu groaned.

I blinked at her, and then suddenly remembered where I was, who I was. I fell to the *tatami*, which still reeked of pickled ginger, and began to apologize for my rudeness.

Chiyome-*sama* interrupted. "Come, Risuko. We shall let Kee Sun and Mieko care for the lieutenant. You will come and explain yourself to me."

I looked up to answer, but she was already striding away. I scampered after her out of the guesthouse and into the bright cold of the courtyard. The Little Brothers fell in on either side of us. I wasn't sure whether they were protecting her, keeping an eye on me, or both.

I felt, in fact, very much as I had that first day, stumbling along beside her palanquin away from our village, from my home, and from my life.

———

We marched back to the great hall, empty now except for Aimaru, who stood at the bottom of the narrow stairs that led up to Chiyome-*sama*'s rooms, shifting from foot to foot. His usually bright face was dark and troubled; he looked away from me as we approached.

"This puppy can go back to guarding the guesthouse," Lady Chiyome barked, nodding her head at Aimaru. "With Mieko and Kee Sun caring for Masugu, I don't think anything can go wrong there that hasn't already. You two," she said, gesturing to the Little Brothers, "keep an eye on things down here. I don't wish our conversation to be... interrupted." She began to stride up the stairs. "Come, Risuko."

I followed. Halfway up the stairs I turned back. The Little Brothers had faced away, watching the doors. I drew a deep, unsteady breath, turned, and fled upward.

By the time I entered Lady Chiyome's chamber, she was already kneeling at her desk, mixing ink in a small bowl. I found myself coming to a stop in the doorway with one foot in the air, the memory of my one previous visit to her rooms rendering me as cold and as still as if I'd been encased in ice.

"Much easier simply to climb the stairs than the outside wall, isn't it, my Risuko?" said Chiyome-*sama* without raising her gaze from whatever it was that she was writing. "And if you've been invited in, there's no point in trying to hide. Especially in the middle of the doorway."

I stumbled forward and knelt before the desk. "Chiyome-*sama*," I said, trying to keep the trembling whine out of my voice, "this humble servant could never, ever try to hurt Masugu-*san*, or search his rooms, or—"

"I know," she said, and then gave her dry, rasping laugh. "Another humble servant. Just what I need."

"Yes, Chiyome-*sama*."

"Kano Murasaki," she addressed me, very formally now, and with no laughter, "answer me: why are you here?"

"In... your room?" She raised a carefully drawn eyebrow. "Oh. I am here because you wish me to become a shrine maiden, Chiyome-*sama*."

"And?"

"And... And a *kunoichi*."

"And what, Kano Murasaki, is a *kunoichi*?"

"A *kunoichi*..." In my mind's eye, I could see her writing the word that first afternoon at Pineshore, her brush slashing across the paper. "A *kunoichi* is a woman trained to kill, Chiyome-*sama*."

She gave a quiet grunt. "Close enough." From beneath her desk, she drew a length of red silk with white edging—an initiate's sash. "Red is the color of weddings. White is the color of death. A *miko* is married to that which cannot die. A *kunoichi* is married to her duty. And to Death." She held the sash out to me.

Dumb and terrified, I stared at it.

She snorted and let the silk fall to the floor before me. "In the first place, I must admit, I can't see you turning the guesthouse over like that—it doesn't seem like your style at all." She leaned forward, her gaze impaling me. "In the second, I saw your face when you spotted that poem. Either you're the greatest liar I've ever met—and I have met some very accomplished ones, young Kano—or you had never been inside of those rooms before, and they had been searched by our clumsy fox demon at least twice before last night. Close your mouth, child. You look like a frog waiting for flies."

I snapped my jaw shut, but couldn't bring myself to lower my gaze as I ought.

"Pick up the sash, Risuko." Lady Chiyome's voice was warm—for her.

I stared down at it.

"Put on the initiate's sash, Kano Murasaki," said Chiyome-*sama*.

My fingers heard the order and obeyed.

When it was knotted around my waist, Lady Chiyome sighed and said, "Your father..."

I did not dare to look up.

"*Mukashi, mukashi,* long ago, when you were just a baby, there was a great battle in a valley not far from this. My husband commanded Takeda-*sama*'s heavy cavalry at Midriver Island. They were routing the Uesugi and their allies, driving them at last from Dark Letter Province. Only one island of resistance stood—troops lent by the Uesugis' ally, Lord Oda."

I looked up.

Lady Chiyome's gaze was still directed at me, but she was looking elsewhere. "Your father... Kano Kazuo faced Mochizuki Moritoki sword to sword, there on the battlefield. Kano Kazuo prevailed." Her eyes regained their usual sharp focus, but they were dew-rimmed. "Though my husband fell, the Takeda nonetheless won the day. The Uesugi and their allies were shattered." She sniffed, looked away and then looked back again. "For some time after the news arrived—after Kee Sun came back and told me—I hardly left the walls of this room. One day, my servants came, telling me that a lone samurai was approaching on horseback. His swords were bound across his horse's back, but they were worried for my safety. I bade them open the gates to him. I did not particularly care for my own safety, you see."

I waited for her to continue.

"It was your father, of course. He told me that he was sorry for my loss, but that my husband had died with honor. That it had been an honor to face him. That... That a battlefield is not generally a place of honor."

I found tears beginning to spill from my own eyes.

"I spoke with him for some time. He spoke of you, of his family. Of how in taking my husband's life, he had felt as if he were taking yours."

A sound began to whistle up from my throat. I did not have any sense that I was making it myself.

"I reminded him of the Buddha's saying: All life is sorrow. All that lives, dies. The same forest gives birth to the tiger and the deer. Who kills and who is killed are one."

We sat there for some time, she and I. The old woman and the young girl. She weeping silently, I keening. Each of us mourning what we had lost long before.

31—Taking Up the Blade

I stumbled down from Lady Chiyome's apartment, tears and memories leaving me blind, and so I walked into the Little Brothers at the bottom of the stairs. The larger one gave me his customary blank look, and then turned back to face the entrances—the front door and the door to the kitchen.

The other Little Brother smiled. From behind his enormously wide back, he drew two bound bundles of bamboo. Each of the bundles was slightly curved, and seemed to have a handle at one end.

"Swords," I whispered.

"Practice swords," said the Little Brother with a nod and another grin. "Since you are now an initiate, it is time for your proper training to begin."

When the Little Brother held out one of the swords, however, I stood there frozen like river-grass in winter. "Murasaki-*san?*"

"I... I cannot. I cannot." I looked up into his frown—the same frown he'd been wearing when I had arrived in Masugu's rooms that morning. That morning? It felt as if that had been a memory from a previous lifetime. "My father... I—"

"Murasaki-*san,*" said the Little Brother, his voice low. "Our lady wishes you to learn to defend yourself. You are Chiyome-*sama's* servant."

"I live," I said, my tongue thick, "at Chiyome-*sama's* pleasure. But I cannot kill. I will not." I knelt and touched my forehead to the cold wood. "If our lady wishes this humble servant killed for her disobedience, this humble servant will gladly die."

The Little Brother hissed. "Get up. Don't... There is a difference between learning to defend yourself, Risuko, and killing people."

I looked up; his broad face was creased with concern. "I know what the *kunoichi* are. I know what it is Lady Chiyome expects me to do."

He grimaced and shook his head—whether to deny what I was saying or to clear his mind I did not know. "Do not be so sure. Your father would have wanted this, I think. Take up your sword."

"Little Brother. Sir..." I stammered.

"To learn with a bamboo sword how one defends oneself is not to kill." He held the sword out to me. "Take the sword."

I thought of my father. Wrapping away his blades.

Hand trembling, I took the handle.

The leather-wrapped hilt fit in my fingers as if it had been created created for no other hand but mine. I stood there, my feet spread, the bamboo practice sword held before me. Without thinking about it, I had taken the first position in Mieko-*sensei's* dance. Of the sword exercises that *Otō-san* used to do every morning out in the courtyard, right up until that last morning when he was summoned by Lord Imagawa. I stared at the bundle of tightly-bound pieces of split bamboo, seeing in my mind's eye the impossibly bright steel of Father's *katana*.

My vision flared.

"Well done, Risuko," said the Little Brother. "You have taken the first position. Good. Now, let us begin."

And he led me through the whole of the exercise—the dance—and as always, I knew each move before the last was finished. After all, hadn't Usako and I mirrored *Otō-san* in the mornings, each us holding a stick of pine or a stalk of bamboo as he swept his sword through each of the parries and cuts?

I can remember us standing in the shadow where the roof is low, by the kitchen, both of us mirroring him. I remember *Otō-san* pretending not to see us.

Soon, I had followed the Little Brother through the exercise four times— once facing in each of the cardinal directions: East, south, west, and north.

The Little Brother bowed, and I bowed back. I felt as if quicksilver were swirling through my innards. "This," he said, "we call *The Sixty-four Changes.* Mastering these positions, you will learn to wield a sword in balance, attacking and defending while still remaining rooted to your center. Each position combines the five elements, the two energies. All flow from the first position, *The Two Fields.*" He took the initial stance, his feet spread wide and his sword before him. "You should feel planted, as if your legs extended deep into the earth."

He walk around me, adjusting the stance with the tip of his sword—moving my feet further apart, making sure my knees were bent, but not too much, showing me how to hold the sword neither too high nor too low, but with the hilt just at my navel.

Finally satisfied, he stepped opposite me and took the pose again himself. "The next stance we call *The Bamboo Bud.*" He stepped to one side with his right foot, bringing his blade up to match the diagonal line from his left foot to the crown of his head. "This position allows you to redirect the force of an opponent's downward cut with no harm to yourself or to your blade—like the young bamboo, you bend, shedding the attack, but do not break."

If it hadn't been for his size, and for the wooden sword in his hands, he might indeed have looked a bit like a shoot of bamboo sprouting from the forest floor.

I mirrored him, and once again, he adjusted my stances until I met his standard.

"Last for today is *The Key to Heaven.*" He stepped toward me, lifting his right foot and knee in exaggerated fashion while raising the sword high above his head, and then bringing leg and sword down with a thunderous bellow.

I blinked, staring down at the wooden sword, which he held a fingernail's width from my chest.

We had gone through these movements while following Mieko-*san*. I had watched our father practice them. And yet watching them one by one...

I stood there, my hands once again shaking.

"Risuko," said the Little Brother, stepping back and gesturing for me to imitate him, and I started to try to tell him that I couldn't, but his big, kindly face shone on me, remorseless and relentless. I gulped down a whimper, stepped forward, and slashed down half-heartedly with my bamboo sword.

Why, I do not know, but as I did so, the image that floated through my mind was of the chicken that I had trapped, just before Toumi wrung its neck, its strange, demon eyes boring into my soul.

"Good," said the Little Brother, smiling. "Again."

I repeated the motion—the lunge forward and the downward slash of the blade—over and over until it felt more like working in the kitchen than anything else: *chop, chop, chop....*

"Good," said the Little Brother again. "You have done well for today. Tomorrow, we will work on the next three forms. You may go to the kitchen now."

———

I found myself some time later in the kitchen, one of the long, sword-sharp cleavers in my hand, chopping up *daikon* because although I needed to

be moving, there was nowhere for me to go. I was thinking about the movements of Mieko's dance. Of how they would feel with a blade in my hands.
The Two Fields—balanced and ready. *The Bamboo Bud*—moving to the
side and bringing the blade up to block an attack at one's head. *The Key of
Heaven*—a swift cut downward....

"That's enough radish I think, Bright-eyes." The voice surprised me, and
my eyes suddenly took in what I had created while my mind had wandered: a
pile of sliced *daikon* that flowed off of the cutting table like slabs of snow from
hemlock boughs. Startled, I looked up.

Kee Sun was grey-faced; his scars seemed even paler than usual.

"Is...?" So much had happened that morning that I couldn't even think
how to finish the question.

"Masugu's goin' t'be all right. Be off his feet for a while, mind. But yeh
and Serpent-girlie did good. And my tonic did the job, right enough."

"Serpent?"

"Ayup. Mieko, as yeh call her. Beautiful as a snake, twice as calm, but just
as deadly if yeh step on her, right?" He winked.

"Oh. Is she still...?"

"Nope. Off in the Retreat with all of the rest of them but you, the lady,
and us men-folk." I must have looked concerned, because he held his hands
up. "Yehr friend with the moon-cake face, Aimaru, he's watchin' Masugu.
Keepin' him talkin'."

The memory of Masugu's fingers on my chin—of his babbling—flashed
through my mind.

Kee Sun smiled. "Don't think he's asked Moon-cake to marry him yet.
But yeh never know."

I felt the blood rushing to my face.

"Nice sash yeh got there, girlie." He began pulling some herbs from the
rafters and dropping them into a large pot of chicken stock that was just
beginning to boil over the fire.

"Uh. Thank you, Kee Sun-*san*." I picked up the knife that I had been
using, and then put it down again. I wanted desperately to forget the sash and
all that it represented—*married to death and that which is deathless.* "So. What
are we making for the mid-day meal?"

He grunted. "We? *I'm* brewin' another batch of tonic, and then I'm
headin' back to care for Masugu." He grinned at me. "Yeh're making rice, and
servin' it with some o' the smoked eel from the storeroom. Oh. And radishes,"
he snickered, pointing at the pile on the cutting table.

"I?" I gasped. "All alone?"

"Well," he said, "guess yeh're an initiate and all now. So I'll send Moon-cake over t'help yeh. Though I'm thinkin' he'd rather be talkin' to Smilie, right?"

"Thank you, Kee Sun-*san*." I was so pleased that I wouldn't be preparing the meal alone that I didn't even mind him making fun of my friends. A question occurred to me. "Kee Sun-*san*? Did they—? Did Masugu-*san* really ask Mieko-*sensei* to marry him?"

I watched his shoulders bunch—a grimace or a shrug, I couldn't be sure. "I tell yeh, Bright-eyes. Men and women? A bloody mess. Every time." And that was all that he said on the subject.

———

Not long after Kee Sun had left with another dose of the spicy-scented tonic, I found myself standing in the middle of the kitchen, holding the long stick that Kee Sun kept to shoo away the rats. Gripping it in both hands like a sword. Like a samurai's *katana*.

Could I? I wondered. *Could I be like Mieko and the rest? Could I be like Father?*

I was in the starting rest position, feet spread, sword in front of me, balanced. *The Two Fields.* I stepped to the side, bringing the stick up at an angle as if to parry a downward cut. *The Bamboo Bud.*

I heard a noise behind me and whirled, not even thinking, bringing the stick above my head and down...

Down onto Aimaru's head. *The Key of Heaven.*

The stick snapped, leaving me holding just a stump.

I can't tell you who was more astonished, Aimaru or me. "I... I'm *so sorry!*"

"I'm all right!" Aimaru said, falling to his knees. "I'm all right! You didn't hurt me." He touched his hand to the top of his head, where a dark bruise was already starting to rise. He shook his head and added with a grin, "Well, not too much."

"*I'm so sorry,*" I repeated, clutching the shattered end of my erstwhile sword to my chest.

"What...?"

"I didn't... I was thinking about the dance, Mieko's dance, and my father's sword exercises, and, and I am *so sorry,* Aimaru!"

He dismissed that apology with a wave of his hand and staggered to his feet. "I'll make sure never to sneak up on you."

"I could have hurt you!"

"With this head?" He grinned at me a bit blearily and looked down. At first I thought he didn't want to look me in the eye, but then I realized that he was staring at my new sash. "You're... an initiate."

"Yes, I'm an initiate. So you can talk to me." I took a breath, trying to block out the thought of what I had just done. "I'm sorry." I tossed the bit of stick away. "I... I have to make the mid-day meal for everyone."

"I know," he said. "Kee Sun asked me to help you."

"Great." I tried to think what jobs I could give him. The small barrel by the stove that held rice was nearly empty. "Do you think you could get us some rice from the storeroom?"

He frowned. It still wasn't an expression that I was used to seeing on his open face, but had been seeing more and more.

"That's all right," I sighed. "Here. If you can watch the fire and make sure that it stays hot enough to boil that big pot of water, I'll go get the rice."

Now he smiled. "I can do that, Murasaki-*san*."

I picked up the longest shard of the stick that had broken over Aimaru's head and ran to the storeroom by the stables. As always, there were rats in the stores, glaring at me as if I were the intruder. I slashed at the closest with the broken stick (*Key of Heaven...*), and they all scattered, gone before I could pull back the stick for another swing.

"We should have a cat," I grumbled, trying to still my trembling. There was a half-empty sack of rice against the right-hand wall, and I grabbed it. It was only once I'd lifted the sack to my back and was almost back to the kitchen that I realized that it had taken all three of us to carry a full sack on the day of our arrival at the Full Moon.

I suppose all that rock-carrying is good for something after all, I thought.

———

As we prepared the meal, Aimaru told me what little there was to tell about Masugu—which wasn't anything I didn't already know. He asked me how I had earned the sash, and I had to admit that I didn't have the slightest idea.

And of course neither of us had any idea who could have poisoned the lieutenant—though I told him about Mieko's suspicious behavior. He seemed more relieved that Lady Chiyome didn't suspect me than anything else. "Someone must have been looking for... something."

"Yes," I murmured, "but what?"

Aimaru shrugged and prodded the fire. "Well, they searched there before. And the stables."

I had forgotten about that. "And maybe in Lady Chiyome's rooms. Though why they'd want to do that, I have no idea." It seemed like a good way to ensure a very painful death.

"Well," he mused cheerfully, "whoever it is can't have found anything, or they wouldn't have almost killed Masugu-*san*."

He was very quiet when I told him what I had realized about the nature of the *kunoichi*. That they were nothing but killers.

"Oh," he said, ladling out the rice. "I thought it might be something like that."

"I won't do it. I'd rather die."

He smiled at me—that sunny, open smile. "All that lives, dies, Murasaki-*san*."

"I know that. People keep telling me that. And... Just Murasaki. Or Risuko. Please, Aimaru."

He nodded, the smile undiminished.

We distributed the meal around the compound. Only Chiyome-*sama* and the Little Brothers ate in the great hall. Kee Sun was with Masugu-*san*, and the rest of the Full Moon's inhabitants were in the Retreat. The red of their robes, which I had always associated with good luck, now seemed instead to be the stain of blood.

———

As we were cleaning up after the meal, Kee Sun returned, looking even more tattered and grumpy than usual. "Got one of those Little Brothers sitting with him now," he said in answer to the question that neither Aimaru nor I had voiced. "He's past the worst of it—he's sweatin' the poppy juice out at this point, and the tonic'll help that."

He must have seen my relief, because he added, "Mind, he's goin' to be weak as a puppy till after the New Year, I shouldn't think. No goin' around kissin' young ladies for him!"

Aimaru blushed, even as he smiled his usual smile. "We served the meal to everyone, Kee Sun-*san*."

"So I noticed," chuckled the cook. "And nobody else poisoned that I've heard tell! Yeh'll do, yeh'll do. Now get outa my kitchen with yeh, Moon-cake. The other of them Little Brothers is waitin' to give yeh a lesson."

Aimaru obeyed immediately, bowing to Kee Sun so that the bruise on the top of his head showed and smiling at me for just an instant before disappearing out the door.

"Did yeh break the rat-chasing thingee, Bright-eyes?"

"I..." I picked up the remains of the stick I'd broken over Aimaru's head

"And would yeh breakin' it have anythin' to do with the lovely bruise atop Moon-cake's head?"

"I can't," I whispered.

"Can't?"

"Can't..." I waved the stub of my pretend sword. "Can't."

"Huh." Kee Sun plucked the handle from my hands and tossed it into the fire. I watched the pine smolder and then catch flame.

My eyes filled as I watched the sword handle burn. "My father..." I choked down the thickness in my throat. "My father... last thing... he said to me... 'Do no harm.'"

"Huh."

"When Lord Imagawa... wanted him... to be a samurai... again."

Sharpening and wrapping his swords, then putting them away. Putting on his best scribe's robes. Bowing to *Okā-san*, who was trying not to weep, then to my sister, and finally to me. He had turned and left, but I had run after him. He stopped, just past the old cherry tree that grows over the little shrine to the forest spirit. I had wanted him to turn, but he had not. I had wanted to touch him, to pull him back to the house, but I could not. '*Otō-san!*' I had called.

His back straight, his feet at shoulder width—*The Two Fields*. Then—in the quietest voice imaginable, Father had said, 'Do not follow me. Do not follow my path.' He had begun to walk again, but before he had taken three steps he had stopped again, his face still away from mine, and had said, in a terrible sob, 'Do no harm, Murasaki. No harm.' And then he had walked away.

While this scene played itself out in my memory, Kee Sun cut up ginger for the soup. The scent was sharp and sweet and hot, and I found myself thinking that perhaps smells could be like herbs, balancing our elements; I know that I felt dark and sour in that moment, and the smell of the ginger was like a tonic.

I watched the flame licking at the stick so that it looked like a snake.

"I met yehr father," said Kee Sun.

"I know. Lady Chiyome said."

"I saw him fight. Saw him fight the Old Soldier at Midriver Island. He was a warrior, yehr daddy." Kee Sun dropped mushrooms and slices of radish into the soup. He gave a thoughtful grunt. "Now yeh know, seems to me, just walking across a field, yeh do harm—to the grass and the ants and such."

I sighed. "I know."

"And I'd've thought, if a body had a blade and the way of usin' it proper," he went on, measuring handfuls of dried onion greens into the broth, and then stirring with his long-handled spoon, "that protecting folks that didn't have swords and such from bandits and the like would be doin' less harm then standin' aside and doin' nothin'."

I stood there, crying, wiping my eyes and my nose with the sleeves of my jacket. "But... The *kunoichi*..."

"It's true. They kill now and again. Serpent-girlie?" He whistled. "Yeh'd be dead and yeh wouldn't even know it, and she'd be out o' the house with a smile and not a hair outa place and no one the wiser till yeh hit the ground. But some? Some of 'em have the talent o' findin' things out. Take Flower-girl that teaches yeh the music." He gave a snort. "Not a killer, that one. But she's very good at makin' menfolk very happy and talky, so's they tell her all the things they're not supposed to, and when she's gone, all they can remember is how much she made 'em laugh."

"But she... Sachi said her hunting...?"

"There's huntin', yeh see," said Kee Sun, lifting an eyebrow suggestively. "An' then there's *huntin'*."

"Oh."

"And some of 'em are good at keeping folk from gettin' hurt. Dressed up like a serving girl if they want, or a cook, or a lady's maid, or a nun, and no bandit watchin' some silky lady go by in her little box is goin' t'think that our girlie is ever a bodyguard, but that she is, and a good one."

"Oh."

I walked over and peered into the pot.

Kee Sun leaned down and took a deep whiff of the steam from the now-simmering soup. "Yeh'll be glad t'hear that Masugu was askin' about yeh."

"He was?" I sniffled.

"Ayup. Durin' one of the times when he wasn't sleepin'. Seemed quite put out that yeh'd been snoopin' on him and Serpent-girlie from atop the Retreat." Kee Sun turned and winked. Seeing my face, he sobered and turned back to the soup. "Kept talkin' about the chimney. I think he was worried yeh'd fall."

I actually laughed at that.

"And as I was walkin' back to strain the soup before yeh got back, I ran into Ghostie-girlie tryin' to sneak in to see him. All flustered and pink she got, too, when I caught her. Told me it wasn't her moon time yet, and she just wanted t'see that the good lieutenant was all right." He snorted. "Told her he was sleepin' fine, and that she was too late anyway—he'd already asked yeh to marry him." He chuckled, and I tittered along with him, even though I had already heard too many jokes on that subject.

I walked over and looked into the enormous pot. The vegetables looked delicious—red, brown, white and green in the clear, golden broth. Perfect. I took a deep whiff. "Kee Sun?"

"Hmm?"

"Doesn't it smell a little... bitter?"

He grunted and took a sniff. "Huh. Perhaps. A bit. Must've overcooked the stock. A bit o' garlic'll take care o' that. Mince some up for us, Bright-eyes."

Without even thinking about it, I went over and found a garlic bulb and the small chopping knife. I had that garlic reduced to fine bits in no time— and I wasn't even feeling sorry for myself as I did it. I brought him the bowl into which I'd scooped the garlic.

He took it from me and poured it into the pot. He inhaled deeply. "There yeh go." He motioned me closer. "Take a sniff now."

I did. "Mmm."

"Right!" he said, rubbing his hands together. "Grab us the big tureen there, and all o' the bowls." Quickly, he transferred most of the soup into the big serving bowl—the tureen, as he always called it—and covered it with its flat lid. The bowls stacked easily on the lid. "Now, let's see if all o' that rock carryin' has done yeh any good. Can yeh pick that up without droppin' it?"

Carefully I lifted the big bowl, and all of the crockery.

He hung a huge serving spoon from one of the handles. "There yeh are. Now bring that out to the Retreat and to the guesthouse. I'll serve the lady and the Little Brothers." He gave me a smile, his scars twisting, and opened the door to the outside, letting in a blast of chill wind. "Get on with yeh! Don't let that soup get cold! And I'll wait t' eat till yeh're back. A body shouldn't eat alone."

"*Hai*, Kee Sun-*san*," I said, and carefully made my way out into the rapidly gathering gloom of the winter evening.

32—Chicken Soup

Snow began to fall again—light, tiny flakes that seemed to appear from nowhere. I struggled to keep the soup from sloshing out of the tureen and the bowls clattered and threatened to fall every time my feet slid on the slick gravel, but I managed. Soon I was at the Retreat. I knocked on the door.

A familiar whisper answered. "Yes?"

"Emi!"

She sighed. "Hello, Murasaki. Do you have our meal?"

"Yes! It's chicken soup."

I heard several of the women inside groan with hunger.

"Open the door," I whispered, "and I can help you serve it out."

"Oh," Emi said, sounding uncertain. "I think you're just supposed to leave it."

I kept my voice low; I didn't want anyone but Emi to hear. "But I need to bring the tureen to the guesthouse to feed Aimaru and Masugu-*san*."

"Oh." I heard movement inside, and the door opened—just a crack. The air inside was hot and stale. I saw a dozen grumpy faces looking toward me. Emi stepped out, finishing wrapping herself in a jacket to to keep out the chill. The women began to press toward the door.

"Stop pushing, ladies. Line up!" said Mieko, and line up they did.

Emi and I knelt. I spooned out the steaming soup into a bowl, and Emi passed each in to one of waiting women inside.

"So," I whispered, "what is it like?"

"Like?" Emi grumbled.

"The Retreat?"

She was silent for a moment. "Boring."

"Oh."

Then she turned toward me and her eyes sparkled. "Anything exciting happening out there?"

"Uh," I gulped, spilling a bit of broth onto the step that was serving as our serving table, "I hit Aimaru over the head with a stick."

Emi laughed—bright and happy, like a dog's welcoming bark. "I wish I could have seen that!"

"But—!" I spluttered. Toumi was scowling from the barely-open doorway, waiting for her meal. I filled the bowl that Emi was holding, and she passed it up to Toumi, who took it with a grunt and began slurping the soup, still watching us as she walked away. I lowered my voice again. "I thought you... liked him."

"Shh!" Emi's face fell, not into its usual frown, but into a grimace of shock.

She handed a bowl out, then sighed. "Anyway... What were you doing with a stick?"

"It was the one we use to chase rats. I was... pretending it was a sword."

"Oh." Emi's eyes narrowed. "Murasaki?"

"Hmm?"

"Your sash."

Not wanting to say the words, I lifted the red and white silk.

Now Emi's eyes got wide. "How—?"

"I think," I whispered, looking past her into the room full of women dressed in red and white, "that I got it because I told Mieko-*san* what *kunoichi* were. That they are—" *Assassins. Killers.* "—soldiers."

Emi nodded, passing a bowl up to one of the women. "That makes sense," she murmured quietly. "That's why they have us doing all of the slaughtering and butchering."

I hadn't thought of that. The teachers had said that what we had learned from Kee Sun would help us as *kunoichi*. My stomach contracted.

Emi grunted. "But what about the dancing and singing and writing and such?"

Laughter bubbled through the doorway. It appeared the Horseradish girls were teasing Toumi.

"I think," I whispered, "that we're going to be spies too, some of us. Gathering information."

"Oh!" Emi nodded. "That's why we dress as *miko*! So we can go anywhere and no one notices us!"

That too made sense. Shino pushed her way in front of Fuyudori and demanded another bowl. I was going to refuse, but Emi shook her head. "I'm stuck in here with her for the next few days. It's not worth aggravating her."

Next Fuyudori came forward. "Good evening, Risuko-*chan*." She smiled her too-sweet smile. "Do not feel too badly. You will be here with us soon enough."

Emi, who was facing away from Fuyudori, crossed her eyes; it was all I could do not to laugh as I poured the head initiate's soup into the bowl that Emi was holding. "Yes, Fuyudori-*senpai*," I managed to say.

"Lovely," said Fuyudori, taking the bowl. She peered down into the soup. "Turnips?"

"Radishes," I answered apologetically.

"Oh." Her shoulders drooped, and she walked away, sniffing at her bowl.

I poked at Emi with the ladle, and she actually smiled. "Fine," I whispered, spooning out her bowlful of soup.

"She's been impossible all day, wringing her hands and weeping about the lieutenant. I thought Mieko was going to strangle her." Emi's brow furrowed. "Actually, from what you're telling me, that might have made for a much more useful lesson than playing music badly."

I considered that for a moment. I think that Emi meant it as a joke, but somehow, it didn't seem terribly funny at the time. "Kee Sun said that he had to send Fuyudori away from the lieutenant's rooms."

"Oh!" said Emi, her voice excited even as her face remained glum. "She was so worried about Lieutenant Masugu that she snuck out not long after you brought the rice this afternoon. Sachi actually had to hold Mieko back, or Mieko would have skinned her."

"Huh." I put the lid back on the tureen.

"Wait," Emi said, lifting her bowl to her lips. "You could stay and have your meal with me."

"All right." She stood and stepped into the doorway. I knew her well enough by then to know that the sadness on her face was neither habitual nor feigned. "It'll be boring without you. All they want to do is complain, eat or sleep." She started to close the door, but turned back toward me. "Say hello to the lieutenant. And, uh, to Aimaru." Her nose and cheeks were already reddened by the cold, but now a pink flush rose up her neck.

"I will," I answered, but she had already closed the door, slurping at her soup.

——

When I got to the guesthouse, Aimaru was far happier to see the soup tureen than he seemed to be to see me, but even so he smiled when I extended Emi's greeting to him.

"Is your head all right?" I asked. The bruise on his forehead was the deep purple of maple leaves.

He grinned as he touched his hand to it. "Oh, yes. It doesn't hurt." He winced. "Much."

My stomach sank as I passed him his bowl. "I'm so, so sorry, Aimaru!"

He chuckled. "Don't be. That was really amazing, the way you did that. Where did you learn?"

"I..." I was about to deny having ever learned anything about anything, but I realized what a pointless effort that would have been. "When I was little, I would watch while my father practiced with his *katana*. And sometime I would follow him, with a stick instead of a sword. I guess I actually learned something."

"I guess so!" He rubbed his neck and laughed. He sat and began to slurp his soup, but looked up. "If you see Emi..."

"I will offer your greetings," I said, and noticed with interest that his neck pinkened in very much the same manner as Emi's had.

Turning toward the sliding door to the bedroom, I felt myself hesitate. The room where I had argued with Mieko and Lady Chiyome, where I had watched Masugu himself nearly die—the idea of going back in there terrified me.

The chaos in the room, courtesy of what Lady Chiyome had called the *kitsune*, the fox spirit, made me shiver with apprehension, wondering if perhaps a malevolent demon was in fact among us. *Nonsense*, I told myself, sliding open the door just a bit with my left hand and then opening it the rest of the way with my right—just as Mother always taught us to do. I entered and knelt, the tureen in my hands.

Masugu-*san* lay on his bed, his eyes just barely open. The sleeping robe that he wore was damp with his sweat, and the room was stale with the scent of his perspiration, as well as the barely perceptible odors of vomit, of the burnt mugwort, and of the pickled ginger that I had spilled, just on the spot where I was kneeling.

"Mu-saki," he rasped through chapped lips. At least this time he knew that I was me and not Mieko. His hand, which was on top of the blanket, motioned feebly: *come.*

I shuffled over on my knees. His face was pale, but not as grey as it had been the day before. "Would you like some soup?"

He made a face—it was just like the face Usako used to make when *Okā-san* tried to feed her *okayu*. She was the only baby I ever knew who didn't like rice porridge.

"It's good for you," I said, ladling out a bowl—just as Mother used to say to my sister.

"Ginger," he said, turning up his nose, and I couldn't blame him. That day, he'd probably had more ginger shoved down his throat—and up his nose—than he'd eaten in the entire year.

I held the bowl up to his lips. "Kee Sun says that it helps sharpen the senses and fight off the effect of the poppy. Just a sip."

He took a sip, but still made a face, and I couldn't help it: I laughed. "No being fussy! Are you a samurai or aren't you?"

He gave me a weary look of disgust, but took another slurp from the bowl that I continued to hold before him. He swallowed, grunted, and lay back. "Bitter."

I sniffed at the soup. Under the delicious smells of the ginger and garlic, the bitter tang that I'd noticed before was still there. "I thought so too. Kee Sun thinks he may have let the stock simmer too hot or too long or something."

He grunted again. Taking a faltering, deep breath, he raised his drooping eyes to mine. "Mu-saki."

"Yes, Masugu-*san*?"

"Chimney."

"Chimney?" I remembered in a flash crouching on the wall above the Retreat's chimney the night before in the driving snow, listening... "Oh. Oh, Masugu-*san*. I'm so, so sorry, I didn't mean to overhear—"

"No." He shook his head with some effort. "No." He raised a finger and pointed at me. "Chimney."

I sighed. "Yes. I... I climbed the wall. I heard a noise and I thought perhaps someone was trying to sneak into the Full Moon, so I climbed up above the Retreat and I overheard you and Mieko-*san* fighting."

He actually managed to flash a bit of a smile. "Not fight..." He chuckled, a dry, dead-leaf chuckle, and pointed at me. "Sq'rrel."

I knew that he was teasing me because I'd been climbing again, but I couldn't help but feel mortified.

"Mu-saki..."

"Yes, Masugu-*san*?"

"Go... chimney." His burst of energy was fading; he fell back against his bedroll, and his eyes began to close.

"Yes. I went up by the chimney." I really wished he wouldn't keep bringing that up.

"No. Chimney. Go."

"You...?" I peered at him. He was struggling to stay awake; I wondered if he were beginning to suffer from one of the poppy-induced delusions again. "You want me to go back to the chimney of the Retreat?" Perhaps he wanted me to listen to what the women were saying? If Emi was right, I didn't think that anything that they might be talking about would be of interest—especially to a man.

Even so, he gave a tiny, relieved smile and nodded. "Go. Chimney... Roof." His chest and face softened as if he were melting into the bed. "Snowbird... Fox..."

Kitsune. That sent a shiver through me. Perhaps the lieutenant was possessed?

"Scroll," he said—or at least that's what it sounded like. "Go...."

At that moment, there was a crash from the front room; shocked, I turned to see Aimaru slumped against the wall. His soup bowl was shattered on the *tatami* below his limp hand, bits of mushroom and tofu and porcelain all dripping into the mat.

I gasped, and so did the lieutenant. *"Poison!"* he hissed.

I turned. His eyes now were wide. Masugu grabbed my hand. "Soup... poison..."

Now my eyes were wide. "Oh! Oh, no! Masugu-*san*, I would never—!"

"No," he groaned. "No. *Kitsune.* **Kitsune.**"

I nodded. I understood him, even if what he was saying made no sense. "The fox spirit poisoned the soup?"

He nodded.

My heart racing, I looked at Aimaru, who was still as death on the floor, and then at Masugu, who was weak; could two sips of poisoned broth finish the fox spirit's assassination attempt? "I'll get Kee Sun," I cried. "He'll help!" I hoped desperately that the cook had in fact waited for me to return before he ate; he could save Aimaru and the lieutenant....

I stood, and the bowl that I was holding spilled to the *tatami* but I paid it no mind. I was thinking that I had just served every one of the women in the Retreat from the same tureen. I remembered Emi closing the door, sipping at her bowl... I began to stumble out.

"Mu-saki!" Masugu's groan stopped me. I turned. He was clenching his hands, as if trying to keep himself awake. *"Chimney. Roof. Go!"*

"Go... to the chimney?" I answered, incredulous.

"Yesss," he wheezed, and collapsed onto his back in a deep, dead faint.

33—Smoke and Stone

For the second time that day I was running across the courtyard toward the great hall. This time, however, I was not stumbling after Lady Chiyome. To whom, I realized, Kee Sun had fed the same soup.

Could Kee Sun be the *kitsune*?

I stopped, mid-sprint, panting in the dark, winter evening. *No,* I thought. *He's crazy, but if he'd wanted to poison us, the Full Moon's cook could have done it any time.* And, as Lady Chiyome had said about Mieko-*san*, he'd have done it without making a mess of it.

I ran the rest of the way to the kitchen; I had no hope that the cook wouldn't already have served Chiyome-*sama* and the Little Brothers. When I burst into the outside door to the kitchen, he was just where I expected him to be: sitting at the work table, with two lidded bowls of soup laid—one for him, and one for me.

"Poison!" I gasped.

He blinked at me, then down at the bowls. He swept the lid from one of the bowls, sniffed, and then snarled in Korean and spat on the floor. "Bitter. You said it was bitter, Bright-eyes." With a look of panic on his face, he sprinted into the dining hall; Chiyome and the Little Brothers where slumped over the head table, their soup spilled on the ground. Lifting our mistress's head, he used his thumbs to open her eyes. "Chiyome! *Chiyome,* can yeh hear me?"

She let out a kind of snort and said something unrepeatable.

Kee Sun gave a bark of relieved laughter. Placing her head gently back on the table, he checked the others quickly—they too seemed to respond. Then Kee Sun ran back into the kitchen, sweeping past me and stumbling over to where the herbs were hung. "Bitter," he muttered, looking along the rafters for the herb that had been used to poison the soup. "Bitter. Bitter."

The poppies were still there—but they would have smelled sweet. He pointed up at an empty space on the beam. "Whew!"

"What?" I asked.

"Why'd anyone use *that* to poison folk?"

"What?"

He turned as if just remembering that I was there, shaking his head to clear it. "Ah. Corydalis."

"Corydalis?" The root from which Mother used to make tea before her moon time. The root out of which he'd been making Emi's tea. "Is that... dangerous?"

"Well..." Kee Sun rubbed his hand through his mop of grey hair. "It'll make'em all sleepy and boneless, and I suppose it'll give folk an awful headache, if she's used all of it. The men-folk especially!" He started to grin, but suddenly his relief disappeared. "Bright-eyes, tell me—how much did yeh feed Masugu?"

"T-two sips! I swear!"

He sighed, "Well, that's all right. Shouldn't oughta harm him, though he's in no fit state..." Turning away from me, he started to grab herbs—what was left of the ginger after all of the day's tonic- and soup-making, mugwort, black tea, green tea, and a box of precious ginseng.

I, however, was thinking about what Masugu had been trying to tell me before the corydalis put him back to sleep. *Chimney...* "Kee Sun! Do you need my help for a few minutes?"

"What?" he grumbled, dumping the stimulating, *yang* herbs onto the cutting table. "Well, I could use some help feedin' this t'everyone, but no, I can get this prepared quick enough. Yeh need to go t'the privy?"

"The...? *No!* No, Masugu-*san* wanted me to go up to the chimney of the Retreat—I don't know why, but he made me promise as he was passing out."

"Huh," grunted Kee Sun, chopping madly away. The kitchen filled once again with the sharp smell of ginger and the earthy tang of ginseng. "Maybe whatever it is she's been lookin' for's hidden up there. Smart place for a man to hide a thing."

"Oh." I thought back—Masugu asking me if I'd visited his rooms, the night of the first snow; Lady Chiyome telling him the fox spirit had been looking for something...

I remembered that night of the first snow, Masugu walking away in the direction of the storehouse, I had thought, tapping a sealed scroll against his own shoulder. *Not toward the storehouse,* I realized: *Toward the Retreat!*

"Kee Sun-*san*, I need to go get it before the..." I stopped at the door and turned. "Why do you keep calling who did this *she?*"

He laughed again, sharp and bitter this time. "'Cause I know it's not me that's done it, and the other men in the Full Moon are all asleep. I'd never believe such sloppiness of a *kumiho*—a fox spirit, as yeh call it. And in this weather, I don't think it's someone come in from outside o'the wall over and over without anybody knowin', do yeh? Though if it's one of the girls who's worked in my kitchen, I'd like to remind her of a lesson or two in how to handle herbs proper!"

"Oh," I said. "I see." And I did. It occurred to me in that moment that it couldn't be Emi who'd done this—or Toumi either, for that matter. All of us knew poppy by sight—and if we'd wanted for some reason to poison the inhabitants of the Full Moon, there were herbs that we'd have known to use before grabbing the corydalis at random from the rafters. "I'll be right back," I called, and waved, but Kee Sun was already bent over the table, tossing herbs into the long-handled wok, and filling the kitchen with their rich scent.

Growing up, I had always been the one who insisted loudly that there were no such things as spirits and demons, that they were just something that Mother made up to scare us with. But as I sprinted behind the great hall, I felt the presence of the *kitsune*, in spite of Kee Sun's certainty: the fox spirit, lurking in the shadows, laughing, the tips of its nine tails whipping, threatening, taunting, just beyond the edges of my vision.

Why does the kitsune *want the scroll?* I wondered as my feet slapped the hard, frozen dirt. *It must be something important, to go to all of this trouble to try to hurt people. And she*—Kee Sun now had me thinking of the poisoner as a *she—must be getting frantic.*

When I got to the Retreat, before I tried to climb, I went to the front door. It was open; Emi lay snoring, her cheek pressing against the cold stone threshold and the shards of her soup bowl still clutched in her hand. I would have found it funny: she always fell asleep so quickly under any circumstances that I could imagine her dropping off in mid-step, on the way to warn us of the poison. But I was worried that she would freeze, out in the winter night, or cut her hands on the shattered porcelain. I removed the pieces of the bowl, pushed her with some difficulty into the Retreat where the other women were strewn about on the floor like blown dandelion seeds, and closed the door.

Then I walked around to the far side of the building where the stone chimney butted up against the back corner of the Retreat. There didn't seem to be any crevices there—certainly none large enough to hide a scroll in. Looking up, I saw a trickle of smoke drifting from the covered top of the chimney and swirling, dancing with the falling snow. *Perhaps,* I thought, *he hid it where he could be sure that no one could find it.* Another thought gave me a guilty sense of righteousness: Or perhaps he hid it where he knew only I could find it. Reaching up, I began to scale the rough stone of the chimney.

There were plenty of handholds there, and so, cold and icy though it may have been, I quickly made my way up to the roof of the Retreat, scrambling up onto the dense thatch before I'd even started to breathe hard. There was a huge mound of snow blanketing most of the building, but there at the back, close to the compound wall, the wind and the heat from the chimney kept the roof more or less clear.

I scrambled along the stone base of the chimney; just above me I could see the top of the Full Moon's wall, where I'd knelt and listened to Masugu and Mieko's argument (not fight, he'd said). I couldn't see the scroll, nor any obvious cranny in the chimney in which to hide it.

Chimney.... Roof, he had said. I had assumed that he had meant that he had hidden the scroll—or whatever it was that I was looking for—in the side of the chimney, somewhere at roof-level. What else could he have meant?

Peering down, I considered the possibility that he had hidden the scroll at ground-level. That seemed unlikely—it was too easy a place for someone to find the scroll, and I would most likely have seen it when I was down there. Inside of the Retreat? No. In the first place, I couldn't see Masugu-*san*, who always tried to be so extremely proper, sneaking inside of the Retreat—except to meet Mieko. In the second, he had very clearly said *Roof,* which meant that it had to be outside.

I searched the surface of the chimney again; no loose stones, no crevices, and no place to hide anything larger than a pebble. I couldn't imagine that even a demon would make all of this trouble over a pebble.

Trying to think, I let my eyes wander up, watching the smoke trickling out from under the chimney's slanted cover.

The chimney's roof.

I stood. For a man of Masugu's height, the chimney roof would have been within reach. For me, however, it meant a little more climbing. *Not a problem,* I thought with satisfaction, and shimmied the small distance up and found a good foothold so that I could reach up under the chimney roof's soot-smeared eaves. There was a small ledge out of sight there—just right.

My fingers danced along the hot, grimy wood. At first I found nothing, and I began to worry that if the lieutenant had left a paper scroll there, perhaps it had been burnt to ash. But just before I reached the far corner, my fingers touched something warm, hard, and round. I grasped it and pulled it down.

It was a metal cylinder—the letter case that I had seen Lady Chiyome with that first day at Pineshore; the letter case that Masugu had poked me with our first night at the Full Moon. The end was closed with a seal marked with three ginger leaves.

Grinning, pleased with myself, I slid back down to the roof. The snowfall had broken for the moment, the clouds had parted to expose the black night sky and snowflake stars, and bright moonlight turned the entire compound silver as trout scales.

As I sat, preparing to make my way down to the ground and return to help Kee Sun revive everyone, I looked down at the cylinder in my hand. *What is in it?*

Perhaps it was simple curiosity. Perhaps the presence of the trickster spirit had infected me. Without even considering, I pulled open the end of the case and tapped it twice, sliding the enclosed scroll into the palm of my hand.

If I had anticipated some formal letter or contract, such as my father had often prepared for Lord Imagawa, I was disappointed. It wasn't parchment, but thin rice paper. Even before unrolling it, I could see that it was a drawing. I unrolled it and was bewildered by a swirl of color that didn't seem to make any sense. I started to roll it up again—perhaps if I showed it to Kee Sun—

A flickering, golden light from the direction of the great hall caught my eye.

It came from high up on the building's side wall, a glimmering square of light set between the black half-timbers that ran up the middle of the wall: the window of Lady Chiyome's chamber, light wavering as if someone had lit a small fire there, a lamp, or—much more likely—a candle. That struck me as odd, since Chiyome-*sama* was almost certainly not well enough to have gone back up to her room, and I couldn't imagine that Kee Sun had gone up there on his own. As I scowled up at the window, I saw a small flame—a candle indeed—and then a flash of white that seemed to fill the frame. A head. It turned, showing me a fine, brittle face.

Fuyudori stared back at me, and her expression was that of a predator stalking its prey.

Stalking me.

34—Falling Fast

uyudori's eyes locked with mine across the space, and the light from the candle in her hand made them flash red.

Then her gaze shifted downward, and I could see that she had spotted the letter. The drawing. A smile formed on her thin, red lips: a wolf's smile. Or, rather, a fox's. She looked hungry. She looked very much as if she were about to devour me.

"*Kitsune*," I gasped, and though I know that she couldn't have heard me she blinked, and the smile grew.

Fuyudori. *Winter bird. Snowbird*, as Masugu had said. *Ghostie-girl*. Kee Sun had laughed that she'd snuck out of the Retreat, desperate to make sure that Masugu was all right, but no—she'd snuck out to finish the job and find the scroll. And to make sure that the rest of us couldn't interfere, she'd tried to poison us. And no wonder she'd used too much poppy with Masugu, and then corydalis rather than something more effective this time—Fuyudori couldn't tell radishes from turnips or pine from hemlock. She probably couldn't be bothered to care. Rage filled me and then terror, in part because it seemed awful not to care, and in part because I realized that she truly didn't care—not what happened to Masugu, nor what happened to Chiyome, and certainly not what happened to me.

Then the snow began to fall again, like a white wing sweeping between us, and I could not see her.

The spell broken, I began to move. My first instinct, as always, was to climb—to get up onto the Full Moon's exterior wall and then to escape to the forest.

I knew, however, that I couldn't leave Fuyudori alone in the compound where she might hurt all of the people whom she'd drugged. I had to warn Kee Sun and the others. I had to stop her. Against my instincts, then, I clambered down the chimney. I started to sprint back toward the kitchen, along the space between the great hall and the wall, hoping to reach Kee Sun before Fuyudori could.

As I approached the corner of the building, however, a shape appeared out of the snow-thickened gloom: not the cook's scarecrow silhouette, but a shape that shone in the dark, clad almost all in white, with splashes of what I knew to be red that looked all but black in the murk. "Good evening, Risuko-*chan*," said Fuyudori. "How lovely to see you."

"You're wearing a *miko*'s robes," I said, though there were a dozen more urgent thoughts in my mind.

"A *kunoichi*'s." Fuyudori took a step toward me, and I stepped back; we both froze. Fuyudori laughed her annoying little chirp of a laugh. "I thought it appropriate, given what I was going to be doing tonight, that I marry myself to Death, if only for the evening."

The compound wall was plastered there; there was no way that I could climb to safety that way. And the great hall's timbers were set too far apart here at the back for me to gain any purchase on such a cold evening. I was fairly certain that Fuyudori could outrun me. "We're close to the kitchen," I improvised. "Kee Sun will hear you."

"I rather think not," she tittered.

"He didn't drink any of the soup you poisoned."

"No." She started to step toward me; I stepped back again. Once again, we froze in place. "However, I believe that Kee Sun will be resting quite soundly for some time." When I gave a surprised grunt, she laughed again—not the bird-chirp titter, but a low, hunter's chuckle. "It's true that I'm not terribly good with herbs. They all look the same to me, you see. However, I was always quite good with the pots and pans." From behind her back she drew what I recognized by the outline to be the long-handled wok.

"You... hit him?"

She chuckled again. "Oh, yes. This wok makes a most satisfactory ring when it strikes a hard skull like Kee Sun's." She twirled her weapon in her hand. "I saw that you were wearing an initiate's sash when you served out the soup that I'd added the poppy to. You know what it is that that old witch has been training us to be. Well, there are others who are better at singing and dancing than I, but I promise you, none of them can kill half as well."

Mieko can, I thought, but said, "Except poisons. You're terrible with poisons. Nearly killed Masugu when all you wanted to do was drug him so that you could search his rooms, and now you thought you'd given everyone poppy—overdosing us so that you could kill us, you thought—but all you put in the soup was corydalis. It's put everyone to sleep for a bit, but they'll wake up soon." I was lying—I didn't know how long the drug would last, but I was certain she wouldn't either. "All you'll have done is take away their cramps."

I could feel her body tense. "Then I shall have to work quickly," she said, and began to move toward me.

All uncertainty or anxiety replaced by terror, I ran.

I had a lead of perhaps ten strides to begin with, but I could hear her feet slapping against the frozen earth, and I knew that her longer legs would close the distance between us before long. My first thought was to get back to the Retreat's chimney, climb onto the roof, then over the wall, and then hide out in the woods; I might freeze to death, but I knew that Fuyudori would never be able to catch me there.

Unfortunately, I had the image of her pulling me down from the chimney, beating me to a pulp and taking the damned letter that had caused all of this trouble from my bloody, broken hand. The women in the Retreat itself might or might not have awoken, but I couldn't risk trapping myself in there if they were still unconscious; my mental image now included not only my battered body, but those of Emi and the others.

I turned the corner of the great hall and began sprinting toward the storehouse—perhaps the rats would bite Fuyudori—when I heard her take the corner close behind me. My lead was down to three or four strides now, and I knew that I would never make it to any of the doors before she caught me and beat me to death. In my mind, terror gave way to anger—Kee Sun's anger, actually. *That's no way to use a good wok!*

The bulk of the huge hemlock blotted out the moon for a moment, and I swerved toward the tree. Fuyudori squawked as she slipped on the icy ground, trying to turn with me. For a moment I thought that I had done it—that I would be able to reach the tree and climb into its safety before she could reach me, but her relentless footsteps began to pound behind me again. I sprinted to the far side of the tree, using the massive trunk for protection.

I was a squirrel. She was the fox. She would start to try to run around the tree, and I would run in the same direction, keeping its bulk between us. She would reverse direction, trying to surprise me, and I would change course and thwart her. This was to my great advantage—I could hear her all the better—but I knew that, like a squirrel, I would run out of endurance if we kept this game up. "Why?" I gasped when we had come to an uneasy pause, each trying to wait until the other committed to one direction or the other.

"Why?" She too panted; I could imagine her tongue lolling out of the side of her mouth, though I was sure that Fuyudori would never allow herself to do anything so unladylike.

"Masugu... All of us..." I stared at the letter case, still in my hand. I was thinking of Lady Chiyome's interrogation that morning. "The letter... Who... are you doing this for? Takeda-*sama*—"

I had been about to say that Lord Takeda would track Fuyudori down and kill her; Masugu and Lady Chiyome said that he was a great leader, but I was quite sure that he was far from being a terribly merciful man. Of course, I was quite sure too that no one from outside of the compound would ever know it if Fuyudori managed to kill us all and escape into the snow-choked mountains. By the time that we were all found, we would all look just the same: bones. How would anyone know who was who, let alone who was missing?

Fuyudori, however, was following another path altogether. "Takeda-*sama*," she spat. "He is why."

"Lord Takeda?"

"Beast!" she snarled. "Monster. These idiot rabbits call him *The Mountain,* but he's nothing but a monster. His troops destroyed my village, killed everyone, left me for dead. Thought I was dead. Stuck under my mother's body." She gave what might have been a sob or a growl. "*Two days.* Then Lord Oda's troops took the valley back. They were burning the bodies, and one of the soldiers saw me move; pulled me out of the fire." She tried to rush around the hemlock and catch me, but I was still listening, and kept to the far side. "That's when my hair turned white. *Ghostie-girlie,*" she snapped, mimicking Kee Sun's bouncy burr perfectly. "Lord Oda himself met me; he likes prodigies, you see, and I was twice rare—I'd lived when I should have died, and I was a young girl with white hair. Thrice rare, since I was possessed with the demon of revenge; I wanted nothing but to kill the Takeda who had done this to me."

"My father faced the Takeda," I murmured. "He said that they were a terrible foe."

"Your father. Now there was a brave warrior! Ordered to kill a bunch of brats, and he couldn't even manage it! Pathetic!"

I knew that she was trying to taunt me, to get me to make a mistake, but I couldn't help the flood of anger that came up from my belly; I could feel the world turning red again as it had that afternoon with Aimaru. Now, however, I had no weapon, and I knew that Fuyudori would not hesitate to grab me and—"My father was a brave man!"

"Oh, yes," Fuyudori taunted. "The very model of a samurai. Or so everyone thought."

"He was!" I cried. My fingers clenched, one hand closing on the letter case, the other on the deeply creviced bark before me; I could smell the earthy scent of the tree mixing with the bitter scent of the snow, which was falling thickly now.

She merely laughed. "*Please.* Ordered to attack a party containing Lord Imagawa and Lord Takeda's nephews and nieces and he was too *weak!* And rather than pay the honorable price by taking his own life like Toumi-*chan* and Emi-*chan's* fathers, he left in disgrace to be scribe, a common scribe!"

Father, sitting there beside the fire, transcribing a marriage contract. There is honor too, he sighed, in humble service. "No! He... He had his own children! If he had died it would have killed us!"

Fuyudori chuckled. She was moving slowly around the trunk now, trying to close the distance stealthily. "Emi-*chan* and Toumi seem to have managed."

I moved slowly away from the approaching sound of her voice. "They lived on the streets of the capital!" I was shaking—fear, cold, anger, and fatigue were all taking their toll. "And my sister had just been born!"

"How awful for you."

"He couldn't sentence us to death any more than he could those other children!" I could see *Otō-san* making that choice: putting our lives and those of the Takeda children above even our family honor.

"'*Those other children,*'" mimicked Fuyudori, sing-song. Then she gasped in delight. "You mean... you don't know?"

"Know?" I peered behind me; the Retreat was perhaps thirty strides away. I thought of breaking for it—climbing the chimney perhaps, or the timbers at the corner—

"They didn't tell you!" Fuyudori laughed again—a full, delighted laugh this time, though it sounded just as terrible and as terrifying as before. "Well, of course the old witch always loves to play her games. And *he* wouldn't say a thing, now, would he?" Her laughter echoed in the snow-muffled quiet.

"What?" I began to step away from the tree. If I could get a good distance before she discovered... "Who wouldn't say a thing?"

She laughed again—cackled really, and the sound raised the hair on my arms. "Masugu, of course!"

I stopped creeping, just a bit more than an arm's distance from the tree and, in spite of myself, stepped closer, as if hearing better would make what she was saying more sensible. "Ma—? Masugu?"

Fuyudori cackled on. "Takeda Masugu!" My hands clenched on the tree's bark again. "Son of Takeda Nobutatsu, half-brother of that monster Takeda *Shingen—!*"

She launched herself around the tree, the wok held in both hands above her head, ready to deliver *The Key of Heaven—*

But I was already out of reach, scrambling up onto the lowest of the hemlock's branches. Relief flowed through my limbs as she stared up at me, eyes and mouth wide. Then she screeched in frustration and slammed the tree with the wok—there were stains on it; *Not Kee Sun's blood, please don't let that be Kee Sun's blood,* I prayed. The metal pan did indeed ring out quite musically.

Nonetheless, I was beyond her grasp, and could wait until some of the others woke and could corner Fuyudori and lock her away—

With an explosive snort, she tossed the wok out into the snow that had begun to collect beyond the cover of the hemlock. Glaring up at me, she clutched at the uneven bark and began to climb.

Fuyudori was no squirrel, but she was very strong—always the first to finish with the stone-carrying exercise—and she pulled her way slowly and furiously up toward my perch among the lowest branches.

My stomach felt as if I had swallowed a large, frozen rock. I gawped at her in shock until she had climbed almost half way up the base of the trunk.

And then I bolted—straight up. From limb to limb I scuttled, higher and higher, so that the trunk was swaying in the wind and the limbs were barely thick enough to hold my weight.

At last, I reached a place where there was no further to go. The trunk itself was thinner than my wrist, and the branches merely twigs. The whole treetop danced as I tried to put as much distance as I could between myself and the madwoman below.

"Do you know," she shouted up from below, "you really are a fantastic climber. It will take me a while to get where you are. But I will get there. You might as well save me the trouble and come down."

"No!" I screamed.

Fuyudori laughed—the same condescending, tinkling laugh that she'd humiliated the three of us with our first day at the Full Moon. "Suit yourself. I'll be there soon enough. Don't freeze; it would be awful to have to pry the letter case from your icy fingers."

I clutched the metal case to me and whimpered, trying to think of what to do—where to go. "HELP!" I shouted, but my cry was met only with silence, and with Fuyudori's laughter.

"Do you honestly think anyone is going to help you, Risuko-*chan*? They're all unconscious, or maybe, if I'm lucky, I've killed them. That old witch and her idiot bodyguards and her imbecile cook. Masugu, the fool, and Mieko, who thinks that she's so special, and all of the rest. Even your little friends. Perhaps I'll light the buildings on fire once I've finished with you, and then no one will escape. Yes, that would be fitting: me, a woman, destroying Lord Takeda's little army of women, of sneaks and killers, as if I were burning out a wasps' nest. Yes. I think perhaps that I shall." Her face appeared among the foliage below, grinning, mad, feral.

I clung to the top of the tree, quivering with cold and fear, with no idea what to do to save myself.

On Fuyudori climbed. As she did, she gasped, "After all, they slew all of *my* allies—the Oda scouts who were trying to get my messages back to the capital. I was *so* angry when it was Masugu who came back through that open door, and not Lord Oda's soldiers, ready to *kill you all!*"

I began to weep, I will not deny it. I considered throwing the letter case away, but then she would simply kill me and go to retrieve it. "What is in this letter?" I howled down at her. "Why are you willing to kill us to get it?"

"I don't know," she snarled back; she was struggling as she came to branches that could barely support her weight, which was considerably greater than mine. "All that I know is that it is Masugu's mission to deliver that letter, and if Lord Takeda wants that to happen badly enough to risk his own nephew, then it is worth killing all of you to stop it." She had reached the level just below my feet; when she tried to climb one branch further, it snapped beneath her foot, and she had to cling to the thin trunk to keep herself from tumbling down to the frozen ground below.

We both remained motionless there for a few breaths, hugging the tree for sheer survival.

"Give me the letter," she spat.

I whimpered, but shook my head. "N-no."

"Don't play games with me!" she shouted and shook the tree trunk. Being higher, my perch swayed more than hers, and Fuyudori suddenly began to smile. "Want to fly, Risuko?" she asked, and began to rock the tree. We began to swing wildly from side to side, and I could see that I was swinging out past the branches below.

Soon, I knew, either the force of the tree whipping me back and forth would shake me loose and send me tumbling out into the dark, or the top of the tree would snap. Fuyudori might go with me, but I would be just as dead either way.

I wanted to be brave, to be like Father, accepting death as a stage along the journey, but how could I? I was young and frightened—terrified. "STOP!" I bawled. "Please, please, please stop!"

"All right," said Fuyudori, panting. She stopped, and the top of the tree slowly found its way back to its natural position. "Now, Risuko, give me the letter."

I trembled there, clinging to the treetop, trying to urge myself to refuse—for my family's honor, for the people of the Full Moon, for my friends.

My hand, however, extended down toward the white-haired demon, the monster, whose face seemed to glow with exultation as she reached up for the letter. Fuyudori was standing on tip-toe, one hand barely clutching a thin wisp of a branch as the fingers of the other stretched out to take her prize from me.

I knew that, as soon as she had the letter, she would kill me, but I couldn't stop myself.

Her fingers closed around the end of the metal case and tugged.

My fingers refused to let go.

Why? Cold, perhaps. Or panic. Or rage. Or sheer madness. But strong though she may have been, Fuyudori was fully extended, and couldn't pull the letter from my clutches.

"LET GO!" she demanded.

For a moment, I fought, and we became locked in the oddest, deadliest game of tug-of-war that I had ever participated in. Fuyudori's muscles strained, her face contorting so that all of her loveliness was gone. "LET! GO!"

"All right," I said, and I did.

For a moment, triumph flared on Fuyudori's face as she held up the letter case. That look was instantly replaced with desperation, however, as she overbalanced, and then with sick dread as the tiny limb beneath her right foot gave way, and she fell back, away from the tree trunk, eyes wide, mouth wide, tumbling backward into the dark, falling through the branches of the hemlock that she had thought was a pine, snapping branches loudly on her way down until she hit the hard ground with the thud of an overripe peach falling to the courtyard below.

Blossoms on the ground...

No blossoms up there at the top of the enormous old hemlock I was clinging to, cold twisting my fingers, terror teasing my gut.

Snow flakes around me, appearing from nowhere, falling to nowhere. Silence: the proper sound of falling snow.

And death waiting below.

No blossoms.

Soldiers falling fast...

For months after that night, only one dream disturbed my slumber: the sight of Fuyudori's wide eyes, her soundless cry, her white hair streaming as she fell backward, away from the tree and into the darkness.

———

I made my way slowly down from the top of the tree. My fingers were trembling and raw, my arms and legs all but strengthless from the ordeal. I wept, my nose running until tears and snot soaked through the front of my thin jacket, making me feel even colder and—if it were possible—more miserable.

I did not want to reach the bottom. I did not want to see what had happened to Fuyudori. A part of me dreaded finding her shattered body; another part imagined that I would find a nine-tailed fox, smirking and laughing at me when I reached the ground, ready to punish me for daring to try to trick it so.

When at last I reached the bottom-most branch of the tree, however, that was not the sight that awaited me.

Lady Chiyome stood, leaning against Kee Sun, whose head was encased in an enormous bandage. Which one of them was holding up which, I could not have said. The Little Brothers, moving stiffly as I had never seen them move, were arranging a white sheet over a shape below. Fuyudori's body, I realized.

Emi stood there, swaying, along with Aimaru—who was holding his head—and Toumi, the Horseradish girls, Sachi—all of the women. Even Masugu was there; there was no question however, that Mieko was the one who was holding him up. However unsteadily, he was at least standing, wrapped in several robes.

I must have gasped because suddenly all of their gazes flashed up at me. I wanted to hide; I felt as if my failure, my cowardice, my shame were all too obvious to all of them, and my tears and sobbing redoubled.

Chiyome-*sama* shuffled over to the base of the tree and squinted up. "Well," she wheezed, "I thought I knew what I was getting when I bought you. Serves me right."

Then she knelt unsteadily and bowed. Deeply. Touching her grey, wild hair to the earth.

Astonished, I gaped at the others. Perhaps the corydalis had affected the lady's mind?

They all seemed as surprised as I was, but one by one—or, in the case of Mieko and Masugu, two by two—they followed her example.

The last two standing were Toumi and Emi. Toumi grunted and started to sneer, but looked over at the sheet covering Fuyudori's body and then up at me. She gave me a curt nod, and then she too knelt. It was not as deep a bow as the rest had given, but it was—aside from Lady Chiyome's—the one that most overwhelmed me.

Emi smiled. *Emi smiled.* She mouthed the words *We heard* and *Thank you.*

And then she too bowed before me at the foot of the hemlock tree as the snow settled softly to the ground.

Epilogue—On the Ground

All of the inhabitants of the Full Moon shuffled to their rest, the corydalis still thickening the blood in their veins.

We turned our backs on the covered body of Fuyudori. Several of us made our way back to the great hall. Some to the dormitories.

Nobody went to the Retreat.

I couldn't stand to go anywhere where there were others. The chill of what had happened made me shiver even more than the biting cold of the winter night. I couldn't think of sleeping—of dreaming.

I shuffled and shivered my way toward the bathhouse, which had always been a warm, cheerful place for me, in spite of the hard work that Emi, Toumi and I did there. And it was untainted by any memory of Fuyudori the *kitsune*. Fuyudori the *kunoichi*. Fuyudori the would-be assassin.

When I slipped out of the snow, which was beginning to fall hard, and into the little building, I reveled in the warmth before noticing that there were two people already there: Emi and Aimaru.

Her face was grim, but then it always was. His face was ashen, making the bruise that peeked out from under his hairline look almost black in the candlelight. Yet he was smiling. "We thought you might come here."

I stared at them blankly.

"The tubs need to be cleaned," said Emi, as if this were the most sensible statement in the world. Which, in some ways, it was.

Together, the three of us began to drain the tubs in preparation for cleaning and refilling them.

Once we were scrubbing at the walls of the two wooden tubs—Emi and Aimaru in the cool tub, me in the hot—I began to stop shivering.

By the time we began filling the tubs again with buckets full of snow, I was actually sweating.

We laid the firewood for the next morning and sat back against the walls of the bathhouse, pleasantly exhausted.

I peered over at them. They seemed to be careful not to look at me—nor at each other. "How much did you hear?" I asked.

"Not much," said Aimaru with a shrug.

Emi cocked her head. "Enough. We heard her talk about you giving her some kind of letter." She gave a quick gasp. "So she was the one! That's what she was trying to find in Masugu's room!"

"And in the stable," Aimaru added, nodding.

"Yes." I wiped a drop of sweat out of my eye. "Only she had no idea what the poppy juice was going to do to Masugu, and then tonight she thought the corydalis root was dried poppy."

Emi actually laughed. "Good thing for us!"

"Yes."

"So..." Aimaru shifted uncertainly. "What was this letter she was looking for?"

"I don't know," I muttered. I'd been trying not to think about the thing. "Oh! I've still...!" I pulled the now-flattened roll of rice paper out from between my jacket and my undershirt, where I had shoved it when I was on top of the Retreat. We all stared at it.

"We should—" began Aimaru.

"—return it to the lieutenant," finished Emi.

We all continued to stare at the paper.

"It doesn't look like a letter," I said.

They both nodded.

"Maybe," Emi began slowly, "we should check. To be sure that it's the same one."

Now we all nodded, even though I knew—and was sure that they knew—that it couldn't possibly be any other piece of paper than the one I'd pulled from the letter case.

I leaned forward and unfolded the paper on the floor. Emi took one end and held it down, and I held the other. It wasn't big.

"It isn't a letter," said Aimaru.

No, it wasn't. It was a drawing. Some squiggles in black, and then squares in different colors—blue, red, and white. The paper had been stained by moisture, but the ink did not seem to have run. The blue and red squares all had what looked like arrows pointing from them toward the white squares. In the bottom corner a crest was stamped in red: a three wild ginger leaves, like shovels. It made me think....

We all squinted down at the paper.

"It looks like..." Aimaru said, biting his lip.

It made me think of sitting in Lady Chiyome's rooms, the night that I'd climbed up the outside wall. Looking down at...

Emi gave a grunt. "It's a map."

Yes, it was a map. Of course! As soon as Emi said that, I realized that it looked a lot like the map I'd seen Lord Imagawa and his general looking at the morning that I met Lady Chiyome. "But what of?"

"The provinces around the capital," came a sharp voice from my shoulder.

I spun around, clutching the map to my chest.

Toumi was standing, her face lumpy as if from lack of sleep. "A battle map, I think."

"I..." I started to talk, but couldn't think what to say.

"We found it," said Emi. "In the snow. I showed it to Murasaki because we didn't know what it was."

Toumi just shrugged.

I stood, as did Aimaru and Emi behind me. I clutched the paper to my chest. "I..."

Toumi's dark eyes did not rise to mine. "Kee Sun has the others cleaning the kitchens, which they hate. I'm supposed to help you. But it looks like you're done."

"Yes." I held my breath.

"You're an initiate." She was squinting at my now-stained sash.

"Oh." My stomach felt cold again, in spite of the warmth. "Yes."

"Huh."

"I..." I leaned forward so that she had to look into my eyes. "It's because I found out what *kunoichi* are. We think that's the test."

"Huh." She scowled at me as I stood straight again. "What *kunoichi* are?"

Over my shoulder, Emi whispered, "Assassins. Spies. Bodyguards."

Toumi's eyes widened. Even now, I am not certain whether it was because of what we had just revealed to her, or that we had told her at all—that we had showed her that trust. "*Assassins?*" She spoke the word with something like reverence.

"And spies," I sighed. *No harm....* "And bodyguards."

Toumi's face fell into a relaxed smirk. "I'd like to see you as a body-guard. Mouse."

I felt the heat rise in my face, but I answered her in kind: "I'd like to see you as a spy!"

She snorted.

Emi hummed almost happily. "That would leave me to be the assassin."

"I think that's the Matsudaira crest," said Aimaru. We all blinked. "On the map."

I lowered the paper from my chest. The ginger-leaf seal lay in the corner where the blue squares were congregated. Once again, the stones on the map in Chiyome-*sama*'s room came to mind. "Yes. I think that the blue... are the Matsudaira. And I'm sure the red are the Takeda." Then I waved at the white squares ranged along the end of what had looked like a long thumb, but which I now saw clearly as Lake Biwa, near the capital. Father always said the lake was beautiful in the springtime. "And these must be Oda-*sama*'s troops."

Toumi gulped. Even she could see it. "So Matsudaira-*sama* wants the Takeda—us—to help him... *attack* Lord Oda?"

Lord Oda. Who had dishonored our fathers. I almost told them then. I almost asked if they knew....

"But I thought the Matsudaira and the Oda were on the same side." Emi rested her chin on my shoulder, peering at the map. *Battle of white and scarlet...*

"So are the Takeda," Aimaru pointed out.

We all stared at the map again.

"If... Matsudaira-*sama* is trying to get Takeda-*sama* to attack Oda-*sama*... Perhaps Takeda-*sama* is doing the honorable thing and warning Oda-*sama*?"

"Maybe," grunted Toumi.

Emi gave a snort of frustration that made the rice paper flutter in my fingers. "Then why's Masugu-*san* staying here all winter, instead of riding as fast as he can to the capital?"

"I don't know," I said. In fact, it didn't make any sense.

Toumi wrinkled her sharp nose. "Maybe we're better off not knowing. Lords. Knowing their business is bad news."

Aimaru murmured, "The monks always said, 'Knowledge without under-standing is like soup without seasoning.'"

"Though I could have done without the seasoning in this evening's soup," grunted Emi.

We all agreed with that.

"Let's give this back to Masugu," said Emi. I rolled up the map, and we all trooped out the door—including, to my surprise, Toumi, who shuffled along sullenly.

"Don't want you two hogging all the credit," she said

———

Imagine a nation at war with itself.

Not so very hard to do in a time when ambition, greed, and fear gallop like unreined horses from heart to heart, from home to home, from town to town. The great lords play their games of conquest as if moving stones around in a huge game of Go, but instead of a lined board, they play upon the land itself, and instead of pebbles, they position, capture, and sacrifice living men.

And women. And children.

Mute, we gave the map to Mieko, who was watching Masugu sleep. *Serpent-girlie.* She promised that she would keep it safe and return it to him.

None of us spoke as we stumbled blearily into our dormitory. We had nothing left to say.

Mai and Shino were sleeping in the head initiate's room. Each was apparently unwilling to allow the other the honor of sleeping there alone.

Toumi and Emi fell into their bedrolls and were asleep almost immediately. I followed soon after, too tired to think, to worry.

I dreamt no dreams that night. None at all.

To be Continued in

Bright~Eyes
Seasons of the Sword #2

Coming Soon!
Find out more on Risuko.Net

Follow on:
twitter.com/RisukoKunoichi • risuko-chan.tumblr.com
facebook.com/risuko.books • instagram.com/RisukoKunoichi
risuko.livejournal.com

THANK YOU FOR READING Risuko!

I hope that you enjoyed this first tale of Murasaki's
adventures. If you did, please tell your friends what you
thought. Word of mouth is an author's best friend—and I'd
like to think you'd be doing your friends a favor too! You can
share an honest review on your blog, post a pic on Instagram
or Snapchat or a link on Facebook, or leave a review on
Amazon (risuko.net/amazon)
or Goodreads (risuko.net/goodreads).
If you do write a review, please let us know where and when
by sending the web address (URL) or a screenshot to
risuko@risuko.net
When you do, I'd be happy send you a download code good
for any audiobook at Audible,
the world's largest audio library!*
Thanks again!

David Kudler

* While supplies last, of course! And yes—that includes the Risuko audiobook.

Sneak Preview:

Bright-Eyes
Seasons of the Sword #2

I meant to take the knife that Mieko was holding out to me, the handle toward my hand.

I meant to. But I couldn't.

"Risuko," whispered Mieko, her eyes locked on mine. The rest of the Full Moon's girls and women were also staring at me.

My eyes flicked toward the pig, which struggled against its bonds, squealing.

We were outside the Full Moon's kitchens, next to the well. The pig was stretched out, its legs tied to four heavy pegs that Emi, Toumi, and I had hammered into the still-frozen packed earth.

What stopped me, what kept me from being able to take the long, narrow blade from Mieko-*san*'s hand, wasn't that the pig was in distress. Its squeals knotted my stomach, but I had slaughtered animals for the kitchens before—chickens, rabbits, even a goat.

But this animal had been dressed in a samurai's battered armor, with a helmet over its head. And all I could think...

Through the long, snow-bound winter, Mieko and the other *kunoichi* had used this armor to teach us its weak points—to show us where even the most heavily armed warrior was vulnerable. As we stabbed under the armpits or between the front and back plates with daggers, it hadn't seemed real; the armor had been on a kind of straw dummy, like the ones we used to put up next to the rice paddies to keep the birds away.

But screaming and straining, the pig was no dummy. It looked like a person, almost. It looked like a samurai. Like...

I looked down and shook my head. "I can't," I mouthed.

Mieko started to say something, but then shook her head and held the knife handle out to Emi, who frowned, but took it.

I ran.

———

I was still running—past our dormitory, past the white length of the great hall—when I ran into Lieutenant Masugu. Or rather, I ran into his horse, Inazuma.

"Going for a climb, Murasaki?" The lieutenant was leading Inazuma by the reins.

I blinked up at him and shook my head.

"I haven't seen you climb since... In a while." His eyes were small, concerned half-moons under his helmet.

I blinked again. "Are you leaving, Masugu-*san*?" Inazuma carried a pack of supplies, and Masugu was dressed in a full set of armor—not his usual shining black armor with the four diamonds of the Takeda emblazoned on his chest, but rather a battered brown set with the white disk *mon* of Mochizuki— the Full Moon.

He was dressed, in fact, very much as the pig had been.

I couldn't hear the squealing any more.

The lieutenant nodded. "It's time to go."

"You're not going to wait for Lady Chiyome to return?"

Now he shook his head. "She knew I needed to leave once the passes to the west started to clear. She won't be surprised."

I wrapped my arms around myself. "I... We will miss you." *Mieko*-san *will miss you the most*, I thought, but thought it best not to say.

"Well, it shouldn't take me more than a month to get to the capital, deliver my... the map you returned to me, and get back here. No time at all." He smiled and patted my arm. His horse whickered impatiently. "Besides, Inazumi wants to run."

I nodded.

"Say, don't you have a lesson? Shouldn't you be with the others?"

My gorge rose, but I stared up at him. "Did you know that if I were to slip a very sharp blade up beneath the back of your helmet, I could push the tip just under your skull and sever your spinal chord?"

Masugu's face froze.

"Mieko-*sensei* was teaching us to do that. On a pig dressed in armor."

"That... would be very effective."

"I couldn't do it."

"No," he sighed. "There is a purpose for your being here, Murasaki-*san*. I do not know the reason that Chiyome-*sama* brought you to the Full Moon. I do not know the reason that the gods brought you, Emi, and Toumi here— but there is one." He squeezed my shoulder. "Learn what Mieko and the rest have to teach you."

I pleaded, "I don't want to be a killer."

"No," he sighed again. "Neither do I. And yet I am a Takeda warrior. It is my duty. We live in dangerous times. If I were not to fight to protect our provinces and our people, how many more would die?" His sad smile reminded me of the one that Mieko gave me so often. "You are a samurai maiden, Kano Murasaki—the daughter of a warrior. You too have a duty."

Now he had me crying. "I'm no s-samurai. My f-family was stripped of its honor." *Otō-san, walking toward the Inagawa castle. Walking toward his death. "Do no harm."*

"And yet your duty remains. If I know anything about your father—or his daughter—I do not believe that any power on this earth would take that away." He squeezed my shoulder again and swept the tears from my cheeks with a gauntleted finger. "In the meantime, Murasaki, why don't you forget about knives and samurai and duty for a bit. Climb."

I nodded and gave him a smile, though it was the last thing I wanted to do. "Thank you, Masugu-*san*. Come back soon."

"As soon as I can, Murasaki-*san*. Take care."

As the lieutenant led Inazuma toward the front gate, I scrambled up into the lower branches of the enormous hemlock that grew on the eastern side of the great hall.

It wasn't until I threw my leg over the biggest of the branches, waving at Masugu as he mounted and rode out onto the ridge beyond the gate that Fuyudori's ghost came to visit.

Not her actual ghost. Angry though the white-haired girl's spirit must have been, we had performed all of the proper rites for her. Her body had been burned and the ashes buried in the icy ground behind the compound. We had left out a bowl of rice and a cup of sake at our meals. (They had been small ones, though—no one felt she deserved more.) No one had spoken her name. It had been longer than the forty-nine days it would have taken for her spirit to reach the next world.

But sitting there on the branch, feeling the wind stirring my hair, it was hard not to remember sitting on that same limb, watching her climbing after me, furious. Murderous.

I took a deep breath and did my best not to think of her.

Already, Masugu-*san* was only half visible, disappearing over the edge of the ridge down the path that led to the valley and the road west, toward the imperial city.

I waved again, though I knew he would not see.

It was nice to be up in the tree again. Nice to feel the wind. Across the valley, the mountain peaks were still covered in snow, but lower down all was green — a deep, living green, broken by flashes of silver where streams poured the melting snow down into the valley.

The ridge top too was green. Fresh shoots pushed up through dead, grey grass. White wildflowers inked the field.

I stayed there for the rest of the lesson. A small moment of bliss.

"You staying up there all day, Mouse-*chan*, or are you getting your mousy behind into the kitchen to help make dinner?" Toumi glowered up at me from the corner of the great hall.

"Can you see anything interesting?" asked Emi. She too was frowning— but then, she always frowned.

"I was waving goodbye to the lieutenant."

"Oh. He's gone?" Emi's frown deepened into a pout.

Toumi made a retching sound. "Come on. We had to bleed the stupid pig. You get to butcher it."

When I blanched, Emi said, "Killing it was very easy. And put the animal out of its misery."

"I know," I whispered.

"Then why didn't you just kill the stupid thing, *baka!*" growled Toumi.

"I couldn't help..."

"What?" Both girls walked below my branch.

I closed my eyes. "I couldn't help thinking... of whose spirit might inhabit the pig."

"You... *What?*" Toumi gaped up at me.

"I couldn't help but think... that it might be... I don't know. Fuyudori. My father."

"Oh," said Emi.

Toumi gave a harsh laugh. "Unbelievable! Seen you kill enough chickens and bunnies. Do you go around worrying about crushing your father when you step on *ants?*"

Again I felt the blood leave my face. "I... I will *now!*"

"*Baka-yarō!*" Laughing once more, Toumi shook her head. "Come on down here, Mouse. You've got your dad to cut up."

"*Toumi!*" whispered Emi.

I took another breath, trying to steady myself, trying to find that quiet bliss again, and looked back out at the green and white landscape.

Over the edge of the ridge, where Masugu-*san* had disappeared, there seemed to be a hazy wave rising. A wave of vertical lines tipped in steel. Spears. Dozens, Many bearing blue flags showing the wild-ginger leaf *mon* of the Matsudaira.

"Uh... guys?" They both looked up at me. Now, instead of feeling bloodless, I could hear the blood pounding through me. "I think we're being invaded."

To be Continued in

Bright-Eyes
Seasons of the Sword #2

Coming Soon!
Find out more on Risuko.Net

Follow on:
twitter.com/RisukoKunoichi • risuko-chan.tumblr.com
facebook.com/risuko.books • instagram.com/RisukoKunoichi
risuko.livejournal.com

Glossary

-chan—Child

-ko—Ending meaning that the word is a girl's name or nickname

-sama—My lady or lord (honorific)

-san—Sir or ma'am (honorific)

-senpai—Senior student (honorific)

baka-yarō—Complete idiot (offensive)

daikon—A large, white, mild radish

go—A Chinese game of strategy

hai—Yes

hanyak—(Korean) Herbal medicine

hiragana—phonetic script used for foreign terms and for emphasis (equivalent to italics)

ichi—The number one

Jizō-bosatsu—The Buddhist saint (*boddhisatva*) of lost children; he is often portrayed with a blank face and large sleeves in which he protects the children

katakana—phonetic script used for most words

katana—A samurai's long, curved sword

kanji—Chinese ideograms; over three thousand of these non-phonetic characters are widely used in Japanese writing

kimchee—(Korean) Pickled cabbage, often spicy

kitsune—A mischievous, nine-tailed fox spirit

ku or *kyu*—The number nine

kumiho—(Korean) Mischievous fox spirit (similar to a *kitsune*)

kunoichi—"Nine in one"; *a special kind of woman*

Kwan-um—(Korean) The Buddhist saint (*boddhisatva*) of mercy and beauty; called Kwan-yin in China and Kannon in Japan

miko—Shrine maidens; young women who assist at Shintō festivals and ceremonies

mizutaki—A hot-pot dish made with fish, chicken, or some other meat

Mochizuki— "full moon"; the clan of Lady Chiyome's late husband

mogusa—Mugwort; formed into pellets, burned (with the lit end away from the flesh) as a stimulant and as a way to celebrate childrens' aging during the New Year festival

mon—The emblem of a noble house (like the European coat of arms)

Mukashi, mukashi—"Long, long ago" (traditional beginning to Japanese folktales, similar to "Once upon a time")

no—Of or from

Otō-san—Father

Okā-san—Mother

Risuko—Squirrel (a girl's name or nickname)

samisen—A long-necked, five-stringed instrument, similar to a guitar or banjo

sensei or *-sensei*—Teacher (honorific)

Shintō—The native religion of Japan; Shintō believes that there are many gods or spirits (*kami*) inhabiting different parts of the natural world, and is frequently practiced side by side with Buddhism

shakuhachi—A long flute carved from bamboo

shōgun—The emperor's warlord

shoyu—Soy sauce

tatami—A straw mat that is traditionally used to cover floors in Japan

torī—A large arch or gateway usually found at Shintō shrines or temples

wakazashi—A samurai's short sword; traditionally used for defense and for committing ritual suicide (*hara-kiri*)

Wihayeo—(Korean) Cheers!

yang—(Chinese) The male force

yin—(Chinese) The female force

Characters

Note: In Japan, as through most of East Asia, tradition places the family name before the given name. For example, in Kano Murasaki, *Risuko's proper name,* Kano *is her family's name and* Murasaki *her given name—what English speakers would call her first name.*

Residents of the Full Moon:

Risuko—Proper name: Kano Murasaki. Called "Squirrel" and "Bright-eyes." Novice.

Lady Mochizuki Chiyome—Mistress of the Full Moon.

Mieko—Lady Chiyome's maid. *Kunoichi*-teacher, *miko*-dance master.

Kuniko—Lady Chiyome's maid.

Tarugu Toumi—Called "Falcon." Novice.

Hanichi Emi—Called "Smiley." Novice.

Aimaru—Servant.

Little Brothers—Servants.

Lieutenant Musugu—Takeda warrior.

Sachi—Called "Flower." *Kunoichi*-teacher, *miko*-music teacher.

Fuyudori—Called "Ghostie." Head initiate.

Mai—One of the "Horseradish Sisters." Junior initiate.

Shino— One of the "Horseradish Sisters." Junior initiate.

Kee Sun—Cook. Korean.

People in Risuko's hometown:

Okā-san—Risuko's mother. Proper name: Kano Chojo.

Usako—Risuko's sister. Proper name: Kano Daini.

Otō-san—Risuko's late father. Former samurai, turned scribe. Proper name: Kano Kazuo.

Naru—Pig-keeper.

Karoku—Woodgatherer.

Kenji—Boy. Played with Risuko and Usako.

Irochi—Egg-man

Major Historical Characters:

Takeda Shingen—Lord of the Takeda clan of Worth (*Kai*) Province. Called "The Mountain" and "The Tiger of Kai." Allied with the Oda and the Matsudaira

Oda Nabunaga—Most powerful lord (*daimyo*) of Japan, controlling the capital in Kyōto and the military government headed by the warlord (*shōgun*). Head of the Oda clan of Rising Tail (*Owari*) Province. Allied with the Takeda and the Matsudaira.

Matsudaira Motoyasu—Lord of the Matsudaira clan of Three Rivers (*Mikawa*) Province.

Imagawa Ujizane—Lord of the Imagawa clan of Serenity (*Totomi*) Province

Ashikaga Yoshiaka—Hereditary warlord (*shōgun*) of Japan. For all intents and purposes Oda Nabunaga's puppet since Oda-*sama* took contol of the capital.

Place Names

I have translated most of the place names in the book; after all, the names aren't exotic to a speaker of Japanese! The translations are my own, and sometimes aim more at a poetic than a literal translation of the name.

There is in fact a town called Mochizuki in Nagano (what used to be Shinano or Dark Letter Province). It is not very far from Midriver Island (Kawanakajima), the site of several of the greatest battles of Japan's Civil War era. I couldn't help but set the estate of the Mochizuki family there. The estate itself, however, is entirely of my own imagining.

Serenity Province—Totomi

   Pineshore—Hamamatsu-shi, Totomi Province

Three Rivers Province—Mikawa

Quick River Province—Suruga

Worth Province—Kai

Dark Letter Province—Shinano

   Full Moon—Mochizuki, Shinano Province

   Midriver Island—Kawanakajima, Shinano Province

Great Eastern Sea Road—Tōkaidō

Rising Tail Province—Owari

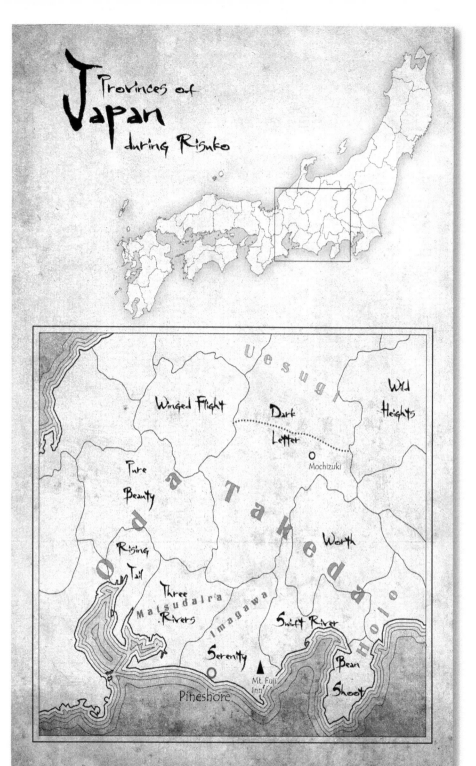

The Full Moon

Well

Retreat

Kitchen

Great Hall

Initiates

Baths

Nunnery

Storehouse

Bull Pen

Guest (Masago)

Stables

Tea House

Acknowledgements

There were many, many people who helped me as I wrote this book. It may take a village to raise a child, but it seems to take an army to write a historical novel.

First, I must thank Julia Nations and her students, who were the first test audience for this book as I was beginning to write it. Their thoughtful questions and their persistent requests over subsequent years to know *what happened next* were a wonderful inspiration to finish the story.

Sarah Jae-Jones was kind enough to try to help me understand how a Korean accent might sound to the Japanese. Don't blame her for the way Kee Sun talks, however. That's all from my peculiar imagination.

Dr. Diane Monteil shared her wisdom in the use (and abuse) of traditional Asian herbal medicines. She was both patient and good-humored in the face of all of my questions about poisons (as well as their antidotes), about traditional treatments for premenstrual syndrome, and about the concept of the five elements, the five flavors, and the five colors.

Brenda and Donal Brown read the book long before it was finished and provided both their wisdom and their apparently bottomless enthusiasm, which sustained me through many of the darkest passages in my journey to complete Risuko's tale. They also introduced my book to Danielle Svetcov (see below), for which alone they deserve literary Elysium—if they hadn't already earned it in a thousand other ways.

Kristine Ball and Amy and Anschel Burke also provided invaluable early input.

Once I had completed the first drafts of the manuscript, a group of early readers provided incredible feedback, spotting inconsistencies, narrative dead ends, and typos, poking me when I needed it, but also telling me what worked, which I sometimes couldn't see. This book would not be as readable as it is without the assistance of Sherry Baisden, Ryan Blood, Alison Coulthard, Victory Davidsmeier, Stephen Gerringer, Sarah Grant, Justice Hardman, Alithea Howes, Diana Lee, Laurie Lockman, Giovanni Martelli, Ania Mieszkowska, Liz Ottosson, Ken Schneyer, St. Margarets, and, most especially, Aleta Johansen. Each of these folks is a wonderful writer in his or her own right; I'm honored to have benefitted from their thoughts on my own prose.

Danielle Svetcov, my agent, took my book on and promptly did what every author needs but no author wants: she showed me where the story lagged, and how to make it much, much better. Her insightful and incisive critiques showed me that I needed to cut a major-but-distracting secondary character, as well as a needless prologue and epilogue. (Once I had made these as well as a number of the other excellent cuts and changes that she suggested, I had managed to add four thousand words. I'm still not sure how that happened!)

The Tuesday Night Mill Valley Library Authors Group, led by the wonderful Caitlin Myer, helped me think through some of those changes. The book in your hands—particularly the prologue and the section about Risuko and Toumi's escapade on the switchback—is there because of their input.

The Risuko Beta Team provided incredible feedback as I was completing the book. A heartfelt *dōmo arigatō* to Lyndsey Lowe (who came first), A.D. Madden, Amanda, Breanna Kelly, Breanna Manlick, Carson Smith, Casia Courtier, Cherrie Walker, Crystal, Dawn Kearns, Dilara Çelik, Elizabeth Fields, Fabienne Gilbert, Gabrielle Nadig, Helen Thompson, Isis Erb, Jaime Andreas, Jo Metivier, Jossie Marie Solheim, Judit Casedemont, Kelley, Kizzi R., Lauren Skidmore, Lucie Boisgard, Melody A., Nikolett Nagy, Racheal, Rachel Stansel, Rebecca A.W. Lovato, Sheri Olshan, Tanya Grech Welden, Ventureadlaxre, Yasamin, Yu Xuan, and Zoe Plant.

Without the Kickstarter supporters who backed *Risuko*, this book literally would not have been published. To Heather Albano, Craig Allen, Andrea, Margot Avery, Candice Bailey, Rachael Barcellano, Roger Beckett, C Carter, Crossed Genres, Isaac "Will It Work" Dansicker, Don, D-Rock, ebuckle@gmail.com, Benjamin Ellefson, Don, Beth & Meghan Ferris, Mattia Forza, Christine Gengaro, Stephen Gerringer, Sylvia-Michelle Hostetter, Alithea Howes, John Idlor, Karpov Kinrade, Alexander John Aristotle Kimball, Ania Mieszkowska (again!), Empress Diana and Imperial Princess Amara of the Most Illustrious Lee Dynasty, Lennhoff Family, Anika Loeffler, magycmyste@gmail.com, Breanna Manlick, Sam Mickel, Joy Mundy and Tony Navarette, mywayhoff11@aol.com, Kira Newman, Ripley Patton, Roman

Pauer, Cara Melia Pico, Jason Png, Ritske Rensma, Roy Romasanta, Rachel S., Riccardo Sartori, Ken Schneyer, Sueatducksfoot, SwordFire, Robert Walter, Susan R. Woodward, Heesung Yang, Seow Wan Yi—you are angels in every sense of the word.

I must of course thank my middle school English teacher, who happens also to be my mother, Jackie Kudler. She read more drafts of *Risuko* than anyone (well, almost anyone—see below). Her fine eye for detail and narrative through-line was as helpful now as it was when I was thirteen—and much more welcome.

My wife Maura Vaughn was on a literary quest of her own through much of the time that I was writing this novel; her book on text analysis for actors, *The Anatomy of a Choice*. Nonetheless, she read every rewrite of each chapter, providing her thoughtful insight, her patience, and her astonishing sense of story to the task, day after day. Joseph Campbell says in *The Hero with a Thousand Faces* that each would-be hero has the assistance of magical helpers as he or she wanders the indescribably difficult path of adventure. I know who my magical helper was and is, and I am honored and blessed to have her for a partner.

Last and greatest is my debt to my own two daughters, Sasha and Julia. They were my inspiration; they were also my first audience. When I began writing *Risuko*, they were young—in Julia's case, too young to read the book on her own. Nonetheless, I read new chapters to each of them, even once they had grown well past the age when they needed to be read to. They are now both young women, wonders in their own rights, with amazing futures before them. I hope that I have captured half of their spirit in Murasaki and her friends.

Also from Stillpoint/Atalanta
Winter Tales

The Seven Gods of Luck

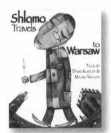

Shlomo Travels to Warsaw

How Raven Brought Back the Light

BY

David Kudler & Maura Vaughn

DAVID KUDLER is not afraid of heights. He just has a healthy respect for depths. "I'm as surprised as anyone," he says, "that I've written a book featuring a girl who loves to be as high up in the air as possible." An editor and author, he lives just north of the Golden Gate Bridge with his wife, actor/teacher/author Maura Vaughn, their author-to-be daughters, and their (apparently) non-literary cats.

He is the founder, publisher, and editor-in-chief for Stillpoint Digital Press. Since 1999, he has overseen the publications program of the Joseph Campbell Foundation, for which he has edited three posthumous volumes of Campbell's previously unpublished work (*Pathways to Bliss*, *Myths of Light* and *Sake & Satori*) and managed the publication of over sixty print, ebook, print, audio, and video titles, including the third edition of the seminal *Hero with a Thousand Faces*. He is honored to serve as the vice-president for the Bay Area Independent Publisher's Association (BAIPA). He also blogs on books and publishing for Huffington Post.

Risuko is his first novel. His children's picture books *The Seven Gods of Luck*, *Shlomo Travels to Warsaw,* and *How Raven Brought Back the Light* (the last two co-written with his wife Maura Vaughn) are available as the Winter Tales. He is currently at work on *Bright-Eyes,* the second book in the Seasons of the Sword series, as well as six Kunoichi Companion Tales (for newsletter subscribers).

For more information about David Kudler and his writing, visit

risuko.net

You can also follow him on social media:

twitter.com/dkudler • davidkudler.tumblr.com
facebook.com/risuko.books • davidkudler.pinterest.com
davidkudler.livejournal.com

Made in the USA
San Bernardino, CA
04 January 2018